The Ninth Curse

K. J. GILLENWATER

ISBN-13: 978-1544149240
ISBN-10: 1544149247

This book is a work of fiction. The names, characters, places, and incidents are products of the writer's imagination or have been used fictitiously and are not to be construed as real. Any resemblance to persons, living or dead, actual events, locale or organizations is entirely coincidental.

Cover art design by The Cover Collection
http://www.thecovercollection.com

First print publication: September 2011

CHAPTER ONE

Joel Hatcher grabbed the Greater Portland phone book from the derelict booth at the gas station, flipped it open and searched for the heading *Curse Removal*.

Finding nothing under *Curses*, he flipped ahead to *Spiritualist*. He scanned each ad listing, overwhelmed by choices—palm readers, tarot card specialists, mystics and astrologists—and one that said curse removal.

"This one," said a quiet voice from behind him. "This is the one you want."

He looked over his shoulder. No one was there. A streetlight flickered and buzzed. Great. So now he heard voices too. As a cursed man, though, was he so far from insanity? He shivered at the dark path his thoughts took. He needed to focus. There was no voice, only his own mind struggling to find a rational solution. To make a choice based on nothing solid, nothing real.

His gaze centered on that one listing.

Madame Eugenie—Palm Readings, Spiritual Guidance, Curse Removal.

He ripped the page out of the book, opened his cell and punched in the number. He hoped she had late hours. Very late hours. He glanced at his watch. Midnight.

When he caught sight of the pustules all over his wrist he had to look away. The oozing, cracked skin disgusted him. Made him hurt more. He tugged his sleeve down.

Five rings.

Six rings.

No answer.

Pick up.

On the seventh ring, a chipper female voice filled his ear. "Madame Eugenie…"

"Hello? I need help. Can you help me?" Joel ducked his head. It had started to rain. He headed toward his car parked by the gas pumps.

"…is here to help you with your spiritual needs. Twenty-four hours a day. Leave a message, and she will get back to you soon."

"*Goddammit.*"

Beep.

A homeless man, drinking from a bottle hidden in a paper bag, strolled by with a shopping cart. Joel pulled up the collar of his denim jacket and turned away from the streetlights, but a car drove by and the headlights illuminated his face.

The homeless man locked eyes with Joel. His face lit up with horror, and he dropped the bottle. It hit the sidewalk with a smash. The man took two steps backward and stumbled over the curb.

Joel stepped forward to help.

"Get away from me." The old man held up a defensive hand. "Don't touch me."

As he backed away from the frightened man, Joel spoke into his cell, "This is Joel Hatcher. I need your help. Could you please call me…?" He heard a click on the other end of the line.

"Hello? Are you there?"

The homeless man yelled for help, pushing his cart down the street at a full sprint.

Joel ran toward his car. "I need to see you. Now." He scanned the dark gas station to make sure no one else watched.

"Who is this?" asked the woman on the other end. "Have you been to see me before? My appointment hours are between eight and..."

"You said on the message twenty-four hours a day." Joel tucked his cell phone under his chin and slid into the driver's seat. Bluto meowed at him from the backseat.

"Yes, well, for my regular clients I am..."

The cat meowed more piteously. Joel reached back, grabbed the carrier and set it on the seat next to him.

"Is that a cat?"

In his rearview mirror the homeless man continued to run, now down the middle of the street, his shopping cart abandoned. "I can't live like this anymore." Joel adjusted the mirror. "I need help." After two days, it wasn't any easier to look at himself. Sores covered his face, neck, even his hands. He looked like the victim of a nuclear holocaust. And the pain. Like fire across his skin, flaring up from an uncomfortable sunburn to raging flames.

"Do I know you?"

"No."

"And you need help with what?"

"A curse...curses. It's too hard to explain over the phone."

Madame Eugenie paused on the other end of the line. "I have room tomorrow at nine thirty, if you'd like to stop by then..."

"I'll be there in five minutes." Joel smoothed out the yellow phone-book page on his dashboard. "775 Orchard Boulevard, right?"

"You can't come to my house *now*, are you crazy?"

He shifted his car into reverse and backed away from the gas pumps. "You're going to help me now. Not tomorrow. Not next week. Right now." As he shifted back into drive, the phone slipped from his shoulder. Orchard Boulevard was only a few miles away.

"If you show up at my door, I'll call the police." He could barely hear her voice.

The moment the cops saw his face, his arms, his hands, they'd put him in quarantine, and he'd die there with no chance to fix this curse. A modern-day leper. He hardly looked human anymore.

He pressed the gas pedal to the floor. He gritted his teeth as a flare of heat traveled down his legs, as if someone held a flaming torch to his thighs.

"You hear me? The police!"

He didn't have time to explain, didn't have time to allay her fears.

He took the last turn so sharply, his tire rolled over the curb. But he'd reached Orchard Boulevard. Help waited only a few houses away. Once she caught sight of him, she would either panic and not let him in or maybe, just maybe, she would pity him. Maybe she'd encountered someone else like him. A stirring of hope in his chest pushed him to drive faster. Bluto made one last meow, then settled in his carrier.

Gen hung up the phone. The urgency in the man's voice chilled her. Most of her clients came to her looking for guidance, for help in making difficult decisions in their lives. A palm reading over a soothing cup of tea in the afternoon. Not this. She shook off a feeling of dread.

"Who was it?" Adam asked.

His voice was only a whisper now, but it grew stronger all the time. He'd been such a comfort to her over these last few months. A voice in the dark of night when she felt so alone. Just enough Adam in order to pretend nothing had changed.

"Some man." Her heart sped up at the memory of those words: *You're going to help me now.* So desperate. "Not one of my regular clients. He said he needed my help. He's on his way over." She headed for the stairs. "I need to make sure Mother didn't wake up. She'd be frightened if she knew I was letting a stranger in so late at night."

"Let him in." Adam appeared next to her, startling her. She hadn't yet gotten used to his quick movements.

This wasn't like him. He usually couldn't wait for her clients to leave, for her to spend more time alone with him. She glanced right through his transparent body at the clock. "It's midnight."

"Let him in." This time, Adam's voice was like a caress.

"Why do you want me to do this? I don't understand."

He reached out to slide his hand along her neck, but his fingers passed through her flesh. The sudden shock of cold made her suck in her breath.

"It's okay, you don't need to worry. I'll keep you safe." His face leaned into hers. His eyes were pale, watery. "You will let him in because he can save me."

Any doubts she had about opening her door to a strange man in the middle of the night left her head. This was Adam. Her husband. The man she loved. It had been so long, she'd almost forgotten the angled planes of his face, how one ear sat just slightly higher than the other, how with one look he could send her blood boiling. She wanted that back. Forever.

In life, Adam had been her rock. The one who protected her and made her feel safe. He wouldn't let any harm come to her. "I'll let him in."

775 Orchard Boulevard was a run-down house with peeling yellow paint and a sagging porch. A darkened neon sign hung in the window—the outline of a hand with PALM READING above it and TAROT CARDS underneath.

The porch light glowed brightly, though, and Joel took that as a good sign. Looked as if she was willing to let him sit on her porch. Now all he'd have to do is convince her to let him inside.

"I'll be right back," he said to his cat. Bluto's scarred face appeared near the door of the carrier. Joel scratched the black cat's head with the tip of one finger. At least animals weren't afraid of him. They didn't care what he looked like.

Bluto gave him an answering meow.

"Chicken and giblets when I get back. I promise." The street was empty.

One streetlight flickered, on the verge of blinking out. He pulled his baseball cap low over his eyes.

He pressed the doorbell and waited either for a cop car to pull up or for Madame Eugenie to scream bloody murder. The ding-dong echoed inside the house. It was quiet. No footsteps. No creaking floorboards.

He knocked.

"It's all right, Gen."

She peeked out the window. A man, face hidden by a baseball cap, stood on her porch. "Are you sure?" Her hand trembled as she held back the lace curtain. How could this stranger help save her husband? It didn't make any sense.

Adam stood right behind her. She could imagine his warm breath on her cheek. "Yes. Trust me." His voice was soothing.

"How can this man help you?"

The hair rose on the back of her neck. She knew he hovered even closer to her now. She wanted to do what he asked, but she was still frightened. Where was the courage she used to possess before Adam died? The adventurous spirit he'd loved? Somehow in losing him she had lost herself too.

"Open the door, Gen. We need him. He's the one we've been waiting for."

Adam. Her gentle Adam. She missed his hands soft on her body, lips warm on her throat. If the strange man outside could bring her husband back to her, then she would let him in.

She reached for the doorknob.

"He's the one." The sensitive flesh along her jaw prickled at his ghostly touch. "I promise you, he's the one."

"Are you Joel?" asked someone behind the door.

"Yes." Joel stepped closer to the door and away from the bright lights on the porch. "Can you please help me, Madame?"

"You can drop the 'Madame'. Just call me Gen." The door remained closed between them. "What kind of help do you need?"

"I told you, curses. I'm cursed." He rested an arm on the doorframe. "I thought I could do this myself, but I don't have the notebooks anymore. I threw them away."

"What notebooks?"

"They came in a package. A letter and a bunch of notebooks. I thought it was trash. I threw it out... I'll explain if you just let me inside."

"Why do you think you're cursed?"

He rubbed his knuckles across his belt buckle. "Look out the window."

"What?"

"Just look at me."

"Okay..."

Narrow window panels framed the door. A slim hand brushed a lace curtain away. A face appeared—a very young face. Not what he expected. When she caught a glimpse of him her eyes widened. He tilted back his baseball cap to let her see the sores.

"Oh, my God. What's happened to you?"

To hear sympathy in someone's voice after three days of suffering, three days of loneliness, was more than he could bear. "Please. Help me."

Her face disappeared. The lock turned. Madame Eugenie, spiritualist and curse remover, let him inside.

CHAPTER TWO

"You look too young." Joel sat on a tiny padded chair in the small living room. A large poster of a palm, its parts and lines dissected, hung above the fireplace. "I expected someone older." *And not quite so pretty.*

Madame Eugenie had short blonde hair, a heart-shaped face with wide-set brown eyes and wore a long skirt, which swirled about her slim legs as she walked.

She removed scarves from a few fringed lamps and rearranged chairs that formed a circle in the middle of the room. "I had a healing this afternoon. You'll have to excuse the mess." She avoided looking at him.

When she passed by with another chair, he grabbed her hand. "Can you help me?"

She bit her lip, her face flushing, then gently pulled her hand out of his grasp. "I'm not sure. Tell me how this all began."

"A little over two weeks ago. I got a package in the mail. A box. No return address. Inside I found a letter telling me I was the next in line…only one of two left in the family…and I was cursed."

She fluttered about the room. He couldn't keep his eyes off of her. She moved like a nymph. She blew out several blood-red candles, snapped on the lights and took a seat on an antique chaise lounge. "And you believed this letter? Is that why you came to me?"

With her deep brown gaze focused on him, he lost his train of thought for a moment. "No—I didn't believe it at first."

The young woman nodded.

Joel rubbed his thumb in the palm of his opposite hand. The motion caused the sores to ooze and send out stings of pain. "I'm a software tester. I don't do this kind of stuff."

"What kind of stuff?" Gen tucked her legs under her skirt and rested her elbows on her knees.

"The supernatural. Witches, curses, werewolves..."

"Who said anything about werewolves? Was there something in the letter about that?" Her pink lips curled down in a pout.

He smiled at her response. "No, I...I just meant all that crazy nonsense. I don't believe in any of that. At least, I thought I didn't."

"Until the letter came."

"Exactly."

"So, have you always looked like this?" She nodded in his direction.

Joel tugged his sleeves down over his wrists. "That's why I'm here. This happened three days ago. I woke up like this."

"Do they hurt?"

"It comes and goes." As he said the words, his scalp felt like it was on fire. He yanked off the baseball cap and set it in his lap.

"So this is part of the curse you were talking about?"

"Yes." He reached in his jacket pocket and pulled out a crumpled sheet of lined paper. "This is all I have left." He offered it to her.

She leaned forward and gingerly took the paper from him. "What is this?" She wrinkled her brow and squinted at the writing on it.

"Part of the notebooks. I threw them away the next day. But this one piece blew out of the box and landed on my windshield. It's all I have. Don't you see? Those notebooks, they had everything I needed...the answers." The anguish he'd carried with him for the last few weeks burst out. "He gave them to me, and I just threw it all away."

Gen read the paper aloud, "'The curses. Unsure how many curses. Perhaps nine judging from the history. First was unnoticeable to me. Unlike some of the others. Matches with all family members. Curse number one, Loss of Livelihood. Thoroughly researched. Possible to combat. Requires one skilled in lifting curses. Ask for a banishing ritual. Wear amulet for protection.'"

"And that's exactly what happened. The day after I received the box, the day after I threw everything away, I got fired."

Gen glanced up at him. "A lot of people get fired."

He kept on. "Nine years at the same company. I was the best tester they had. Worked overtime when everyone else went home. It didn't make any sense. At first, I didn't make the connection. I just didn't think…"

"What amulet is he talking about?" Gen turned the paper over, as if that would hold the answers to her questions.

"I found a necklace in the bottom of the box. A piece of junk."

"And where is it now?"

"There was a fire."

She read from the front of the page. "'Curse number two. Trial by Fire.'"

"I came home, and my whole house was on fire. Three fire trucks. Smoke billowing out the windows. And the heat. The heat was so intense. I lost everything. Except Bluto."

"Bluto?"

"My cat. Well, he's my cat now. He was a stray. Used to feed him out on my back porch every night. He's out in my car."

She nodded. "And the amulet?"

"It was in my kitchen. It's all gone now. It was just a hunk of rock on a chain."

"What color rock?"

"Black. Kind of shiny. All pointy."

"Sort of like a crystal?"

"I guess."

"Magnetite."

"What?"

"Magnetite—very commonly used for protective amulets. Sounds like this distant relation of yours knew what he was talking about."

"There's nothing left in the house. Nothing." Joel wanted to rest his head in his hands, but he couldn't stand the feeling of those pustules on his face. The dripping, disgusting sores. He slipped his baseball cap back on his head.

Madame Eugenie watched him, taking in his pathetic appearance. How hard it must be for her to look at him.

She read more from the paper. "'Curse number three. Painful Pox.'"

"And here I am." He pulled up his sleeves to reveal the third curse covering his body. The curse anyone could see. Something he couldn't hide, couldn't run away from. "I thought I could handle this. When I figured out it was real—that the curses were real—I thought I could fix it on my own." He tugged the sleeves back down. "I thought I could do some reading and find a way to stop this. But I don't think I can. Please tell me you can do something...some magic or potion or whatever."

"Magic? I'm a palm reader, a psychic. Not a magician." Gen set the paper in her lap and wiped a strand of hair off her forehead. She got up from the chaise lounge. "Would you like a cup of tea?" Pushing through a beaded curtain at one end of the room, she disappeared from view.

He called after her, "Your ad said 'curse removal'. That's why I called you. Why did you let me in, if you can't help me? If you don't believe me?" He thought about his car out front that held everything he had left in the world. A cat, a suit jacket and a pair of dress shoes. In a few weeks, he would be out of money with maxed-out credit cards and nowhere to go.

Gen stopped on the other side of the beaded curtain. Joel hadn't been what she expected. Over the phone he'd sounded like a raving lunatic. She'd had her share of the mentally ill find their way to her door, but Joel's suffering was real. All over his body. Could he really be cursed?

Adam hovered near the doorway.

She made her way into the kitchen, walking through the transparent body of her husband. She shivered at the sensation. "I can't do anything for this guy."

He followed her as she prepared hot water for the tea. "I can help him, and he can help me."

"I don't understand. What does he have to do with anything?" She set two cups on a tray.

Adam floated up behind her and wrapped his ghostly arms around her waist. "A cursed man's blood is a powerful thing."

His touch was like a whisper, a gossamer strand—there one minute, gone the next. She imagined him whole again. Arms to hold her. Lips to kiss her. The warmth of his chest against her back as they lay tangled in bed together.

His words sank in. So Joel really was cursed?

"His blood instead of mine?"

"Yes," he hissed in her ear. "A cursed man's blood…" Adam's voice echoed in the room. The Resurrection Spell was wearing off again. He was losing form. The only way to bring him back would be to perform the ceremony again, but this time he wanted her to use Joel's blood. "Use the spell oil to cure him, and he'll give you anything you ask."

Adam disappeared.

Gen entered the room with a small silver tray. Two cups of steaming tea, a sugar bowl and a little pot of cream balanced on it. "When I looked out the window and saw you on the porch, there was something in your eyes." She set the tray on an upholstered footstool and looked up at him.

"Excuse me?"

"You asked me why I let you in." She added sugar to one cup. "That's why. You were lost. You needed help. I couldn't turn you away."

"Not very smart for a woman who lives alone." He took the tea cup and saucer she offered. She appeared to be as fragile and fine as her tea set.

She ignored his comment. "I'm more of a palm reader, a spiritual guide, rather than an expert in curses."

He took a sip of the bitter tea to be polite and set the dainty cup and saucer on the table next to him. "Are you trying to say you can't help me?" He thought he'd found the right person to help, but maybe he would be forced to surrender to the curses one by one and suffer the knowledge his brother would be next. He knew he wouldn't survive the last curse. Even if he could bear the other eight that came before. A blistering flare of heat enveloped his back, and he cried out, arching away from the chair.

"Are you all right?" She leapt up and rushed over to him. Her hands hovered, as if she were afraid to touch him. "Let me get something. I'll be right back."

Still groaning in agony, Joel leaned forward on his elbows. When a wave hit like this, he had to just grit his teeth and wait for it to pass.

Moments later, she knelt at his side. "Let me put some of this salve on you. It might help ease the pain."

The burning sensation on his back traveled up his neck. He could anticipate when and where new sores would appear on his skin. He imagined the pustule growing, bursting open. Three days into it. Four days left. Then the next curse, and the next one, and the next one.

Jesus.

He thought of Matt, his younger brother, in the same painful, horrible position. The young man whose tuition he could no longer afford. It was more than he could bear.

He nodded, assenting to her treatment. It couldn't hurt to try.

She unscrewed the top of an old Vaseline jar, its label faded and oily. "This has been on the shelf in my kitchen for ages. I use it for burns." She scooped up a quantity of the opaque, yellowish cream inside the jar and spread it liberally across the back of his hand. He was grateful she didn't flinch or shiver in disgust when she touched him.

Her hands were small and quick, spreading the cool of the cream which cut the heat of the sores. Not completely, but he felt minimal relief. He sniffed it. "Seems to be helping. What's in it?"

"Old family recipe." She shrugged. "This is the last of it." She held up the jar. It was half-full. She spread the salve over the sores on his arms, working it into the ruined flesh. He didn't want her to stop.

"Can you unbutton your shirt? Seems like your back is really bothering you."

The blissful feeling of the cool cream on his body motivated him to follow her orders. He didn't care so much now if she saw him. He knew the sores were worse than the last time he looked in the mirror.

When he got to the final button, she gasped. "Oh my God, how can you stand it? How can you possibly stand it?" She scooped up more salve and spread it on the bared skin of his chest. He closed his eyes for a moment. After days of hiding and only having a cat for company, a sympathetic ear and a woman's touch was too much for his battered body. He couldn't ignore her hands on his skin.

"Not like I have much of a choice." He eased out of the shirt, slipping it off one shoulder and then the next. The open wounds stuck to the fabric in some places. He peeled the material off each one, wincing. "Doctor told me I must have been out in the sun too long. Told me to try aloe vera."

"You went to the doctor?" She worked the cream up his chest and onto one shoulder. Her hands, like birds, flitted from sore to sore.

"The first day. When I woke up and had these...*things* on me." He didn't want her to stop. This little bit of relief gave him back a small piece of sanity. "I still didn't believe. The curse, I mean."

"I'm so sorry..." Gen continued to spread the salve without even glancing up at him.

"Sorry?" He laughed bitterly. "*I'm* sorry. I'm sorry I didn't listen. Didn't believe. I had all the answers in that damn box, and I just threw it away." Letting his anger take over helped get his mind off those caressing hands.

"We'll figure this out. I'll help. I've never worked on a curse like this before, but there might be something…"

He touched her arm. "Thank you." The gratitude welled up inside him. A stranger was willing to help. A complete stranger. That must mean something good, shouldn't it? That must mean he could beat this. That there was hope.

CHAPTER THREE

Gen sipped her tea. The now-empty Vaseline jar sat on the tray next to the sugar bowl. "Don't you have any family? Anyone you can go to?"

"Just a brother." Joel carefully adjusted his shirt back onto his shoulders. His thinking had cleared now that her hands no longer touched him and the pain had disappeared. "He's just a kid. A sophomore at the University of Washington."

"I see." She set her empty teacup on the tray.

A creak echoed from the entryway.

Gen looked up. A smudge of worry darkened her brow. "Come. Quickly." She grabbed Joel and dragged him by the hand through the beaded curtain into the unlit dining room beyond.

"Why?"

She pressed him into a chair at one end of the table. "Shh. Please just stay here and be quiet. I don't want to worry my mother. If she sees you here…"

He could barely see in the murky darkness.

"Gen. Where are you?" A wheezing sound drifted into the dining room. "I heard voices. Did you make me some tea?"

Gen gave Joel a hard stare then passed through the beaded curtain. "Mama, what are you doing up? It's late."

At the far end of the sitting room, through the beads, a thin woman in a nightgown clutched a blanket around her bony shoulders. "I told you. I heard voices. Are you deaf?"

"I'm just cleaning up…from this afternoon." He could understand why she wanted him to hide. A stranger was in their house late at night, and he looked like a walking disease. He kept quiet.

The old woman took Joel's chair. His half-empty teacup still sat on the table. She picked it up, sniffed at it and set it back down. "You're serving tea to the dead now, are you?"

Eugenie's back was to him. Her body stiffened at the words. "Mama."

"I told you, there's no use to it. It's been too long."

Gen cleaned up the room. She scooped his teacup off the table and plunked it on the tray. "I don't care what you say." Her voice had changed from quiet and soft to scratchy and high-pitched. "I'll find a way to make it work."

"It won't work, Gen. Do you really want to spend the rest of your life cooped up in here?"

"Stop it, Mama. You don't know everything…you don't know…"

The older woman sat back in the chair. "I know that you can't change what's meant to be. How much longer are you going to keep this up? How many more months?"

"I can't just give up." Gen's voice had quieted to a whisper.

Her mother got up from her chair and took a seat next to her daughter. "Come to bed. Sleep will help you forget."

Joel wanted to get up from his chair and help. He was a burden. She clearly had problems of her own. Serving tea to the dead? What did Gen's mother mean by that? Before this curse, he never put much stock in the supernatural. But now he looked at things with new eyes. What was Gen trying to hide?

"Leave me alone, Mama. Please. I'll be fine." She prodded her mother

17

toward the entryway and the stairs beyond. "I'll be upstairs soon."

Her mother hesitated for a moment, then touched her daughter's shoulder. "Don't stay up too late, now." She shuffled toward the stairs, wrapping the blanket more tightly around her thin body.

Joel sensed movement behind him. A touch of a hand or a brush of a shoulder. But when he turned to look, nobody was there. He shivered. This house gave him the creeps. Especially after what Gen's mother had said.

"She's gone," Gen said, her voice thick with unshed tears.

Joel shook off the odd feeling and held open the bead curtain. "Maybe it's better if I go?" He ducked his shoulders and tucked his chin to his chest. Knowing how much he looked like some horror-show nightmare, he couldn't help himself.

Her face was flushed, her eyes red, but she flashed a bit of a smile.

Gen dabbed at her eyes. "What? No, no, I don't want you to go. All that...with my mother? It's nothing. Typical mom-daughter stuff."

"You don't need to explain...I just don't want to get in the way. And it *is* late."

"I thought you wanted my help."

At her words he became aware once again of the painful sores covering his body. Back at the gas station it had seemed so simple. He could conquer this curse thing just like a glitch in a software program. Find the cause, root it out. Make the broken program whole again.

Gen had been the way to that fix, but now he realized she wasn't just some code he could insert. "It seems like maybe you have a lot going on." Just because he'd shown up on her doorstep and she'd let him in was no reason to expect she'd drop everything and help him.

"I need this." She twisted the fabric of her skirt in her fist. Lines of determination creased the sides of her mouth. "I need something else to think about right now. I want you to stay."

Joel scanned her heart-shaped face, trying to get a read on her. "All right." Maybe the sores that wracked his body distracted him from the truth—he could've sworn she was lying to him. But why would she do that?

"Good," she said. "Then let's begin."

"Let's begin?"

"Yes. A curse is something very powerful, a very ancient kind of magic. Going back as far as Roman times. Whoever laid these curses on your family was likely a witch of the highest order. Well-versed in the lore and in binding. A curse tends to be laid upon an individual, not a family. The power needed for a family curse… Is there anything you remember from the notebooks your relative sent to you? Any information about where or when this curse was laid?"

"I wish I could tell you something. I read the letter inside the box then set it out for the garbage. If it weren't for that single page from one of the notebooks—"

"You would have no idea what to expect." Gen picked up the sheet of paper he'd handed her earlier. "But you have the list, and this will help us."

She read it, this time announcing each one. "Loss of Livelihood, Trial by Fire, Painful Pox, Curse of the Mute, Bone Chill, Unquenchable Thirst, Blindness, Fatal Touch, Death Curse."

Joel shivered when she read the last one. He'd read it over and over since the sores appeared, and he'd started to believe. Wondering what each one would be like was a curse in itself. "And you know how to help me with these?"

"I can try. I have a book…" She didn't elaborate.

A flare of heat seared across his abdomen. "Goddammit." He clutched his arms around his middle. "I can't live like this."

"Relax, let me get some more tea, and then we'll try one of the oils." She swished through the beads and headed into the kitchen.

"Your mother almost ruined everything." Adam leaned against the kitchen counter with arms crossed.

Gen was surprised to see him again. He must be stronger than she thought. Each Resurrection Spell brought him one step closer to full restoration. "She's not well, and she worries about me." Her mother had an inkling, perhaps, of what she'd been dabbling in, but Adam's presence had been her secret. She wasn't ready to reveal how she was trying to fix her mistakes, make things right.

"You need to keep a better handle on her."

He was Adam in some ways, but in others...

She thought about Joel waiting in the living room and how serious his situation was. He had problems she couldn't even begin to help. But Adam would know. He'd been the one who taught her some of the secrets of black magic. "Tell me how we're going to cure him," she said.

"First, don't forget the blood. I need the blood."

"Okay, yes, the blood." She didn't mind taking some of Joel's blood if she could cure him. It was a very complex curse, but she had faith Adam would know what to do. "And then we cure him, right?" She cranked up the stove and set a fresh pot of water on it.

"No."

His answer gave her pause. This wasn't what she'd agreed to. "What do you mean, no?"

"We keep him."

She stared at him. "We can't keep him, for God's sake. You can't just kidnap a man off the street."

Adam floated to her. His hand pressed against her mouth, quieting her. "Shh, it's okay. You want me back, don't you?"

She nodded. His hand was like a brand of ice.

"You want us to be together again, right?"

Her eyes were hot with unshed tears. She looked into her husband's bloodless, transparent face. She'd missed him with a sharp, terrible pain she didn't want to feel ever again.

She nodded again. If Adam wanted her to choose, she'd choose him every time. She tried to separate her pity for Joel from her logical mind. If Adam needed Joel's blood, that should be her first and most important task. Healing Joel would be second.

He took his hand away, his face now inches from hers. "Then we keep him. Don't worry. He won't even know it." His body grew less visible. "I'll give you the cure for the Painful Pox, and then he'll trust you. Do whatever you ask." He lifted his hand and stared at it. "I need his blood, Gen." He showed her how his fingers vanished, turning into smoke. "I need his blood."

He disappeared, leaving only a wisp of mist behind.

The pain was intense, crippling. A new pustule erupted on Joel's belly, like a cigarette burn to his skin, with a crawling sensation as the pustule rose up and burst, oozing pus and blood. He reached for the Vaseline jar and hoped some of the soothing salve would be left. Another jolt of pain hit him, and he knocked the jar to the floor. It was empty.

Gen entered with the tray. "Here. Sit. Drink your tea."

He clutched his stomach. "I don't want any more tea." Couldn't she see he was in pain?

"It's cleansing."

"It's crap-tasting hot water." He pushed the cup and saucer away. The constant struggle to stay above the pain, to stay sane, ate away at his patience.

Gen stood there, holding the two saucers with their brimming cups of tea, steam rising. She blinked and set them on the footstool.

"I'm sorry," Joel said. "I'm not usually this touchy."

"It's okay. I understand."

"No, you're trying to help, and I just bit your head off."

She smiled. "Let's skip the second cup of tea. Come with me. There are a few things back here that I want to try."

"Back where?" He followed.

"Don't worry. It's just my pantry."

In the kitchen she directed him to a stool behind a breakfast bar. "I keep all my oils and things in here." She opened a tall cabinet door next to the fridge. Inside were row upon row of small tincture vials, unmarked bags of what looked like tea and a shelf full of candles in a variety of sizes and colors.

"Whoa. That's quite a collection you've got going."

"I don't use it often. Most of my business is the readings." She turned a few of the glass vials to read the labels. "When's your birthday?"

"July thirtieth, why?"

"A Leo…well how perfect is that?" She removed one of the vials from the pantry and set it on the counter in front of him.

"What's this?"

"Hold on a minute. And one more thing we could try…" She turned back toward the shelves. "Jupiter, Moon, Uranus…ah ha." With a flourish, she set another small vial on the counter.

Joel picked it up and read the faded label. "Mars Spell Oil?"

Gen ignored his question and returned to the pantry shelves. "A little bit of incense, and we're all set."

When she set a plastic baggie full of small brown cones on the counter, he asked, "So what is all this for?"

"A healing spell." She unzipped the baggie, took out one of the cones and put it in a small brass dish on the counter. "This is incense. In order for the spell oil to work, its effects need to be drawn out in the smoke of the incense." Uncapping the vial of Mars Spell Oil, she dripped a small quantity of the liquid on the incense cone.

"And this is supposed to make these"—he lifted his sore-covered arms and hands—"go away? Just like that?"

Without looking up from the incense, she said, "Do I sense some lingering doubts?" After lighting the cone with a match, she covered everything with the burner's lid. "*You* called *me*, remember?"

He erased any lingering doubts out of his head. She'd taken him in and given him the cooling salve. Why not trust her cure might work? "If this heals me, then what? What do we do about the next curse? And the next one?" Panic rushed in. The long list of nine curses repeated over and over in his head. He couldn't forget them. Mapping them out in his mind. Week after week a new affliction on the horizon…until…the *Death Curse*.

Her words, spoken so softly, grounded him. "Most of the curses on the list I'm unfamiliar with. The specifics, I mean. But I can do research." As she talked, scented smoke rose from the burner.

"Research?"

"I keep a small library of books." She tugged Joel's sleeve. "Now, put your hands into the smoke."

Doing as instructed, he settled his hands in the small spiral of smoke. The scent made him feel lightheaded, odd.

"Close your eyes."

Gen chanted under her breath. He couldn't catch the words, but they sounded foreign. The scented smoke grew thicker, choking. It seemed an eternity he sat there with his hands poised over the incense burner. Her hand brushed against his. Then again.

"It's done." A note of wonder lifted her voice. She grasped his hands in hers, her excitement palpable in her touch.

Instead of pain, he felt nothing. He opened his eyes. The open wounds on his hands and forearms had sealed up, healed. He turned his hands over in wonder. "How is that possible?" He took the cap off his head. "A mirror. Do you have a mirror?"

Gen blinked at him, her eyes round and wide. "In the dining room."

Joel jumped off the stool and rushed into the darkened dining room.

"The switch is on the wall," she called after him.

He groped for it. A dusty chandelier lit up the room. A mirror above the sideboard reflected his image. His perfect, unaltered image. He touched his face and stepped closer, unbelieving. Instead of red pustules covering his face and neck, he had a few days' growth of brown beard on his chin and cheeks, his eyes were bright blue and free of their bleary redness.

Madame Eugenie was his miracle worker. His healer. His savior.

CHAPTER FOUR

In the mirror, Joel caught sight of Gen. "You did it. How did you do that? I can't believe…I didn't think—"

She came up behind him, studying the reflection of his face, and seemed as shocked as he. "I knew I had the gift, but I never thought I could do something like this." She touched his healed hand.

"Well, you're a genius." He turned away from his reflection. "Thank you for this. Thank you." He reached for his wallet. "What do I owe you?" He thought about his dwindling supply of cash. She deserved every dime he had if she could rid him of this curse and spare his brother the same fate.

Her brow crinkled. "Owe me?"

"Yes, you do this for a living, right? It's a service, and I want to pay you for it." Being healed made him feel lighter than air. As if he could conquer everything.

Her brow wrinkled with some complex emotion. "You don't owe me anything."

"But I showed up in the middle of the night—practically forced my way in here. I must owe you something."

"We can talk about it tomorrow."

"Tomorrow?"

"The rest of the curses. You *do* want my help with that, don't you?"

The lightness departed. This was just the beginning. "What time?"

"Let's say ten."

He thought about the pouring rain outside and how cold his car would be in the forty-degree temperature. But at least he wouldn't be writhing in pain and discomfort the whole night. "You're on."

"Then we can look at the rest of the list. See what we can do."

Next Monday, the fourth curse would befall him. "Maybe we can find a way to end it. Finish this thing once and for all before it's too late." He had every confidence in this spiritualist. She healed his sores. What couldn't she do? She was a miracle worker as far as he was concerned.

"Too late?"

"I mean, before the next curse." She didn't need to know about Matt. Why bring his brother into this? Joel would take care of everything just like he always did. Just like a big brother was supposed to do. He'd always watched out for Matt, and this situation would be no exception. His parents would have expected no less from him.

"I'll do my best." She yawned. "But for now, I think we both need to get some rest." She led him back into the sitting room where just minutes ago he was suffering and in pain.

"All right. Ten o'clock."

"Ten."

At the door, he hesitated. The rain still came down in torrents. His dark car huddled next to the curb, but at least Bluto waited in there for him. He wasn't completely alone.

"Good night, Joel. I'm glad I could help." She extended her slim hand.

He gripped it and gave a quick shake. A business deal. They were cementing a business deal. That was it. As he walked down the front path to his car, though, he couldn't help but rub his fingers against his palm, thinking of her cool fingers gripping his hand and her small pixie face adorned with a slight smile.

25

Gen leaned against the door for a moment. Joel without his sores was more handsome than she'd thought. Dark hair that curled around his ears, bright blue eyes, tall, solid frame. So unlike Adam had been—dirty blond, elf-like features, long, slender hands.

"Did you get it?" Adam's voice was a bare whisper in her ear. The spell had almost worn off. His body was an outline in the dim light.

"Yes." She slipped her hand into the pocket of her skirt and pulled out a handkerchief stained with Joel's blood.

"That's all you have?"

"It should be enough." She'd felt badly enough deceiving Joel. He was suffering, and to take something from him without asking…

"I need more than that. Why did you let him go? I told you, we need to keep him."

"He's coming back tomorrow. He thinks I can help cure him."

Adam laughed. "You can. Clever Gen. He's played right into the perfect trap."

"He's already in pain, frightened. I can't be the one to cause him more harm." She only wanted her husband back. Whole again. Maybe she asked for too much. Bringing someone back from the dead shouldn't be easy. The Resurrection Spell made it sound so simple. Some blood, a bit of his ashes. But over the months she'd begun to realize how much life it took from her too. "You must know how to help him. Why can't you both get what you want out of this?"

"Have you forgotten why I brought him here?"

"You brought him here?" She thought Adam had only limited abilities. He'd seemed tethered to her from the very first ceremony. What else was he keeping from her? "How did you…?"

"It doesn't matter. I found him. He's here to help me, not the other way around. Don't you want me back? Don't you want things the way they used to be?"

Gen picked up a framed photo on the hall table. She and Adam—

smiling, happy, full of life. She traced a finger around his face. He was her whole world. She'd never let anything come between them then…and wouldn't let it happen now. She erased the doubts from her mind. "Yes, you're right. It doesn't matter. Come, let's do the ceremony. Will you stay with me tonight this time?"

A cool breeze caressed her cheek. Adam.

"I'll stay as long as I can."

Gen smiled, tucked the bloodied handkerchief back in her pocket and followed the white ghostly blur of her husband up the stairs. He would stay, and maybe her nightmares would finally leave her.

~ * ~

Me-e-ow.

The slight weight of two cat paws on his chest woke Joel. Bluto leapt to the floor. Joel stretched and worked out a cramp in his neck. Never a very good idea to sleep in a car. He couldn't stretch out because of his height, had no blanket and the emergency brake had poked into his back most of the night. But it was the best sleep he'd gotten in four days. No sores. No painful bursts of heat.

Meow.

Bluto, his one good eye blinking at him in the early morning glare, tapped on his leg with one paw.

"I get it, I get it. You're hungry." He rubbed the sleep out of his eyes and scrounged around in the back of the car for cat food.

When he dumped a small pile on the floor next to Bluto, the cat scooped it up hungrily, purring and swallowing at the same time.

Joel ran his fingers through his hair and glanced at his watch. Eight in the morning. Another couple of hours until his meeting with Gen. He glanced at her house. Last night he'd thought about driving away, parking somewhere else for the night so she wouldn't know he'd slept in his car. But he'd been so tired. After the thrill of being healed—the miracle of the oil and smoke—tiredness had overtaken him rather quickly. Days of suffering had exhausted his body.

His stomach growled. He pulled out his wallet and looked at the bills inside. Fifty-two dollars and some change, plus a Visa card with a dwindling amount of available credit. Everything he had left. The money in his bank account was for Matt. He had to save that. It wasn't his to squander because of his condition. He could make do with very little if he had to. He'd done it before.

In the cup holder sat a carry-out cup of coffee from the day before. He picked it up and sloshed it around. A swig or two of liquid was left. He drank it down, trying not to gag at the cold, overly sweet coffee. One too many packets of sugar and a few too many hours of sitting in his car, but it satisfied the empty space in his stomach.

A skinny guy in jeans and a ratty sweatshirt drove up on a scooter. He pulled into Gen's drive and put up the kickstand. Another customer, perhaps? The guy took off his helmet and hung it on the handlebars.

On his way up the walk, Gen opened the front door. This morning she had a pink scarf wrapped around her head, which overpowered her small face. She wore dangling gold earrings, another long skirt with volumes of fabric and a tank top, which revealed thin, white arms and the curves of her breasts.

After ushering her customer into the house, she scrutinized Joel's car for a second. To get a better look inside, she leaned down. Their eyes met.

Bluto jumped on the passenger seat and butted his head against Joel's thigh, begging for attention.

Gen gave him a confused-looking smile, waved, stepped back inside and closed the door.

"Bluto," he said, scratching the beaten-up cat on top of his bony head, "please tell me she doesn't think I'm a nut." He laughed. "How could a woman who reads palms for a living think *I'm* the nut?"

While he waited for his appointment, he picked up his cell phone. He'd turned it off last night so he could get some sleep.

Two messages.

He switched on the speaker function and set it on the dash while he petted Bluto. The cat dug his claws into his pant leg.

"This is an automated message. Your Wirenet service will be disconnected on…Friday…March…Twenty-first…for nonpayment. If you would like to pay your bill—"

He skipped to the next message.

"Hey, bro. Where are you? I tried calling the house. Anyway, spring break's coming up next week. Thought I would crash with you instead of going to L.A. with Jonesy. Yeah, I know. Spending time with the big brother instead of watching chicks on the beach. Sounds crazy, huh? I've got this project I need to finish, and it just made more sense to come home. So call me."

Matt was coming home next week. Coming home to a house that no longer stood there. How in the hell would Joel tell him there was nowhere to come home to? That he was living in his car and…he couldn't tell him. Not yet. Not until he fixed this mess he was in, got a job, started making money again. He wouldn't fail him. He wouldn't let him know his big brother had screwed things up for him and his future. All because of some damned curse.

Bluto meowed and purred, rubbing up against his hand.

"Wish I were a cat. All you have to worry about is your next meal." He petted the ratty-looking cat from head to tail and cringed when the claws dug in deeper. "We can figure this out, can't we? Daddy's gotta give his cat a home."

Meow.

Bluto agreed and lay down next to Joel in a ball of black fur.

CHAPTER FIVE

"So tell me what you know about your family history," Gen said. She sat on the chaise lounge again with her legs tucked under her skirt, a cup of tea in her hand. "In order to figure out how to end the curse, I need to know more."

Was there any time this woman didn't want to drink tea?

Joel looked down at his teacup and set it aside on the table. "My parents are dead."

"I'm sorry."

"Don't be sorry. It was a long time ago. My mom had cancer. My dad had some heart trouble…"

"You don't need to explain."

Joel was glad for that. His father hadn't been the same after his mother died. He just let the disease take him, didn't even try to fight it. He cleared his throat. "Now it's just my brother and me." He hadn't meant to tell her about Matt, but she seemed so caring, so concerned.

"I see. What I really wanted was some past history. You say you got this box from a relative."

"He said he was a distant relative in the letter. A cousin maybe or a second cousin, whatever those are. My brother and I are apparently the last in the family. The end of the curse. Once I'm dead and…" He couldn't say the words. He couldn't even think about his brother being next in line.

"Let's not think about that part of it right now. If we find out where in your family's past this curse came from, perhaps we can figure out a way to end it."

"You do know there's only a few days before the next curse? By Monday, it's the Curse of the Mute, and I'm guessing we pretty much know what that means."

"That's why anything you can tell me about your family history right now is so important."

A shuffle of footsteps in the entryway interrupted them. "Gen, I told you I need my medicine. It's acting up again."

"Excuse me." Gen swept out of the room, her skirt swirling around her bare feet. "Mother, I'm with a client. Can you just get it yourself? You know the dosage."

Joel explored the living room while he waited. He studied the poster on the wall, the one with the graphic of the hand and all the parts of the palm detailed. He skimmed his finger over the lifeline on the chart, following the curve across the palm and between the thumb and forefinger. Lifting up his palm, he traced his own lifeline. Unlike the drawing, his lifeline faded in the middle, a bare crease in his skin.

"Do you want me to do a reading for you?"

He tucked his hand in his pocket and turned to see Gen standing in the doorway.

"Sorry about that. My mother can be a handful sometimes." She nodded toward the stairs.

"That's all right."

She closed the distance between them and took hold of his free hand.

At first, he pulled away. "Oh, I don't know. I really don't think—" Her fingers were gentle and cool.

"This is an interesting palm. Did you know no two hands are the same?

Just like a fingerprint." She skimmed her index finger across the different lines on his palm. "Aristotle wrote a book on palmistry."

"He did?" The touch of her fingers on his sensitive skin soothed him, like a lover's caress. He tightened his jaw. Why did he feel this connection to her? Why did he trust her so easily?

She gestured to a small table and chairs in one corner of the room. When they both were sitting, she took his hand again and drew it across the table, resting it on the surface. She brushed her hand across his, studying it. "'If the Hand be soft and long, and lean withal, it denotes the Person of a good Understanding, a Lover of Peace, and Honesty.' You have a very nice hand. Very clear and easy to read."

"Was that Aristotle?"

"Yep."

He studied her as she bent over his hand. The bright scarf twisted into a knot at the side of her head, the sweep of her lashes, the earrings swinging with a pleasant jingle. "Does it tell you how this all ends up? Does it tell you about this curse?"

She curled his fingers toward the middle of his palm and set his hand gently on the table. "Palm reading doesn't predict the future. Palm reading reveals your true character. You can't hide from me, Joel Hatcher."

Her last statement made him uncomfortable. He felt naked sitting there. She may say he was a lover of peace and honesty, but she knew so little about him. Did she always trust her palm readings so implicitly? "I never said I had anything to hide."

"True." She paused. He could read in her eyes she had something more to say, but didn't. "But back to your family history. What do you know of your family tree?"

"Not much. I can get you as far back as my grandparents, but that's about it. I don't remember anyone discussing a family curse or anyone dying under mysterious circumstances."

"Then we'll need to go to the library. I really need to get out of this house for a while." She looked over her shoulder toward the stairs. "Come on. If we don't know your history, we won't know how to stop this. 'If you want to understand today, you have to search yesterday.'"

"More Aristotle?"

"No, Pearl Buck."

Joel thought of his brother's voicemail message. About how he expected to come home this weekend for spring break. He needed to have this thing taken care of before Matt got here. Right now Gen was his only hope. "So where's the library?"

"Not too far. And we're taking your car."

Bluto meowed when Joel opened the passenger side door.

"Your cat?" Gen asked.

A blur of black fur jumped over the front seat into the back.

Joel grimaced. "He's a little skittish."

"I can see that." She sat, grabbed the length of her long skirt and pulled it in next to her.

"Until the fire, he wouldn't even let me get close to him." He climbed behind the wheel.

"Did you know in Egypt black cats are considered to be good luck?"

"No. But if that's the case, Bluto's not doing his job very well."

She touched his hand—those cool small fingers again. "But you're alive. You could have very well died in that fire."

"I suppose."

Her hand lingered for a few moments. He didn't want to move. He liked the feel of her hand on his.

A dented Honda Civic with a missing back bumper sat in the drive. "So is that car yours or…?"

"If you can call it a car." She pulled her hand away, and his heart fell just a little. "That's been sitting there for months. Ever since…well, for a long time now."

"Why don't you get it fixed?" He started the car and drove down the street.

"I don't want to," she snapped.

Joel raised an eyebrow.

"I'm sorry. Can we just drop it? I don't mind walking or riding my bike. The store's not too far away." She twisted her hands in the fabric of her skirt. "Turn here, the library's a few miles down this block on the left."

He made the turn. Bluto howled from the back. "He doesn't like the car all that much."

She peered over her shoulder. "So why do you keep him in here, then?"

He didn't want to tell her he was living in his car. "They don't let me leave him in the motel room. My insurance covers the stay, but not any damage my cat might do." She didn't need to know he had no insurance. Three months ago when he had to make a choice between Matt's tuition and paying his insurance bill, it had been a no-brainer.

"It's all right, kitty-kitty. We're almost there," she sing-songed.

Joel pulled into the parking lot.

Bluto jumped over the seat and landed between them.

"Hey, precious," she cooed, scratching the cat between his ears.

"Did you wear pâté perfume this morning? He's not too keen on strangers."

"He's such a good little kitty." Bluto purred and dug his claws into the seat. "My mother used to say I had a way with animals." She gave him one last pat before they got out of the car. "We'll need to get a subscription to FamilyQuest. It's one of those genealogy websites."

He thought about his dwindling cash supply. "How much will that cost?"

"Oh, probably nineteen ninety-nine or something like that."

Twenty dollars. He could dip into his savings and hope that if they could break the curse, it wouldn't matter anymore.

The library on Thursday midday didn't have many patrons. A homeless-looking man sat in the periodicals section reading yesterday's *Oregonian*. A woman with two small boys searched through the children's section, mulling over Dr. Seuss books.

Gen pulled up a stool next to the nearest computer console. "Do you have a credit card?" She typed in the web address.

Joel handed her the one card that wasn't maxed out.

"Joel S. Hatcher. What's the S stand for?" She typed in his credit-card information.

"Simon. If I had been a girl, they were going to name me Simone."

"You don't look like a Simone." Gen smiled at him, then turned back to the screen. "Address?"

He rattled off his address information, thinking about the burned-out remnants of his once cozy home. His parents' home. He would have to call Matt soon and explain about the fire. Explain why he hadn't called. Explain how nothing remained of their mother and father and their life before…

"Okay, we're in." Gen scooted her stool closer to the monitor. "Let's start with your father's side. What was his name?"

"Charles Allen Hatcher. His parents were Rita and Edward."

"Here he is. Born January 1953?"

"That's him." Joel leaned in closer.

"Okay, then, we can print this. Did your relative give you any clue as to how far back this went?"

"I think he said eighty years? Or eighty-five?"

"Let's go with ninety. Just in case. That would be 1919. So we should probably go back to your great-grandparents. It would be their generation." She clicked and typed until she found what she was looking for. "This has both your grandmother's family and your grandfather's family." She selected print.

"Wait a minute." Joel pointed to a branch of the family tree. "See this here? My grandmother's sister? I know I still have cousins in Oklahoma. Alive and well. The letter told me that my brother and I were the last in line."

Gen clicked back to the start page. "Mother's name?"

"Caroline DeVries Hatcher. She used her maiden name as her middle name."

"Got it. What's her birth date?"

"October 1955."

"Born in Calvin City, Oregon. That's not too far from here. Along the coast, right?"

"Yep. She's a native Oregonian. My great-grandfather was part of the DeVries Lumber operation out there."

"The big paper manufacturer?"

"Well, back before my grandpa's day it was mostly lumber. They owned some of the largest timber stands in the state. They branched out into paper in the forties, I think. Right around World War II. My grandpa was just a distant relation. You know a cousin or something, but he owned a bit of stock. Sold it off in the early fifties to put a down payment on his house."

"Nowadays that stock would probably be worth a pretty penny. Well, that makes this research a bit easier. There should be plenty of detailed information on a family with that kind of background."

Gen scanned through the pages of genealogical history and printed up several of them. "We have to pick these up at the front desk."

Joel's cell phone rang.

The young mother in the children's section narrowed her eyes at him. So did the librarian standing behind the counter.

"Um, let me take this outside. I'll meet you in the parking lot."

"All right." Gen shut down the website and headed for the front desk.

Once Joel was out of earshot, Gen sensed Adam's presence.

"You need to go with him to Calvin City." His voice was quiet and breathy in her ear.

She shivered at the sensation.

"I can't go—what would I tell my mother? And how would I convince Joel to let me tag along?"

Only a few people stood in line at the front desk. The man in front of her eyed her intently. Gen turned away from him and pretended to cough.

"Your mother will be fine. Tell her it's for a job. Money. She'll be okay with that. She knows the game. As for our cursed man, he trusts you. Do you really think it will be that hard?"

"He hardly knows me," she whispered. His orders made her uncomfortable. It had been hard enough deceiving Joel last night so she could take some of his blood, but to push herself on him even further? It didn't feel right.

"You cured him."

"With your guidance."

"You have to go to Calvin City. There's something there that we need." An invisible hand touched her cheek. "I need. Would you go for my sake?"

She leaned into his touch. How was it that with just a touch, just a memory of what they used to have, she would do anything for him? Leave behind her better judgment. Had it always been this way with him? "Yes. I would go for you."

"Good," he whispered, his voice growing fainter. "It won't be long now. I promise you."

Joel's phone rang again. He pushed through the glass doors to get outside and away from the annoyed library patrons. "Hello?"

"Hey, bro. It's me."

Matt. He had hoped to avoid his brother's call until he had time to break the news about the house, about spring break. "Uh, hey there. How are you doing? How's class?"

"Did you get my message?"

"Yeah—"

"So is that okay with you? I didn't think you'd mind, but I didn't want to just show up on the doorstep unannounced. I wanted to make sure you stocked up on mac 'n' cheese and beer."

"You're nineteen, Matt."

"The beer's for you, of course."

"Of course. But about next week—"

"Is something wrong?"

Joel didn't have the heart to tell him, so he lied. "I'm actually going to be on a—a road trip." Where did that come from?

"You are? Well, that's okay. I have the keys to the house, I can just hang there by myself. I mean, I've got this huge project to work on, and I can make sure to feed Bluto for you."

"Actually," he said, digging himself an even deeper hole, "I was hoping you'd come with me."

"Come with you? Where are you going?"

Gen tapped him on the shoulder, a small stack of papers in her hands.

"Uh, can I call you back, Matt? I've got to get going..."

"But where's this trip?"

"I'll call you later today."

"But, Joel—"

He hung up the phone. What the hell was he thinking? What trip? Shit.

CHAPTER SIX

Joel tucked the cell phone into his front pocket. What the hell was he supposed to do now?

Gen showed him the printed-out papers. "We should be able to find what we need..." She stopped short. Clearly, he wasn't hiding his feelings very well. "Is everything all right?"

"Yeah, no problem. Just a little issue I need to deal with later on." *Liar.*

"Okay." It didn't sound like she believed him. "Then why don't we go somewhere to sit and look this over."

"Back to your place?"

"My mother is not in what you'd call the best of moods today."

Joel's phone rang. He looked at the screen. Matt again. He switched off the phone.

"Do you need to answer that?"

"It can wait."

"There's a coffee place right down the road."

He'd probably be expected to pick up the tab. The least he could do was buy her a cup of coffee. She hadn't said a word about any compensation for her help. But with only a few dollars to his name, even spending ten bucks on a couple of lattes hurt. "Sure. Coffee it is."

"Great. I'm dying for some caffeine."

If she liked caffeine so much, Joel wondered why she spent all her time drinking herbal tea.

~ * ~

"So it looks like we'll be going to Calvin City."

Joel practically spit out his coffee. "What?"

They sat in a small coffeehouse along a busy street. Since the day was unusually warm for March in the Pacific Northwest, the door stood open, letting in a nice breeze and the sounds of the lunchtime commute.

"We can't do any more with our research." She held up a piece of the printout with pencil markings all over it. Two mugs of coffee sat on the table along with an untouched plate of chocolate-dipped biscotti. "Your mother's side of the family was very much entrenched there. For years. Our best bet is to go there and see if we can find out more. Maybe there's an historical society there. Or someone who might know the history of your family. Looks like up until forty years ago, there were a lot of DeVrieses around there."

"And none anymore?" Saying it aloud gave him the creeps. The whole DeVries family had just disappeared from Calvin City in the late fifties—a few years after his mother was born. Could it really be true he and his brother were the last living members of the DeVries family?

"None in Calvin City, anyway. The local library will probably have more information. It's too far from Portland to have any small town news make it into the city paper. We'd probably spend a heck of a long time searching through boxes of microfiche to find anything. It would be a lot faster to just go there."

There was the road trip. Matt would have to come with them. But how would he explain? Why in the heck would he be traveling to some small city in the middle of the Oregon coast for no reason? With a petite blonde woman who liked to read palms and wear large hoop earrings and scarves. "My brother's going to come with us."

"He is?"

"Yes. And he can't know what we're doing."

"You mean you haven't told him what's happened to you?"

"Right, as if I can just tell him, Hey, I'm cursed. And guess what? You're next on the list." He sat back in his chair and ran a hand through his hair. "He's just a kid. I'm in charge of him. He's my responsibility."

"So when your parents died, you raised your brother alone?"

Joel couldn't look at her.

"And you were just a kid then..." A softness tinged her words.

"We're not talking about me." His jaw tightened. He wasn't looking for pity. He'd had enough of that after they'd buried his father. "We're not telling my brother what's going on because you're going to help me get rid of this damned curse once and for all. End it. He doesn't need to know about any of it. Got it?"

She set the papers on the table and took hold of his hand. "If that's what you want, it's not any of my business to tell your brother. I just wonder how we're going to keep it from him."

Her hands were so small and pale against his. How could it be this slip of a woman could have the power to help him? He curled his fingers into his palm and pulled his hand away.

"Let me figure that one out. You just figure out how to save me—how to save my brother."

"So, when are we going to leave on our little trip?" She picked up a biscotti, dipped it in her coffee and took a bite.

"Saturday morning."

She swallowed. "But that only gives us a couple of days before the next—"

"I have faith in you, Gen." He thought back to the magical healing smoke. The way the sores cleared up in a matter of moments.

"But, Joel—"

"We don't have any other choice." He pressed his thumb into his palm. "This is how it has to work. We wait for my brother, and then we leave."

"All right." Gen held his gaze. "We wait for your brother."

CHAPTER SEVEN

With its red roof and unusual rounded wing at one end, Union Station in Portland looked like a Bavarian castle. In the center rose a clock tower, five stories high. A very impressive structure for such an outdated mode of transportation.

Joel parked his car in the short-term lot. "You wait here." Rain drummed on the roof. "I have to explain to him what's going on."

"I thought you already explained it to him." Gen had surprised him by appearing on her porch that Saturday morning wearing jeans, tennis shoes and a red rain jacket. No flowery skirts. No hoop earrings.

"I explained we're going on a road trip, but I didn't explain why you were coming along. Don't worry, I'll think of something."

She sat in the backseat with Bluto in her lap. That cat had attached to her faster than flies to honey. Gen's mother had been right, she had a way with animals. "Well, go get him then. His train should be pulling in any second."

Tugging his baseball cap lower, he jogged through the storm and into the station. Grateful for the shelter, he looked out at the driving rain. Yesterday's unusual sun and warmth had given way to the typical cold and rain of March. Cold, miserable, gray. Just like he felt. Time was ticking. Less than forty-eight hours remained before the next curse took hold of him, and he was positive now that would happen. He'd suffered enough to know the curses were real.

The squealing of a train's brakes announced the arrival of the train from Seattle. Joel made his way to the platform. Nerves turned his stomach into a fluttering mess.

A trickle of passengers spilled out of the train cars. The six fifteen train from Seattle to Portland on a Saturday morning was not the most popular commute. But his brother took the train every time he came home. When Joel was employed he'd had enough money to pay for Matt's tuition, but not quite enough to pay for a car. Matt had seemed okay with it. Always took their lack of finances in stride. He was a good kid.

Joel caught sight of his brother immediately. Matt was tall, like his brother, and wore his bright red Trail Blazers cap, faded from repeated washings, but still easily visible amongst the small crowd of travelers.

"Matt! Hey, ya. Over here." He waved at his younger brother, a very good likeness of his father with his long nose, thin lips and hollowed-out cheeks.

Matt saw him and gave him a thumbs up, a large duffle bag slung across one shoulder. Probably full of dirty laundry. Even if they were planning to be on the road, Matt more than likely would insist they find someplace along the way to wash his clothes.

"Hey, bro. How've you been?" He clapped Joel on the back. A few days ago, the brotherly gesture would have caused severe pain, but today it was as if nothing had happened to him over the last four weeks. Having Matt here made all the bad stuff seem a million miles away.

"I've missed you, bud." He grabbed for Matt's heavy bag.

"I've got it, old man. Don't want you straining your back on my account. Where'd you park? Let's get this show on the road." They headed toward the stairway. "A trip down the coast, huh? What made you suddenly want to take a vacation?"

"It's more of a working vacation."

"A traveling software tester? That's a new one."

Once up the stairs, they made their way back to the front entrance. The other passengers had disappeared to the luggage area or out into the parking lot.

"Yeah, well, there's a few businesses that use our products, and they wanted to send out an expert to check on some problems with the newest release." His lies echoed in the high-ceilinged vestibule. "I volunteered. I thought if you weren't coming home for spring break—"

"Sorry about that. It was a last-minute thing. Jonesy is kind of a party animal."

Joel raised an eyebrow.

"I mean"—he switched his heavy bag to his other shoulder—"he's just not the type who would understand me backing out of something because I had to stay in the motel room to work on a paper."

"There should be plenty of downtime for you to work while I'm doing what I need to do." Joel was grateful his brother would have something to keep him busy and indoors while he and Gen did their research. "Oh, and I had to bring a coworker along with me."

"Another tester? Who, Dave?"

"Uh, no, not Dave. A salesperson. She's—"

"She? You're bringing a girl along on the Hatcher Brothers' road trip?" He socked Joel in the arm. Hard. "Is she hot?"

"What?" He thought of Gen sitting in the back of his car with Bluto in her lap. In her jeans and rain jacket she looked no more than fifteen. His face heated. "No, she's not…she's a coworker. She's just coming along to deal with the customers. Jeez, Matt."

"Oh, she must be hot. I can read you like the back of my hand, bro." Matt shot ahead of him out the door and into the parking lot. "Where'd you park? I'd like to meet this *coworker*."

Joel ran to catch up. The last thing he needed was his hormone-driven younger brother hitting on his spiritualist. "Matt, wait."

Matt was already loading his bag into the trunk when Joel caught up to him. Gen, her rain hood pulled up over her short blonde hair, stood outside next to him. They were chatting.

God, she better not have screwed up his cover story by talking about some weird mumbo jumbo. She looked nothing like a salesman.

"Hey, guys." Joel tried to catch his breath.

Matt slapped him on the back. "Looks like you're out of shape. Better get back in the gym."

Joel shook off his brother's hand. "I see you met Gen. Best salesman we have."

"Salesperson, I think you mean." Matt winked at Gen. "Yeah, I hope you don't mind if I introduced myself. Since we're going to be spending a lot of time together in the car, I thought I better make friendly." This time, he winked at Joel. Thank the Lord Gen didn't see.

"Matt told me how surprised he was you were bringing a woman along," Gen said. "Says you don't get out much." The rain slowed down to a fuzz, and she wiped stray droplets off her nose.

Joel gave his brother a hard look. "I'm pretty dedicated to my job. I don't have a lot of time to just sit around."

"So socializing is a waste of time?"

Matt quirked a smile at the mild-mannered argument he'd started and opened the front passenger door for Gen.

"Oh, I don't mind sitting in the back with Bluto." Gen popped open the door to the backseat.

"You have her sitting in the back with the maniac? Are you nuts, Joel?" Matt glanced through the rain-spattered window to get a look at the black cat.

"He's sweet," Gen said. "A very good kitty—" She slid into her seat.

"A very good kitty?" Matt gave Joel an astonished glance. "Are you crazy, woman? He nearly scratched my arm off last time I tried to touch him. I'm surprised you managed to get him in the car without being ripped to shreds."

Joel closed the back door once Gen was inside. "He likes her for some reason. She's got a way with animals."

Gen, watching the two brothers through the window, didn't think Joel and Matt looked very much alike. They were both tall—Matt being a few inches taller than his older brother—but the similarities ended there.

Matt had a more solid build, wider shoulders and an angled bony face, but he did have the same kindness in his eyes—eyes that said *trust me, believe me.*

"Two for the price of one," Adam whispered in her ear. He'd kept himself invisible, but she could sense his presence on the seat next to her.

Bluto hissed and hid under the driver's seat.

"Excuse me?"

"We might be able to use them both." He didn't elaborate. "You brought the ashes with you?"

"Of course. They're right here." She patted a large shoulder bag which sat in her lap. "I'm running out of the leaves… And the next curse, I need the cure for it." As long as Adam traded his knowledge for Joel's blood, she would go along with the plan. Both sides won that way.

"Don't worry. I know. It's taken care of."

Adam's presence was gone.

Joel stood outside the car with his brother, anxious to be on their way. When he moved to get into the car, though, Matt stopped him.

"So, this is the high-powered sales chick they sent with you?" Matt nodded at Gen. "It doesn't look like she could sell lemonade in the desert."

"Trust me. She's got some incredible skills." He thought of her cool fingers tracing the lines in his palm. "She's definitely earned herself this trip."

"If you say so. At least she's nice to look at."

"Matt…" His voice rose in warning.

"What? Can't a guy appreciate a beautiful woman? I won't bother her, I promise." Matt climbed into the car, leaving Joel standing in the drizzle.

Beautiful? He never thought to categorize Gen as beautiful. Fresh-faced, maybe. Slender and pretty, perhaps. But there in the rain in her little red rain jacket, he'd noticed something different about her. A vulnerability and a little bit of sadness.

They had a lot of road to cover before dark. It wouldn't be wise to get distracted by a wisp of a girl sitting in his backseat. No, that wouldn't be smart at all.

CHAPTER EIGHT

Calvin City was a small coastal logging community, which had changed its focus from the timber industry to tourism somewhere around the 1960s. Along the DeVries River, down which logs used to traverse from logging camp to the lumberyards, sprang up blocks of quaint tourist shops and restaurants. Their brightly painted clapboard sides reflected the late-afternoon sun. The only non-tourist industry which remained was the DeVries Paper Mill on the outskirts of town. Its sickly sweet smell of wood pulp and chemicals hovered in the air for miles.

Matt had fallen asleep an hour earlier, slumped in the front seat, and Joel and Gen had ridden along, mile after mile, in a companionable silence. Every now and again Bluto would purr or meow to remind them of his presence.

"Have you ever been here?" she asked, staring out the window at the wide expanse of river next to the road.

"To Calvin City? No. I've driven along the coast some. When I was younger. You know, family camping trips, that kind of thing." He caught sight of her in the rearview mirror. Her sharp gaze took in the beauty of the pine trees and the rocky expanses surrounding them. He wished he could do the same, but his mind was on the ticking clock. Each minute they spent driving meant one minute closer to the next curse. He directed his concentration on the road.

"I've been doing some research for you."

"You have?" He flicked a quick glance at her.

"The books I told you about." She traced a slim finger down the window. "I've been looking into the next curse."

Matt mumbled in his sleep and shifted so his head rested against the door.

"I thought we said ix-nay on the urse-cay with Matt around." He nodded in his brother's direction.

"He's asleep."

"Still—"

She sighed loudly. "What I'm trying to tell you is that I may have found a way out of the next one."

"You did?"

"Maybe. If we can find the right ingredients."

"Another one of your oils?"

"No, this one would have to be something stronger. I found a similar curse in one of my books. I brought it with me. It's in my bag." She tugged her oversized bag into her lap.

"And you think we can take care of this? Before Matt has to know?" He followed the road across the bridge and into town.

"I know I can. You just have to have a little faith."

Matt stretched and yawned. "A little faith about what? What did I miss?"

"We're here, Matt. You missed some spectacular scenery." Joel's heart raced at the thought Matt might have overheard their conversation.

"I still don't understand why we couldn't stop at the house for some of my CDs. Where's your luggage anyway, Joel? Do you always go on business trips with nothing but the clothes on your back?"

"I told you, they're fumigating the house for termites." It had been the best lie he could think of. "Most of my work clothes were at the cleaners, and this trip came up unexpectedly. I was going to buy stuff on the road." They drove down the main street, past T-shirt shops, souvenir stands and jewelry stores. "Maybe that wasn't such a good plan."

Gen leaned forward between the two seats. "I'm sure wherever we're staying, they'll have suggestions."

Joel got very quiet.

"You *do* have reservations somewhere for tonight?" his brother asked.

Joel didn't answer.

"Jeez, bro, what the hell? You drag all three of us out to this Podunk town, and no one at work discussed booking a place for you to stay? What kind of company do you work for?"

"Don't be so hard on him, Matt." Gen touched Matt's shoulder. "They threw all of this at us very last minute. It wasn't that well-organized."

Joel was surprised at how smoothly she lied. He gave her a quick glance in the rearview mirror. For the first time, he noticed she had a sprinkling of freckles across her nose.

Matt fumed silently in his seat.

"Place like this, so close to the coast," she said, "I'll bet there are dozens of cute little places to stay."

~ * ~

"So will you be in town long?" A middle-aged woman with iron gray hair and a flowered apron around her plump middle greeted them on the porch of her small bed and breakfast. "We don't get many visitors this time of year."

"It's a business trip," said Matt, hauling his duffle bag up the front steps. "I'm just along for the ride. Do you have a library nearby?"

"A business trip?" She held open the screen door for them. "Up at the paper mill, I'd guess."

Joel brushed past with Bluto's cat carrier. "Uh, yep, the paper mill. Software problems. They called us out for some consultation."

"Whatever keeps them running. Biggest employer in the county. Some say it spoils the land to have them around, but I say whatever keeps this town alive." She peeked into the carrier at the cat and cooed. "Without DeVries there'd be no Calvin City. Well, come in, come in. Don't let my rambling slow you down. You're probably tired after your long drive. You came from Portland, you say?"

"Yes. And the library?" asked Matt.

"Oh, I'm sorry, son, I almost forgot. There I go chatting away. In this business you need to learn to make small talk, but sometimes, like Stan says—Stan's my husband—anyway, like Stan says, sometimes I can get carried away. Not everyone comes to a B&B for the chatter." She laughed to herself. "There's a library downtown. Not a big one, but they just got the Internet there a couple years ago. Federal funding or what have you. Yes, we're very modern now."

"Well, that's good to hear," Matt said. "Really I just need somewhere quiet to work. Maybe a little bit of research."

"Oh, we're mighty quiet out here. That's what we're known for—peace and quiet. And my breakfasts, of course." Once everyone made it in to the foyer, the hostess let the screen door bang closed. "And where are my manners? I'm Stella Connor. You'll probably meet my husband, Stan, later on. He works at the garage on Juniper Street. Well, I guess you wouldn't know where that is, but, anyway, if you had any car troubles, he would be the one to see."

"We'll keep that in mind, Mrs. Connor," Gen said.

"Oh, call me Stella, honey." Her gray curls twitched as she laughed. "Now, let me show you where you're going to stay. Our two nicest rooms upstairs, extra rollaway's in the closet." She gave a look at Matt. "Both with a good view of the ocean. We're just a few miles from Devil's Churn—"

"Devil's Churn?" Just the sound of it gave Joel the creeps.

"Why, don't you know about Devil's Churn? People come for miles to see."

"See what?" Gen asked.

"The ocean. It can be a powerful beast here along the coast. Treacherous waves. Beautiful, really. Very spectacular scenery. If you get a chance, you should really take a drive out there. There are some trails, and some places where you can get down to the tide pools and the caves."

"Caves?" Matt's interest in the conversation grew.

"Oh, my, yes, there's Sea Lion Cave. There's an elevator that can take you down. Back when I was a girl…well, it was a dangerous place. Could only get down there with a rope. Not many were willing to do that. The sea lion can be a very aggressive creature. Anyway, nowadays all kinds of people like to visit."

"I'm not sure if we'll have time to go exploring while we're here, ma'am." Joel was anxious to get up to their rooms and work to solve this family mystery. With the limited time they had, they needed to get settled and talk about a plan of action.

"Well, that's too bad. Call me Stella, please." She grabbed two keys off of an apple-shaped key plaque next to the front door. "No ma'ams around here." She led them up the stairs. "Follow me, and I'll show you to your rooms."

~ * ~

"I'm bored." Matt lay on the loveseat under a bay window in their room. Bluto lay curled up in the middle of the bed, sound asleep.

"I thought you had work to do." Joel had just stepped out of the shower to see his brother sprawled all over what was probably an antique piece of furniture. He nudged his brother's feet off the armrest. "You know, big research project? The one that you chose over a trip to L.A. and bikini-land?" He rubbed an extra hand towel over his head to dry his hair. It was nice to be clean, but it wouldn't be so nice to put on the same clothes he'd been wearing for a week.

"It's too late to get anything started now."

Joel picked up his watch off the bureau. "Six o'clock is late? Boy, they sure don't make college kids like they used to."

Matt tossed a throw pillow at him. "Shut up, bro. College is stressful. Takes a lot out of you."

"I'll have to ask Jonesy the next time I see him." He put on his jeans, which were about ready to walk by themselves. He'd have to ask about borrowing some of Matt's clothes soon, even if his brother had a few inches on him.

"He's cool. He's managed to keep his scholarship and still party once in a while."

"Look, Gen and I need to go out for a business dinner in a few minutes—"

Matt gave him a once-over and grimaced.

Joel glared at his brother. "Do you think you'll be all right fending for yourself and keeping an eye on Bluto?"

Matt picked up a blue binder. "Stella has a nice little reference guide here for her guests. Pizza's right up the road. They even deliver. Can you spare a twenty?"

Joel thought about his almost-empty wallet. It was bad enough having to put the rooms on his credit card. Pretty soon he'd have to worry about going over the limit. "I'm almost out of cash. Think you can cover it tonight? I'll see if I can find an ATM. Hey, I thought your financial-aid package included a stipend?"

"I've got some spring-break money I can use, but you can't blame a brother for trying." He smiled at Joel, like it was all a game to him. Matt squeezed extra cash out of his brother whenever he could. Thank God breakfast came with their stay. At least that was one less thing he had to worry about buying.

"We'll probably be back late. Don't wait up." Joel slipped on his tennis shoes and double-knotted the laces.

"No tongue on the first date."

"Matt..." Joel said in a warning tone.

"I'm just kidding. You have to admit, though, she's pretty cute for a married chick."

"Huh?"

"Wedding ring. Left hand. Or have they changed that tradition in the last ten minutes? My turn in the shower." Matt hopped up from the loveseat and headed into the bathroom. "And there better still be some hot water."

Gen shut the door behind her. The room was pleasant enough—lacy curtains, appliqué quilt on the bed, a gas fireplace against one wall. But she could sense him in here—her husband.

It was too late to turn back. The minute she'd agreed to go on this journey, she knew what Adam expected. More blood. More ceremonies. Each one bringing him closer to what he once was—a living, breathing human being.

A man she could hold close, share secrets with, grow old with. Just like they had planned on their wedding day. She could have it all back again for a little stolen blood.

She sensed movement near the curtain.

Adam. His body appeared slightly more solid than the night of Joel's first visit. Beneath transparent skin, she could see muscle and sinew, bones and veins.

"You've done very well, my darling." He stepped forward, a hand outstretched. "Come, give me a kiss."

His hand felt icy to the touch. After the last ceremony, he'd joined her in bed. She'd missed his arms around her as she slept, and although he couldn't be physical with her in his current form, she drew some comfort from his presence next to her at night. But instead of the warmth she remembered, Adam had been a cold presence. The nightmares still came. Sleep had been fitful.

She took his hand. He enveloped her with his incomplete self. Instead of her hand passing through his body, she could feel a density of cool almost-flesh. Soon he'd be whole again.

She stepped up on her tiptoes, like she had so many times before, and leaned in for a kiss. But this time, her thoughts were not of her husband, but of Joel, the live, warm human being whose body she'd touched, massaging the cream into his chest and back. The look in his eye when she'd cured him, the slight smile of trust.

She shuddered. She shouldn't have thoughts about another man.

Adam was the man she loved. This misty, cold apparition. She pressed her mouth to his, wanting to remember his kiss. The feel of his lips against hers. A bare hint of flesh was enough to give her hope. He would return to her. And once he did, she would never let him go.

CHAPTER NINE

Gen was married? Matt had to be wrong.

Joel knocked on her door, which was right down the hall from theirs.

When she opened it, gone were the jeans and red rain jacket. Instead she wore a bright purple sweater with a matching full skirt. Similar to her palm-reading garb but not nearly as flamboyant.

"Hey, ready for a 'business dinner'?" she asked.

He wanted to get a look at her left hand, but she'd hidden it behind the door. What did it matter if she were married? It shouldn't make a difference. But for some reason it did. "I hope fast food is okay."

"It's not the food, but the company you're with." She smiled.

Better to just get down to business. "Time's getting away from us. We really need to talk about our game plan."

"Game plan?" She frowned.

"You may not be all that concerned, but I only have thirty-six hours before I might not be able to speak."

"Of course I'm concerned. Would I really have come all this way with you if I weren't concerned?" Sincerity filled her brown eyes. "This is not my typical day at work, if you haven't noticed."

"Let's get out of here, so you can tell me more about what you learned from that book."

She held up a black leather-bound book that had seen better days. "I've got everything we need here."

"You think we can find what we need to break the curse?"

"I hope so."

"You hope so?" He leaned one arm against the doorframe. "Great, my future depends on that little book and a lot of hope."

"We'll fix this, I promise."

"Wish I would have found you weeks ago."

"I do too."

Her words had an odd hitch to them. A deeper sorrow behind what she said. He tried to look at her, to gauge her emotions, but she moved past him into the hall.

~ * ~

They sat in a hard plastic booth at a fast-food diner, munching greasy burgers and limp French fries. Less than ten dollars, though, so Joel relished each inexpensive bite.

"Curses are a tricky thing." Gen dipped a fry in ketchup. "They're full of ancient, powerful magic and should only be used sparingly."

"Does cursing a whole family sound like *sparing* to you?"

"I said they were powerful. It can be easy for someone inexperienced to make a mistake, go beyond his intentions."

"So what do we need to do to end this?"

"First we have to deal with the next curse—my book should help us with that." She held up her black book, then slipped it back into her bag. "Then we'll have to do some more research into your family's history."

Joel shook his head. "How are we going to do this? How are we possibly going to find all of this out? A curse from ninety years ago? Laid on what distant relative in my past? And by whom? I just don't see how…" Helplessness engulfed him like a dark cloud.

She touched his hand, and he noticed her ring for the first time. A simple gold band on her ring finger. No diamonds or precious stones. Just a gold band. "So you're married?"

Gen's face clouded over. "I was."

"Then why do you still wear the ring?"

"I don't want to talk about it." She curled her hand away from him and set it in her lap. "Everyone has their reasons for keeping secrets, don't they, Joel?"

He pressed his lips together. "It just didn't seem like…I mean, it was just you and your mom—"

"Can we just concentrate on you right now? You're the one I'm worried about."

A door between them closed. He could sense it. "I've been asking myself for the past few days why you're so worried about me. Why you care so much."

She picked up a French fry and took a dainty bite. "There was just something about you. You reminded me of someone. Someone who's been gone a long time."

"Hopefully someone you liked," he said with a smile.

She laughed, and it was glorious to hear it. A tinkling like a bell. "Oh, Joel. I just want you to take care of yourself. Stay well." She ate another French fry. "By the way, thanks for dinner."

"My pleasure." He tried not to think about how light his wallet had become. "Anything for the lady who's going to save my life." But he couldn't keep his eye off the gold band that glinted under the fluorescent lighting. Who had given her that simple ring and where was he now? What kind of man had captured her heart?

"Research is most important. I can gather the things I need for the next curse, but to stop the whole chain of events will take some work. We have to find out the who and the why. You need to get to the root of the evil before you can pull it out. We might want to stop at the library, see what they have. I also found this brochure at the bed and breakfast." She showed him a glossy rack card with a little red clapboard building on the front. "It's the Calvin City Historical Society. They opened a kind of history museum a few years ago. Might be the place to find just the sort of information we're looking for."

Joel took it from her and flipped it over. Most of the notable exhibits had to do with the DeVries family and the history of the paper mill. "How will this help?"

"We find the source of the curse, and we can get rid of it once and for all."

Joel thought fleetingly of his brother, innocently eating pizza and probably working on his paper. "Thank God I found you."

"I haven't done anything yet."

He held out his hand and turned it over so she could see his unmarked skin. "Just a few days ago, you saved me from the brink of insanity, don't forget." The memory of the burning sores covering his body was still fresh in his mind.

"I've never done anything like that before."

"Maybe it's because you never tried."

"Well, whatever reason it was, I'm glad you're well—"

"For now."

"For now." She took a final bite of her cheeseburger and glanced at her watch. "It's getting late. Your brother will be wondering where you are, and I have some things to gather first."

"What?"

"We spiritualists have our secrets, you know."

"More than just one." He gathered the empty wrappers and soda cups, and placed them on a tray.

She chose to ignore his subtle dig. "I'll meet you on the porch tomorrow. Early. Before dawn." She added some napkins to the heap of trash.

"And then?"

"And then we'll prepare to break the Curse of the Mute."

CHAPTER TEN

Gen stood on the porch dressed in her red rain jacket again. The rain last night had stopped, bringing with it a cold, damp chill. The gray light of dawn barely lit up the foggy gloom. "You look like death warmed over."

"Gee, thanks." Joel rubbed at his tired eyes. Last night he'd come home to a room littered with beer cans. Underage Matt had somehow persuaded Stella to buy him alcohol. This morning he left his younger brother snoring in his cot. He'd deal with him later. "Can we just do this thing?"

"Sure. I've got everything we need here." She held up her oversized shoulder bag. "According to the book, we need a fire. I thought maybe we could go into the woods. Find a place far enough away so that no one would bother us."

"Who's going to bother us at six in the morning on a Sunday?"

"You never know." She led him away from the house. There weren't many other homes at this end of the block. Dense woods surrounded them. She entered the tangle of underbrush and pine trees until they came to a small clearing. Because of the heavy growth of trees, the rain had barely touched this protected spot. The ground was dry.

"How did you know this was here?"

She shrugged. "I did a little exploring before you were up." She picked up bits of kindling and stacked it in a small fire pit she'd cleared away.

"You're positive this will work?" He helped her gather wood, piling it next to the pit.

She pulled a matchbook out of her jacket pocket, struck a match and set it to the bits of dry leaves and pine needles under the kindling. "I never said I was positive about this. I wasn't positive about the healing spell, but it worked." The fire caught.

"So you experimented on me that night?" He dropped the heavier pieces of wood he'd been collecting.

"I didn't say it was an experiment. You came to me for help, I tried what I knew. It worked. You're healed." She poked at the fire with a stick.

"I thought you said your book had a cure for the Curse of the Mute."

"Not exactly." She pulled two plastic baggies out of her pocket. One held some kind of green leaves, the other looked like it held mud.

He caught her by the elbow. "I need this to work, Gen." He didn't mean to sound so desperate, but she was all he had to hold on to.

Gen looked down at his hand holding her arm. He knew he should let go, but he couldn't. Silence hung between them for a moment. Neither of them moved. He wanted to lean into her hair, pull her close. He shook off the feeling and slowly released her. "What's that stuff?" His voice was gruff to his own ears.

Gen stepped back, the connection broken. "St. John's wort and graveyard dust. Although it was wet when I gathered it, so it's more like graveyard mud."

"Graveyard dust? You got this from a cemetery?"

"Graveyard dust is very powerful. The power of the life lost is absorbed into the soil around a gravesite. The St. John's wort is used for banishing evil spirits."

"So there's an evil spirit following me rather than a curse?"

"A curse is almost like an evil spirit come to life. Whoever placed this curse on your family is long gone, but the evil it was created with is still following you. Plaguing the DeVries family beyond the grave." She placed a larger piece of wood on the growing fire. "Evil spirits can wreak havoc on the living…mostly in the forms of curses. This particular ceremony should help protect you against this interference."

"So a panacea of sorts. A ceremony to give me blanket coverage."

"That's what we're hoping for." She took out a pinch of St. John's wort, crushed the leaves in her fingers and tossed them into the flames. The leaves curled and dried under the intense heat, releasing a strong aroma. "Come here."

Her fingers were stained purple from the plant juices.

He stepped closer.

She painted his lip with her fingers. A gentle touch, barely more than the edge of a butterfly's wing brushing against his mouth. An unexpected tug in his gut made him think something more existed between them in that moment. She stood so close to him—he could feel the heat of her body. The urge came over him to grab her hand and kiss it. Run his mouth down those slim fingers, over her palm and to the pulse point in her wrist. He wanted more from her than this light touch of her fingers. He knew that now. He stared at her, unblinking, surprised at this revelation. Her eyes were dark in the dim light of early morning. "To protect your voice." She cleared her throat and pulled her hand away. "And now for the graveyard dust."

He touched his lips and watched as she took a handful of the mud and tossed it onto the now-raging fire. The damp of the dirt caused a puff of smoke. The smell of wet earth blended with the sharp smell of the burning St. John's wort. She stretched her hand into the dense smoke and mumbled something he couldn't understand.

Adam's presence drifted past. The hair on Gen's arms rose with the sensation. She kept her face impassive, focusing on the flames and the thick smoke. Joel couldn't suspect a third person was in their midst.

Her insides twisted from the fevered look in Joel's eyes when she'd touched his mouth. As if dying coals had been stoked back to life. A slow burning that she hadn't felt in so long—

"I need the blood."

The words were a bare whisper in her ear. Like a puff of wind. A soft breeze. She tamped down the strange feelings inside. She had a mission. Her husband needed her help.

"Take it, Gen."

The brush of an invisible hand against her arm startled her. She whispered the words Adam had told her, the ancient words that would cure Joel from the next curse.

"The blood. Cut him and take the blood."

Her heart beat rapidly. She whispered, "How?"

"He trusts you. He'll suspect nothing."

She circled her hands through the smoke.

"Take your knife and do it."

She faltered.

"Do it."

"Give me you arm," Gen said.

Joel had been so intent on watching her actions, her words caught him by surprise. "What?"

With a quick movement, she grabbed his wrist, pushed up his jacket sleeve and sliced a shallow cut in his arm with a pocketknife.

"Hey!" He jerked his arm away. "What the hell?"

Gen closed her eyes and repeated the incantation for the spell. The fire died down. The smoke thinned. She opened her eyes.

"We're done."

His arm dripped blood onto the thick mat of pine needles. "You cut me."

"The ceremony calls for blood." She shrugged.

Her indifference unnerved him. "The least you could've done was warn me."

"You'll be fine. Here." She handed him a bunch of tissues from her purse. "Now we just wait until tomorrow and see what happens." She studied his face for a moment. "Let me get this off." She brushed his lips with her thumb.

He caught her wrist. "That's okay. I can do it." He took the back of his hand and wiped the rest of the juices off his mouth. He couldn't handle the feel of those fingers again. Besides, her surprise slice and dice on his arm peeved him a little.

She kicked dirt over the waning flames of the fire. "Let's get back before Stella notices we've been gone. She doesn't seem like the type who would keep a secret very well." She took the bloodied tissues, balled them up and stuffed them in her bag.

"You noticed that, did you?"

She laughed her tinkling, silvery laugh. "She's probably just a lonely lady."

Joel snorted. As he followed her into the woods and back to civilization, he wondered if this ceremony would work. He pushed the sleeve of his jacket down to cover the fresh cut. He didn't need his brother asking any questions.

When they arrived back at the bed and breakfast, the aroma of frying bacon greeted them. Matt sat in the front parlor, a mug of coffee in his hand. Guess they had been gone longer than they planned.

"Hey, where've you been?" Matt asked. When Gen followed behind him, he raised an eyebrow.

"After last night I didn't even think you'd notice." Joel glared at his brother. "How's the hangover?"

"Shut up. Stella showed me her husband's gun collection last night— rifles, shotguns, a couple of World War II pistols. Stan might have time today to show me how to shoot them. Pretty cool, huh?" Matt drank down the rest of his coffee. "Then I offered Stella some of my pizza, she offered the beer. I didn't want to insult her generosity."

"You know better than that. Dad would've killed me if he knew you'd been drinking." Joel stood over him. "I'm responsible for you." His brother might give him a run for his money once in awhile, but Joel knew he wouldn't let these curses touch him. No matter what it took, he would protect his brother.

"I never asked you to be." Matt got up and shoved past him.

Before Joel could continue the argument, Stella waltzed into the parlor. "I forgot to mention. On Sundays breakfast is served at eight. Stan and I've got church, you know. Nine thirty service. Bethlehem Baptist on the other side of town. We'd love to have visitors." She gave them all a broad smile and wiped her floury hands on her apron.

"That's so kind of you, Stella," Joel said, "but we've got some business to attend to this morning before our meeting over at the sawmill tomorrow." The lies came so easily it scared him. Since his life went down the toilet almost four weeks ago, he'd gotten good at this.

"Business? On a Sunday? Why, that's the Lord's day." Stella shook her head at the news. "What kind of kooky company makes anyone work on a Sunday? Well, you need to call them right up and tell them you can't do it. God is more important than business. Yes, indeed. Do you want Stan to talk to them? He's real good at knocking sense into people."

"That won't be necessary." Considering Stella had shared a twelve-pack of beer with his underage brother the night before, he had to wonder how much she relied on the Lord to guide her in daily life. "We appreciate your offer, but we'll have to pass. Maybe next time we're in town."

A timer beeped.

"Oh, my soufflés!" Stella ran into the kitchen, apron strings flying.

"So where exactly were the two of you this morning?" Matt deftly avoided continuing their discussion about last night.

"I was out for a stroll, and I just happened to meet your brother on the porch when I got back," Gen said smoothly. "So you're planning on putting some time in at the library today?" The change of subject effectively shut down his brother's curiosity.

Matt moved to the sideboard to pour himself more coffee from a fancy, silver pot. It didn't surprise Joel his brother needed more than the usual kick-start this morning. "Yeah, if we're stuck in this town for a few days, I need to get moving. Stella says they don't open until one on Sundays."

Gen joined him and picked up an empty mug. "What kind of project are you working on?"

Joel watched the two of them from across the room, wary Matt would reveal too much to his spiritualist. More than he'd been willing to share with her.

"Geology. That's my major. It's a paper for my Marine Geology class. It's pretty esoteric."

"Try me."

"Well, it's about cretaceous platforms and carbon with a relationship to offshore oil drilling. In a very, very hardly related kinda way. I mean, the idea of studying geological formations, even underwater, for possible oil exploitation has always been a huge focus of industrial geologists, but I want to focus on—"

Gen held up her hand. "Whoa, I think that was plenty. Rocks. Oil. Gotcha."

Matt laughed. "I warned you."

"You think you'll be able to find what you need here?"

"Well, I have most of the major research done. Internet access is really important, but beyond that, I just need a quiet spot to work for many, many hours." He sighed and took a gulp of coffee. "So, how did you get into software sales? You don't seem like the techie type."

Joel had been listening, making sure the topics stayed off anything too risky. But at this question, he intervened. "Hey, why don't we go in the dining room? Smells like breakfast is just about ready." He ushered them both toward the beautifully set table in the adjoining room.

~ * ~

The Calvin City Historical Society Museum looked like a log cabin straight out of the 1800s. It was a small place on a corner in the middle of the tourist-focused downtown. The front windows sported utilitarian white curtains, but someone had planted a garden of wildflowers in front, which softened the hard exterior.

Once Gen and Joel were inside, an elderly woman with a rounded back and a hand-carved cane greeted them. "We don't open until one o'clock." She pointed her cane at the digital clock on the wall above the entrance.

It was twelve fifty-five.

"Can we just have a look around"—he read her nametag—"Mrs. Leach? We're doing a little bit of family research. We won't be a bother," Joel said with a smile.

"The sign says one o'clock." The crotchety woman stuck her nose back in her quilting magazine.

Gen gave it a try. "We're only here for the weekend. We don't have a lot of time, and if you could just—"

The woman looked at Gen over the edge of her magazine. "I can't be bothered with a bunch of questions."

"We understand," said Gen.

"And I don't like it when people touch the glass on the cabinets."

"We'll keep our hands to ourselves," Joel promised.

Her gaze darted over to Joel, and her eyebrow rose into a disagreeable arch. "I suppose. Entry fee is one dollar." With a skinny stick of a finger, she tapped on a plastic box on the edge of her desk. "A donation to the Historical Society. I don't get paid for my time. All volunteer. Donations pay the bills, you see."

This time Gen paid up. She pulled a wallet out of her bag and put a crisp dollar bill and four quarters into the donation slot.

They headed toward the largest display in the building, a history of forestry and the DeVries family.

"Here, Joel. This should tell us something." She pulled out the pages she'd printed at the library back in Portland. "Maybe someone in your mother's family line will be mentioned here." She started to read a plaque of names, which identified members of the DeVries family in half a dozen photos hanging above a glass case.

Joel had more interest in the objects inside the display case. An old-fashioned bandsaw, a remnant of the old logging days, took up most of the space. There were other metal objects he couldn't identify, which didn't have any tags to explain them. Guess that dollar entrance fee didn't go very far in improving the historical society's offerings.

"Look at this." Gen pointed to a black-and-white photo which showed a tugboat surrounded by six burly men. "I think this might be your great-grandfather, right here." She drew his attention to a young man in a floppy, wide-brimmed hat standing on the pier next to the bow of the tug. "It says Wm. DeVries. William. Your great-grandfather. And the dates match. 1932. He would've been eighteen."

Joel leaned in closer to the small, blurry picture. He couldn't tell if there was any family resemblance there. Gen scribbled madly on the papers, which she set on the glass cabinet.

"I said no touching the cabinets." The grim old woman from the front desk watched them with her sunken blue eyes, two flat buttons of color in a pale and pasty face.

"I'm sorry." Gen swept the papers off the cabinet. "Turn around, Joel."

"What?"

"Your back. Let me use your back."

He turned around and rested his hands on his knees. Gen set the papers on his back and used him as a desk. "C.W. DeVries. G. Wortham, J.T. DeVries." She read the names aloud as she scribbled. "We need an extensive family tree to look for patterns."

The scratch of the pen across the paper tickled his back. "Maybe our caretaker could help us." Joel flicked his gaze across the room at Mrs. Leach and her cane. She'd obviously lived a long life. Maybe she would know something about the DeVries family history that wasn't shown in the display cases and on the walls.

"I'm not sure if she'd be willing."

"Why not? We just have to sweet-talk her."

"I think she lost the ability to be sweet-talked many years ago." Gen stopped writing and folded the papers away, stuffing them into her bag. Joel straightened up. "But I guess it would be faster than trying to do this on our own."

Joel took the initiative and headed to the front desk.

"Excuse me, ma'am." Joel smiled at Mrs. Leach.

The older woman pulled her gaze away from her magazine. "Is there a problem?" She looked beyond him as if making sure all the exhibits were in order.

"No, no problems." Gen caught up to him. "I was just hoping you might be able to answer a few questions for us. About the DeVries family."

The woman's mouth set in a determined line.

Gen took up the argument. "I've heard around here no one knows Calvin City like Mrs. Leach. But if you think the librarian might know more than you about the DeVrieses…" The trap had been set.

The woman set down her magazine. A spark appeared in her faded blue eyes. "The librarian grew up in Eugene. She doesn't know a thing about Calvin City. Why, she's likely to tell you the oldest house in town is the Marvin House, but us long-time residents know it was Gene Smith's place on Main."

Joel knew they had her now. He put another dollar in the donation box. "Well, I'm so glad we ran into you, then. I want to make sure we know the true history of Calvin City."

The older woman settled into her story.

"The DeVrieses built this town. Built it out of nothing. Calvin City wouldn't even be a footnote in the book of life if it weren't for Randall DeVries and his family coming to start the logging. Great stands of trees, all around. Just what a growing country needed. Wood. And lots of it. Mr. DeVries knew that this part of the West was destined to start a different kind of Gold Rush—lumber."

Brought to life by their interest in what seemed to be her favorite topic, the woman's back appeared straighter, her skin a little less pale. She pushed up from her chair using her cane and bid them to follow her to the back of the room. "By the turn of the century, 1900 I mean, Calvin City was booming. They named it Calvin City after Randall's oldest, Calvin Johnson DeVries. Here's his picture." She pointed at a large portrait on the wall. "Isn't he handsome? He was in charge of the river, the tugboats, moving logs from the timber stands to town."

"I didn't see him in that other photo," Gen said.

"What photo?" Mrs. Leach asked.

"Oh, the one over there." She pointed where they had been earlier. "Of the tugboat. With William DeVries and some others. William is Joel's great-grandfather."

"Is he now?" Mrs. Leach looked at Joel with a different eye. "I didn't know there were any more DeVrieses left in these here parts. It's been a long time since I've heard that name in this town."

"Oh, but the sawmill, surely—"

"Kept the family name, but some conglomerate bought it years ago. Not a soul there remembers any of the DeVrieses. Not a soul." She grew quiet and kept her eye on the portrait of Calvin DeVries.

"So what happened to them?" Joel needed answers. This woman must know something. She was as old as the hills, and it seemed she had a personal affection for the DeVries family.

She waved a hand at them. "They died off years ago. Years and years. When I was a young girl, things all started to go wrong for the DeVries family. Never quite understood why that family, who had done so much for our town, was struck so hard by the tragedies of life. God should have rewarded such a great family. That's why I'm surprised to hear you had a relative…a DeVries who made it out of Calvin City. That's good to hear. Makes an old woman's heart happy to know." She tapped Joel's shoulder with her cane and hobbled back toward her desk.

They followed after her.

"What kinds of things went wrong, Mrs. Leach?" Gen asked. Joel could hear the excitement in her voice. They were close to finding out more.

Perhaps Mrs. Leach could tell them everything they needed to know, and this could be over by tonight.

"It all started after the war from what I understand. When young Calvin came home from the war, he was different. Not the same happy lad he had been in his youth. The joy, the spark was gone. Like many men who went away to fight, he didn't come back quite the same." She drifted off, lost in her own thoughts. Her eyes blurred for a moment.

The front door opened and a man in his early twenties with stringy blond hair stepped inside. "Hey, Gram, what are you doing? You know you're not supposed to be here."

"I work here, Tommy, you know that. Sundays and Tuesdays one to five."

"Not anymore, Gram, remember? You haven't been on the volunteer list for five years."

"Five years?" The old woman seemed confused. She tapped her cane hard on the wood floor. "But I was just talking to these lovely young people about the DeVries family."

Joel smiled awkwardly at the young man.

Tommy gave them a cursory glance and picked up his grandmother's handbag and her unfinished magazine. "Dad's outside. He's going to drive you back home."

Mrs. Leach's face screwed up in irritation. "We were just getting started, they wanted to talk more about the wonderful Calvin. You remember my stories about Calvin, don't you, Tommy?"

He ushered her toward the door. She hobbled slowly, taking her time with the cane. "Yes, you've told me many times about Calvin, Gram. He was a wonderful guy, gave you candy at the store once. I remember."

"More than one time. He would give me some sweets and pat me on the head. Yes, a wonderful man. Too bad that woman ruined him. You know the one, Tommy? She was a bad sort. If only he'd listened—"

The grandson helped her out the door. "I'll be right back," he said to them before he slipped out the front door.

"Looks like we found a starting point: Calvin DeVries. Something happened there." Gen walked back over to his portrait on the wall. "January 1917, it says here. He was about twenty in that picture."

Joel joined her. "What do you think went wrong with them? And what woman 'ruined him'? What do you think Mrs. Leach meant by that?"

Gen stared up at the picture of the young man with slicked-back hair and a moustache. "I don't know. Maybe that guy Tommy will know something."

"And if he doesn't?"

"Guess we're off to the library. The newspapers. Do you remember how to use a microfiche machine?" Gen skimmed her fingers lightly across the picture frame, still looking at Calvin's portrait. "It's been a few years since I had to use one."

"I think I could manage—"

"I'm sorry about that, folks." Tommy closed the front door behind him. "My grandmother still thinks she volunteers here. Every now and then she wanders off. She has a key to this place hidden somewhere. We've never been able to find it."

Gen turned away from the portrait. "That's all right. She really was full of information."

Tommy took his grandmother's place behind the counter, fiddled with a small portable stereo and turned on a Top 40 radio station. The music didn't quite suit the place. "That's why the Historical Society was so glad to have her here. She's lived in Calvin City her whole life and had a memory like a vise. Now, though—" He shucked off his jacket and set it on the back of the chair.

"Did you grow up here?" Gen asked.

Joel picked up a copy of the weekly, local newspaper and scanned the front page.

"Nah, my dad got out of this place after college. But when Gram got so sick, he moved back. Somehow I ended up here, working at the paper mill. Not great, but it's a job. I'm thinking about moving back to Portland, though."

Joel looked up from the newspaper. "So, how long have you been volunteering here?"

"I don't."

Joel exchanged a look with Gen.

Tommy reached down to change the radio station. Now the stereo spewed out hip-hop. "I'm just waiting until PJ shows up."

"PJ?" Gen asked.

"Priscilla James. We all call her that—PJ. Anyway, since Gram hides the key, I usually wait until someone else shows up. Especially since you're here."

Joel tucked the paper under his arm. "So I guess you don't know a lot about the history of Calvin City?"

"Me? Nah. Why? Did you have a question? PJ should be here in a minute."

"Actually," Gen said, "we were thinking about making a trip to the library. I think we've just about maxed out on information here."

Tommy nodded. "Okie-doke."

After they left the historical society, Joel hesitated outside on the sidewalk.

"I wish we could've gotten more information from Mrs. Leach." Joel folded and refolded the newspaper he'd picked up. "She really seemed to know a lot about the DeVries family."

"Too bad she's not all there, you know?" Gen tapped her forehead. "But at least we have a place to start—Calvin DeVries around 1918 or 1919."

"The woman Mrs. Leach mentioned, we need to find out more about her, if we can." That part of Mrs. Leach's story stood out in his mind. What kind of 'bad sort' was she? "I don't see how a whole family could be brought down by one war-damaged soldier. There's something more there."

CHAPTER ELEVEN

An old post office housed the Calvin City Library. The hours posted told them they only had a short while before closing time.

"Keep an eye out for Matt," Joel said. "He might be here."

"Um, need I remind you we have the only car, and it's not like he would walk ten miles to town."

Joel kept his eyes open anyway. If his brother had somehow managed to convince Stella to give him a few beers, he could coax her into giving him a ride.

"So what should we be looking for?" Joel asked.

He held the door open for her. She smiled and ducked under his arm. "The obituaries. That's the best place to look for the kind of information we need."

Although a bit macabre, he could see her point. If the curses took down the DeVries family, it would stand to reason there might be some mention of unusual causes of death.

"Since your great-grandfather managed to make it out of Calvin City alive, I would say we could limit our research to 1918 to 1938."

"Twenty years of obituaries? That will take us forever."

Gen headed toward an open computer near the front of the library. Two teenage kids huddled around one. An older man looked up books on another. "You forget, Calvin City was pretty small back then. It was a lumber town, but a boomtown. Still developing. It looks like most of the buildings downtown date from the 1920s." She typed in a search. "Which means probably only a weekly paper and not a whole lot of deaths to report."

"I hope you're right."

She hunched over the keyboard, hunting and pecking for the right keys.

He sidled up next to her. Her typing method was painfully slow. "Um, would you like me to take over? I'm a software tester, remember? I can type reasonably well." He almost laughed at the serious expression on her face.

"I can do this." She glanced down at her fingers and then up at the screen, backspacing to correct her errors.

"No," he said, gently pushing her off the stool, "you can't. Here, let me."

She frowned at him, but let him take the helm.

He quickly typed in the parameters of their search, limiting it only to the Calvin City Times. She was right. The list was quite short. In fact, for the first few years, they published the paper only once a month. It wasn't until well into the twenties that the paper cranked out one issue a week.

"Looks like they have this stuff in the stacks," she pointed out. "Before microfiche they used to bind a year's worth of papers. Either they never had the money or the time to convert them to digital files. I hope they haven't deteriorated."

Taking in the tight quarters of the Calvin City Library, it didn't surprise him very much. They probably used every penny they had in the operating budget just to pay the light bill.

Gen scribbled down the reference number of the bound books they wanted. "I think we have to ask the librarian for these. It says 'Special Collection'."

Joel glanced over at the gray-haired matron manning the check-out counter. "Ladies first."

They sat amidst a dusty, disorganized mess of bound books, rotting newspapers and severely out-of-date magazines. Although the items they needed had been numbered and on the shelves in a dim back corner, they had to wade through other abandoned and uncategorized reading materials to get there.

"Forget what I said about digitizing this stuff, they need to spend some money on a cleaning crew. This is ridiculous." Gen pushed aside a tall stack of old *Life* magazines to reach the books they needed. "Here it is. 1910 through 1930, all along this shelf." She took a small stack of heavy, leather-bound books the size of extra-large photo albums. "You take this one." She gave him the book from 1918. "And I'll take this one." She shoved another book under her arm.

He coughed at the dust clouds they were churning up with their searching. "We only have an hour to look through this stuff."

"We can always come back tomorrow."

Joel wished he could make her feel the urgency he did. With his brother tagging along, the invisible clock ticked loudly in his head. What if they'd followed the wrong lead?

"I just want to get this over and done with. I want my life back." Joel sat on a chair with a missing arm and paged through another book of yellowed newspapers. He could feel her eyes on him.

"I know, Joel. I know." For a few seconds, the only sound in the dank basement was the dry rasp of old newspaper as they turned pages. "I hope you know I want to end this just as much as you."

He wasn't sure how that could be possible. She could go back to her life. If he couldn't find a cure for this, what did she care? He was nobody to her.

He winced at that thought. Nobody. It was true. The memory of her cool hands on his body flashed in his head—smoothing cream over his arms, his hands, his chest. He kept holding on to that image as if it meant something. She had only been kind to him, nothing more.

Even though they sat less than two feet apart, Joel felt more alone than ever.

CHAPTER TWELVE

With ten minutes to spare before closing time, Gen announced, "I think I found something."

It hadn't taken long to page through the first few years' worth of obituaries. A handful of lumber accidents, numerous flu deaths and the typical elderly expiring from natural causes filled the short section of death notices. They scrutinized anyone with the last name of DeVries. They'd found only two relatives so far—a woman who died in childbirth and a boy who succumbed to swine flu. Nothing unusual about that.

"What? What is it?" Joel's eyes hurt. The dim light in the cramped basement made it difficult to read the fine, faded black print.

"I need a copy machine. Do they have a copy machine?" She stood, clutching the book in her hand, a page marked with a finger.

"What did you find?"

"A suicide. It looks like it might be Calvin's wife, but we'd need to compare it to a family tree. She seems about the right age."

"Let me see." He held out his hand. She stepped closer, her shoulder touching his arm. He breathed in the smell of dust and her shampoo. She flipped the book open.

"Right here." She pointed to a passage on the page. *"Myra Harding DeVries, 22…"*

Joel read the obituary aloud, *"Myra Harding DeVries, 22. Born September 12, 1897 in Portland, died February 25, 1920. She was united in marriage with Calvin Johnson DeVries Oct. 21, 1919. Her husband preceded her in death on December 27, 1919. She is survived by her mother (Mrs. John Harding) and two sisters (Irene Harding James and Sally Anne Harding). During the last months of her life, Mrs. DeVries was afflicted in such a way that, at times, she was robbed of her mental powers. During one of these episodes, she took her own life. Funeral at Christ Presbyterian Church, February 27th. Interment in Oak Grove Cemetery."*

"I thought maybe that part, 'robbed of her mental powers', might be a clue. I mean, if she were cursed—I could imagine she might kill herself."

Joel counted on his fingers.

"Joel?"

He stumbled over the junk in the basement to the shelf where the bound newspapers were stored.

"What are you doing?"

"I need to find Calvin's obituary. It said here he died in December 1919. We need to work our way backwards, see what it says about his death. That's the only way we'll know."

She joined him at the bookcase, where he scanned the dirty bindings for the book from 1919.

"Got it." He flipped the book open on a stack of old trunks.

"What does it say?" She peered over his shoulder.

"Here." He found the obituaries from the last week in December. "Here it is." What he read chilled him to his core. *"After nine weeks of suffering, Calvin Johnson DeVries was found dead in his bed on December 27th."* That's all he needed to read. The number was too coincidental. Too perfect. And his wife dead nine weeks later. He returned to the papers from 1920. Frantically flipping pages, he found another DeVries death and another and another. Nine weeks, eight weeks, nine weeks. Over and over. People dropping dead right and left with no clear explanation.

"My God," Joel said. "So many of them. So many."

"Calvin DeVries is where it began. We found it, Joel. Calvin's death definitely started it all. We have to find out why. Who. Where. This will be the only way we can end it. Look at this." Gen had been scanning a business article on the opposite page from Calvin's obituary. *"DeVries Lumber Completes Controversial Road."*

"What does that have to do with anything?"

"Read."

Joel scanned the story. "So they built a road to connect Calvin City to Florence."

"Read this part." She pointed at a paragraph later in the story.

Joel read it aloud, *"The Silva family denounced the road saying they hadn't been paid fairly for their property. William Silva claimed DeVries Lumber underpaid him for his land, forced his family out of their home and injured livestock. 'How is a man supposed to make a living? If you don't work for the lumber company, you don't matter to Randall DeVries. Where is my family supposed to go? I can't live on five hundred dollars. I've got three daughters. Who's going to take care of them?' The road was completed this week after two years of planning and construction. The fanfare was less than expected due to the untimely death of Calvin DeVries. The new road opens up a better delivery route for DeVries lumber from Calvin City to Eugene, saving money and increasing the amount of deliverable lumber to the capitol."*

"This might be the key," Gen said.

"What's the key?"

"We've found a family with a grudge. A reason to want to harm the DeVries family."

"But it doesn't say anything about this family being—"

"What? Witches?"

Joel stumbled over his words. "Curse-laying people."

"There's a grudge here. The timing is right, and besides, I just feel we're on the right path."

"Is that your spiritualist self talking?"

"Sometimes intuition works, Joel." She shook her head. "You should trust it more often yourself." She closed the book and set it back on the shelf. "We can do this. We can stop it. I know it. And I think I know who we have to talk to. Come on." She tugged on his arm.

"Where are we going?"

"Mrs. Leach. The woman she spoke of. The one that was a 'bad sort'."

"You think she may have been the one to lay the curse on Calvin?"

"Taking someone's property. Destroying the family home. Maybe that's what Mrs. Leach was talking about. Maybe this woman was from the Silva family."

"How are we supposed to find this Mrs. Leach? All we know is that her grandson is named Tommy and she lives somewhere in town."

"Have you always lived in Portland, Joel?"

"Yes, why?"

"You clearly don't know how a small town operates. Follow me." Gen set the dusty binder full of newspapers back on the shelf and waded through the junk in the basement to reach the stairs.

"Mrs. Leach from the Historical Society?" the stern librarian asked. Her eyes lit upon Joel, but her words were directed toward Gen.

"Yes, we met her this morning," Gen said. "Sounded like she knew a lot about the history of this town."

"Oh my, yes, she was just a gem. A gem, I tell you. It's such a shame the Alzheimer's runs in the family. These last few years her memory's been so spotty. Hard to tell what she's talking about."

"Where can we find her exactly?" Joel asked, anxious to get going.

The librarian set down the stack of books she'd been about to reshelve. "Her son's been keeping an eye on her. Didn't want to move her from her house, you know. Too much of a shock to her system if he'd had to put her in a home. That's what I heard." She leaned in toward them as if she was about to share secret information. "Weak heart," she whispered.

Joel cleared his throat. The woman sure could talk, considering her job entailed keeping other people quiet.

She looked at him over the edge of her glasses. "You can find the Leach place a few blocks off of Main. The big yellow house at the end of Pine. Can't miss it."

"Thank you." Gen smiled.

The librarian nodded and headed toward the nonfiction section.

"So how much information do you think an old woman with Alzheimer's will give us?" asked Joel.

"Why don't we go find out?"

CHAPTER THIRTEEN

Theodore Leach was unmoving as he stood in the doorway of Mrs. Leach's home. "My mother's not well. She isn't up for visitors. How did you get this address again?" The middle-aged man stroked his mustache, his dark eyes missing nothing.

"A friend." Gen bit her lip. Joel held his breath, hoping such a vague answer would get them inside.

"What friend?"

"A good one?" She sounded unsure of her own answer.

"My mother is ill. She's not strong enough to be seeing strangers." Mr. Leach moved to close the door.

"We're not strangers." Joel thought solely of the necessity in talking to this woman to cure him. All politeness, all second thoughts went out the window the minute he remembered this small fact. Without this elderly woman's help, his journey might end here, on the front steps of a yellow Victorian house.

Mr. Leach eyed him suspiciously.

Joel cleared his throat. "We met her at the Historical Society this morning. She was extremely knowledgeable. Seemed to really enjoy talking about the history of Calvin City. Sort of brought her out of her shell."

Mr. Leach's face softened—maybe just a hair. Or was that the setting sun throwing shadows across his face? "She does like to talk about her youth. That seems very clear to her still. She might not remember who I am half the time, but she remembers every single neighbor on this street since the Depression."

Gen picked up the conversation. "It would mean a lot to us if we could talk to her for just a few minutes. That is, if she's up to it."

"Why did you need to talk to her again?" Mr. Leach asked. "Some research project?"

"Family history—genealogy," Joel explained.

"I see." The evaluating stare lessened in intensity. "Your family's from Calvin City?"

"My mother's side. She was a DeVries."

Mr. Leach's eyebrow ratcheted up in a sharp arch. "A DeVries? Really? I didn't know there were any left. We haven't had a DeVries in this town for maybe forty years. The last one died out years ago."

"Died out?" Gen asked.

"Yes, it was one unlucky family."

"Unlucky how?" Joel pressed.

"Well, I guess it can't be that unlucky…because here you are. Guess some of them moved away. You wouldn't happen to have an interest in the paper plant?"

"Uh, no. My grandfather sold his shares years ago."

"That's too bad." Mr. Leach clucked his tongue. "It's one of the biggest mills in the country now. Shares are worth a fortune."

"So would it be all right if we spoke with your mother for just a few minutes?" Gen brought them back to the reason for their visit.

"What? Oh yes, I suppose so. But not too long, now. She tires very easily." He opened the door to let them inside. "You can wait in the front parlor. I'll go and get her."

The house was so large and so old-fashioned that it had a parlor—a cozy area with settees and pretty gilded lamps and stained glass. Big plants in pots near the windows. A wheeled tea cart. As if they'd stepped back through time.

"So there really are no more DeVrieses." Joel knew what that statement meant. Knowing how many relatives in his family likely had suffered from the same curse he did, and none of them had been able to stop it.

Gen must have sensed an underlying terror in his words. "Mrs. Leach is going to help us change all that." Her words were a little too bright. A little too perky. If she had patted his hand, he wouldn't have been surprised. The fake pat. That would be all he needed to believe Gen never thought she could stop this curse.

"Mother." Theodore Leach led Mrs. Leach into the room on his arm. "This nice young couple would like to ask you a few questions."

Mrs. Leach jerked out of her son's hold. "You don't need to coddle me, Teddy. Why do you insist on treating me like I'm about to break? I'm old, not frail." She walked right into the room with her cane, moving with grace and determination.

Joel had a hard time keeping a smile off his face. She was a tough old bird, no matter what her son believed.

Mr. Leach shrugged and left them to their little chat. "I'll be back in a few minutes to check up on you."

Mrs. Leach waved a hand at him. "Oh pooh, Teddy. I can manage a conversation without your help. Why don't you go do whatever it is you do when you're not bothering me." She turned away from her son and settled her faded blue gaze on Joel and Gen.

Gen jumped right into the questions. "I don't know if you remember us—"

"Of course I remember you. Did Teddy tell you I'm forgetting things?" Mrs. Leach asked. Gen shook her head. "Well, he's lying. My mind is sharp as a tack, I tell you. I think he just moved back in here so that he could get a hand on my silver. His wife always liked that set we use at Christmas."

"Okay, then." Gen made a face at Joel. "Um, we were wondering if you could tell us more about that woman you mentioned…the one you said ruined Calvin DeVries?"

"I knew someone would ask me about her some day. The rumors lingered around here for years, but then everyone seemed to forget. I didn't forget. I won't forget. That woman was pure evil."

"What woman? Who was she?" Gen asked.

"Sabina Silva. The farrier's daughter."

"Silva. The same family who was forced to move when they built the road," Joel said. Just like they had suspected. There was a grudge.

"Oh yes, her father was hopping mad about that. I was only a little girl when that all happened, but the bad blood remained between them. Even after Mr. DeVries died."

"Calvin, you mean?" Joel felt they were getting close to something. Gen was right. Intuition could be a very strong thing, if you'd just listen to it.

"Calvin? Oh no, not Calvin. He'd been dead for awhile by then. First it was Calvin…then the wife. Pretty thing she was too. No one knew how or why. And then it all started to happen."

"What?" Gen asked.

"Their luck started to turn. The DeVrieses started to drop like flies. From one illness or another. Some committed suicide. A few sold their shares in the company and tried to get away. Start over. But from what I understand, there aren't any left."

"My mother was a DeVries," Joel blurted out.

Mrs. Leach turned her gaze on him. "So you must be next."

"Excuse me?"

"Next, my dear. You're next. Is that why you're here in Calvin City?" She laughed a dry little laugh. "Did you think there would be something here to find?"

"What aren't you telling us? What about this Sabina Silva? Who was she? How is she connected to the DeVries family?" Joel's voice rose well above a polite, conversational tone.

"Joel." Gen touched his arm.

"No." He shook her off. "She knows something. She remembers something."

Theodore Leach popped his head around the corner. "Everything all right, Mother?"

"I thought it was all over. I thought it had ended years ago." Mrs. Leach regarded Joel as if he were a specimen in a glass jar. "How very, very interesting."

"Did Sabina Silva curse my family?" Joel grew incensed. He leaned forward in his chair. She drew back.

"I think you need to go." Theodore Leach stepped into the room, putting his body between Joel and his mother. "This was a mistake. I would like you to leave now."

"She knows something, and she won't tell us."

Mrs. Leach picked up her cane and rapped Joel on the leg with it. "Yes, a curse. There was never any doubt. No one wanted to believe it, but it was the only explanation. And she was the one. Her family…an unusual family. People always wondered, but until Calvin's death it had only been rumors. But we children believed it. We knew it the minute we walked past the Silva place. Evil. You could feel it there."

"Mother, please. I think you need to lie down." Theodore tried to help his mother up from her chair. "These people are going to make you ill. How dare you intimidate an old woman."

Mrs. Leach fought off her son's protective hands. "I'm not afraid of this man. But *he* should be afraid. He knows what's next. The DeVries family died long ago. You are just a ghost, young man. A ghost from the grave. It's too late for you. Too late." With that, Mrs. Leach pushed up from her chair with her cane.

Joel could barely restrain himself. He wanted to grab Mrs. Leach and make her tell him more. Give him more details. Explain herself. She knew about the curse, but she didn't care. It sounded like no one in this town cared. The DeVries family built this town, made it what it was, but no one liked a success. No one liked the rich man who brought the jobs, the work, the livelihood. Least of all a farrier who had to give up his land to build a road.

But before he could do something rash, Gen held fast to his arm. "Let's go, Joel."

"But she knows something…" He met the eyes of Theodore Leach and knew he wouldn't get any more information.

"That's okay," Gen said quietly. "We have what we need."

"I would like you to leave now." Mr. Leach opened the front door. Darkness had settled in during their visit. A mist hovered on the lawn outside, like a ghost waiting for them. Just like Mrs. Leach thought Joel was. A ghost she had said. He wasn't even worth saving, because she knew he was already dead.

Gen pulled him out the door.

"She knew more than she was telling us," Joel said. "She laughed at me. Laughed at what was happening to me."

"She's an old woman. Did you really think her son would let us ask her anything more after that? You have to learn to control your temper."

"My temper?" He backed away from her. "I'm sorry. I'm sorry if you think I got angry, but I'm in trouble here. I'm dying."

"You're not dying." Gen stood there in the mist with her pink-cheeked face and lithe body, so full of life and promise. It made him sick to think how the last four weeks had aged him, changed him forever.

"Yes, I am. There may be five weeks left to this thing, but I may as well be dead."

"Now you're just being maudlin."

"Maudlin?" He wanted to smash his fists on the hood of his car. Make her understand the fear that choked him. "Do you remember the list? The next curses on the list? I have no idea what half of them will do to me, but I do know that the whole entire DeVries family went mad. Crazy. Insane." He kicked an empty recycle bin into the road. "Why do you think I'm any stronger than they were? Why do you think that I could just sit here, think rationally, act rationally, when this is hanging over my head like a hangman's noose? How sane would you be if you were in my shoes?"

Gen glanced at the dented recycle bin. "What's the point in wasting energy over what *might* happen? Don't you want to take action...figure out what we need to do next?"

He was surprised at the depth of feeling in her voice. He'd thought she was brushing off his worries, but now he could see she was just as scared, just as worried. Could it be she felt something more for him than pity?

That one thought gave him hope. A desire to press on and save not only his brother but himself. "We need to find the Silva family."

"Exactly. Track them down. Find a relative, a descendant. Someone who might know something." An urgency filled her words.

Joel shut off the tap fueling his fear and directed it toward the new idea. "Yes, track them down. You're right."

"But first, we need to get back to Matt. He'll be wondering where we've been."

"Yes, Matt." In their goose chase to find answers, he'd almost forgotten that Matt and Bluto were here, waiting for him. Matt thought everything was just fine. Joel had to get his fear under control. He couldn't let Matt suspect anything. "But tomorrow, we have to find someone from the Silva family. And then..."

"Then, we have something to work with."

Her determination to track down the answers surprised him. She had a way of focusing their energies, distracting him from negative thoughts. He could've used her calm strength years ago after his father's death. She was a light burning bright in the darkness of his soul—a light he didn't want to extinguish. "If we find a descendant, what do we do?"

"I'll worry about that part." Gen grew quiet. "You just worry about staying sane."

While Joel went to unlock the car, Gen popped the dents out of the plastic recycle bin and set it back on the curb. The visit with Mrs. Leach had been very enlightening.

The hairs rose on the back of her neck. Adam must be here. He risked too much by visiting her with Joel nearby.

"I need you tonight," her husband said.

She turned around, but no one was behind her. Adam was invisible again. How did he manage it? Visible one moment, invisible the next. "Tonight? I'm not sure if I can get away." After righting the bin, she pretended to tie her shoe.

"Have a date with Joel?" His voice lowered to a darker timbre.

"No." What was Adam playing at? He was the one who brought Joel into their path. "But he's right across the hall from me..."

"I need the blood. The ceremony. Don't you want me back, Gen?" Invisible fingers stroked the back of her neck.

She closed her eyes and sucked in her breath. "Yes." When he touched her like that she could imagine him alive again. All those feelings rushing back. Overwhelming. Addictive.

Joel called to her from the car, "Hey, you coming?"

Adam slid his cool fingers to her jaw, his invisible hand cupping her face. "Then you will meet me tonight with everything we need."

"I'm running out of the leaves."

"I told you, I'll take care of that. Just meet me tonight." Cool lips touched hers briefly. "There's a cemetery through the woods. Midnight."

"Gen?" Joel gave her a questioning look.

"Tonight. Midnight." Gen finished tying her shoe. A chill ran through her, but she smiled all the same. After tonight they'd be one step closer to bringing him back. Forever.

CHAPTER FOURTEEN

Except for the saw-like snoring coming from his brother, the night was quiet. Joel couldn't get to sleep. He was tired, and he knew it was late—but he just couldn't keep his mind off the next curse. How could he be certain Gen's cure would work this time?

Tired of tossing and turning, he slid out of bed and got dressed. Maybe a walk in the night air would clear his head, help him get some rest. He couldn't do much about his situation in the dead of night. No matter what, he'd have to wait until morning to know if Gen's spell worked.

Gingerly, he slipped past the rollaway bed and the sleeping form of his brother and made his way to the door. When he turned the knob, the hinges creaked. He held his breath, but his brother continued to snore.

Out in the hall, he moved noiselessly down the stairs and into the entryway. A dark figure moved around on the front porch, and he heard voices. The doorknob turned. Joel slipped into the shadows under the stairs. Only one person stepped into the house. Even in the dim lighting, Joel recognized Gen right away. What was she doing out so late at night? And who had she been talking to?

She picked up her large bag, which sat near the front door, and headed back outside. As soon as the door closed, Joel crept forward, curious to find out where his spiritualist friend was headed and who she might be meeting.

Once outside, he saw she was alone. Whoever her companion had been, he'd disappeared. Perhaps he'd been imagining things?

The mist swallowed her up. Coastal fog was common this time of year. The halogen streetlight down the block from the bed and breakfast barely penetrated the thick swirls of fog. He hesitated for a moment. It was really none of his business where Gen was headed, but curiosity began to override any guilt he felt. Had she found an important clue about the curse? Or could she be meeting with someone? If he wanted to track Gen, he needed to move quickly, quietly.

Her steps were determined. Joel trotted to catch up with her, worried he would lose her in the mist if she stepped into the woods. She had no trouble navigating the wilds surrounding the B&B as she had shown him yesterday. She seemed more at home outside in nature than in the civilized world. A waif-like creature of the night, tiny hands pushing at branches and shrubs, her blonde hair disappearing and reappearing amongst the trees.

Joel struggled to keep up. The dark closed in. How could she still see where she was going? But the crunch of her steps on the fallen leaves kept him close enough.

Up ahead she stopped. He heard the squeak of an unoiled hinge. A gate swung open. Gen passed into the clearing beyond.

When Joel slipped through the gate, he knew where she had led him. A graveyard. Probably the same one where she had acquired graveyard dust for his cure yesterday. The gravestones were pale and eerie, rising out of the mists. The fog lifted, and a brilliant full moon shone down, illuminating the cemetery in ethereal light. Joel hunkered behind a large stone crypt, where a limestone angel peered down at him.

Gen moved between the grave markers, touching each one with a light caress. From so far away, he couldn't discern her emotional state, but her movements were stilted and slow. She stopped in the middle of the cemetery and raised her hands to the moon as if in supplication to the quiet, distant rock. A sing-song murmur filled the air. The words were just beyond his hearing. Gen kept her hands upraised and swayed in rhythm to them. A cry escaped her lips, and she fell to her knees.

Joel wanted to go to her, but he instinctually knew Gen did not want to share this with him. It would be an intrusion on her privacy.

From her bag, Gen removed some objects. She set them one at a time on the ground. He was too far away to see what they were.

Gen started a small fire and threw different items into the flame. Each time the blaze grew larger, her words grew louder.

Joel could just make them out now.

May angle sar te merel kadi yag, opre, Adam!

May angle sar te merel kadi yag, opre, Adam!

May angle sar te merel kadi yag, opre, Adam!

She lit a fat yellow candle from the fire's odd, red flame. A shadowy figure stepped out from behind a gravestone just behind her, tall and broad shouldered. A man. He drew closer.

Gen remained unaware this man was mere steps away—

"No!" Joel jerked forward, wanting to protect her.

Gen whipped her head around. "Who's there?"

The shadow man turned too, but evaporated into the mist.

Were his eyes playing tricks on him?

Joel revealed himself. "It's me, Gen. It's me."

"What are you doing here? Did you follow me?" She backed away, keeping the fire between them. "What did you see?"

"A man, I think," Joel said. Her eyes were big and round, her mouth half-opened...like a creature of the night, startled by a human passing through her territory. Her face was ashen. "Does this have something to do with the curses? Who was that...man?"

"Who said I was doing this for you?" Gen kicked dirt over the strange red fire. "Do you have any idea what you've just done, Joel?"

"What *I've* done?" He took a step toward her. "What do you mean?"

"You can't just wander in here…I didn't ask for you to be here. Now it won't work. You've ruined it."

"What won't work? What are you talking about?" As he came closer, he could see her eyes were filled with unshed tears.

"It's personal." She snatched up the things on the ground and stuffed them back in her bag. "Just forget it."

"I don't understand…if you'd just explain."

"I don't want to explain. It's none of your business. Just leave me alone." She brushed past him.

He caught her elbow. "What are you so darn upset about? I can't sleep, and there you are outside talking to someone in the middle of the night. And when I follow you, you come out here…and…and do this."

She tugged it free. "Go back to your brother. Go back to your life and leave me out of it. You don't want to be messed up with me."

"I'm already messed up with you. You made it that way. You came along with us. Helped me with these curses. What am I supposed to do, just pretend I can do this without you?"

Gen stopped her movements. "I'm sorry, Joel. Please don't ask me to explain. I want to help you, but that doesn't mean you get to know everything about me. I have to have my privacy."

"You're right. I'm sorry."

She slung her bag over her shoulder and made her way to the open gate at the other end of the cemetery. "Then let's go back. Let's just get some sleep."

"Wait." Joel caught up to her. "You still haven't answered my question. Who or what was that back there?"

She turned. The moonlight lit up her face, her eyes glowing. She made a little sound, a gasp, like the sound an animal makes when it's caught in a trap.

Joel could sense her heart racing. The tight dilation of her pupils, even in the dark, told him she feared him or feared he might find something out. Lightly, he grasped her upper arm. Her skin was cool. A night wind blew her hair across her forehead, which hid her eyes from him.

Here in this moonlit graveyard, she looked like the limestone angel that had been standing guard over him earlier. All cut angles and hard surfaces. But her skin. Her skin was soft and pliant under his hand. He slid his fingertips over her shoulder, across her collarbone, under her chin and forced her to look at him. "Tell me. He was going to hurt you."

"You didn't see anything. It was a trick of the dark." She tried to pull her chin out of his grasp, but he tightened his hold.

"You're lying."

Gen clutched her bag closer to her body. She blinked back tears. "Please don't ask me to explain."

"Would it really be so terrible to tell me?" He took a step toward her. She didn't move.

"I told you I don't want to explain. It's very personal to me and—"

The emotions she had so clearly been trying to keep in check came flooding out in one quick burst. He couldn't resist. He had to make the tears stop. He let go of her chin, curved his arm around her waist, pulled her close and kissed her. A light, sweet kiss. Her scent reminded him of strawberries and sunshine. He drank it in, wanting to absorb her into himself.

Her mouth opened to his, inviting him into her warmth. He groaned at the invitation and deepened the kiss, their tongues meeting furtively. He moved his hand up to her shoulder and under her jaw, keeping her soft lips against his. When his other hand brushed across the curve of her backside, she put her hands on his chest and pushed.

Gen broke away. "Don't."

He stood there, his arms empty, but still feeling her heat, her softness. Her kiss burned his lips. He touched his fingers there and watched as she made her way to the gate, slipping past its rusted iron bars and into the woods.

Tears fell freely now. At first, she'd thought the tears were for Adam, for the husband she'd lost and still yearned for. But now she wasn't so sure. Joel's kiss had stirred something in her she'd never thought she'd feel for another man.

"He kissed you." Adam barely suppressed the rage in his voice. "What gave him the right to do that to my wife?" He floated next to her, his body pale in the dark forest.

"He doesn't know I still have a husband." She wiped her eyes with the back of her hand. "Besides, I thought you wanted me to stick close to him."

"Not that close." They walked silently for a few yards. "But you're right. This may be a good thing. He has feelings for you. We could use that."

A strange twinge of guilt cut into her heart at those words. *Use Joel. Play with his emotions.* The idea didn't sit well with her. She brushed her thumb across her mouth, remembering the pressure and heat from his kiss. "I'm sorry we didn't finish the spell."

"You still have the blood?"

"Yes."

"We'll find another time." They'd reached the road. Gen stuck to the shadows along the edge, so Adam would be hidden. "Tomorrow you need to go to Cape Perpetua."

"Why?" He'd been giving her mysterious orders since they first arrived here in Calvin City. She'd followed them to the letter without complaint, but now she wanted to know more. Understand why he directed her to do these things.

"Just go. There's something you need to pick up for me."

For a moment she could believe he walked beside her like he used to, his hand in hers. She ached for that to be true once more. For his arms to hold her in a warm embrace. His body entangled with hers in bed. His heart beating in its slow, sure rhythm.

Although thoughts of Joel ran through her mind, she pushed them aside. Adam was her husband—Joel was just a distraction. "I'll do it," she said, as if the words themselves would bring Adam back to her. "I'll do it."

CHAPTER FIFTEEN

When Joel woke up the next morning, something seemed different. He couldn't quite put his finger on it. Instead of yesterday's gray gloom, sunlight streamed in through the window, but that wasn't it. And it wasn't the fact that he had kissed Gen last night and made a mess of things.

His brother was sound asleep. Snoring. That kid must have some kind of septum problems. He sounded like an elephant in heat when he slept.

He rubbed his chin. He needed to shave. His once scruffy growth felt more like a full-on beard. Although he was in lumberjack central, he certainly had no intention of blending in.

A soft knock at the door interrupted his thoughts. He pulled on his jeans, ran a hand through his hair and opened the door.

It was Gen. She appeared fresh and well-rested, not a trace of regret or embarrassment on her face. He stepped into the hall and closed the door quietly behind him. He didn't want to wake up Matt if Gen had something private to share.

"What are you doing up so early?" he asked. No sound came out of his mouth.

Her eyebrows knitted together.

He touched his throat. Panic crept into him. The curse was back.

"Are you okay?" She touched his forehead with the back of her hand as if she were checking for a fever. "Joel, can you talk?"

The ceremony from yesterday didn't work. Why?

"It's nothing to worry about. We'll fix it."

The skepticism must have been clear on his face.

"I know. I tried to fix it yesterday. But we can do something else. I think there's another cure in the book—"

He shook his head violently.

"Why not?"

The door opened behind him.

"Hey, what are you guys doing out here?" Matt scratched his bare chest. "Don't you know how early it is? Breakfast isn't for another hour. Can you keep it down out here?" He stumbled back into the room, his eyes half-closed. He threw over his shoulder, "Hey, bro, I've got a favor to ask."

Joel looked at Gen, hoping she could see the pleading in his eyes.

"Your brother..." she sputtered. "He...he's got laryngitis."

"What?" Matt came out further into the hall to inspect his brother. "When did that happen? When did you get sick?"

Joel shook his head, as if it was just as much a mystery to him as it was to Matt.

His younger brother smiled. "Well, this will be a nice change of pace."

Joel shot him a wary look.

"Now I don't have to worry about Mr. Know-it-all interrupting me all the time. I'll have to do the talking for him." Matt looked thoughtful. "Yeah, make sure everyone understands what my brother is trying to say. Right, Joel?" He clapped his brother hard on the shoulder.

Joel shrugged him off.

Gen tried to hide a smile. "Be nice, boys. We've got a long day ahead of us."

Long day?

Matt got there first. "What do you mean 'long day ahead of *us*'? You two have to do your software magic, and I've got a paper to finish."

"Our meeting with the client isn't until later this afternoon," Gen said. Joel cocked an eyebrow. "I thought we could do some sightseeing." She glared at Joel.

Apparently, she wanted him to agree to this crazy idea.

Joel tried to keep it together in front of his brother, but his thoughts ran wild. How was he going to get away with not talking for a week, much less a day? How could he explain that to Matt?

"After Stella mentioned it, I really want to go see the Devil's Churn at Cape Perpetua. And this will be the only free day we have."

"Why do you want to go out there?" Matt asked.

Joel wanted to know the same thing. Why such interest in this place?

Gen twisted her skirt in her hands. "Well, I read up about it yesterday when we were out. I don't want to miss it. Sounds like quite a sight."

"I've got a lot of work to do," Matt said, "but I think I can spare a couple of hours seeing the wonder that is nature." He gave Joel one last clap on the back and went back into the room. "I'll be showered and ready to go in about fifteen. See you downstairs."

After the door shut behind his brother, Joel frowned.

"I know, I know. Why bring him along? But I thought he might come in handy. If I can't talk to you, he might be the next best thing. He's a DeVries too, after all."

Joel shook his head.

"Don't worry. I just want us to go and do a little snooping there. Find out more about the Silva family. From what Mrs. Leach told us, there could be a grudge there, a reason to want to do somebody harm. And if Cape Perpetua encompasses the old Silva place, there might be some history there we can uncover."

Joel sighed. At least he could still make that much noise. He touched his throat, as if he would find something there. A hole in his neck, an empty space. That's how it felt to have no voice, to not be able to express himself.

And now he had to pretend for his brother he had a week-long case of laryngitis? Gen got lucky with that first cure. A fluke. She knew barely more than he did about this family curse, and his life depended on her help—the help of someone who spent more time reading some mysterious book than living in the real world.

Gen didn't seem to be able to read the defeat he felt. He nodded at her to agree to her plan, but there really wasn't much he thought they would find there. Some pine trees, rocks, ocean. What kinds of clues would there be almost ninety years later? Everything would be swept clean after years of harsh winds and salt-water spray. If there had been anything to find in the first place.

Her hand touched his arm like a will-o'-the-wisp. There one second, gone the next. Just like their kiss from last night. He faced her.

Her brown eyes were so open. No doubt or worry in them. "We'll find out what happened. We'll find out how to help you. I may not have had the right help this time, but I'll figure this out before it's too late. I promise."

He gave her a fleeting smile, the kind of smile a person doesn't mean, that comes with no feeling behind it.

She knew he didn't believe her. Her mouth flattened into a straight line. "I'll see you downstairs in a few minutes, okay?"

He nodded and slipped back inside his room without a noise.

"Adam, where are you?" Out in the hall Gen let her anger boil over. "I want to talk to you."

She sensed him before she saw him. The coolness of his hand on her shoulder. She whirled around to face him. "What did you do to him? Why didn't the cure work?" She'd agreed to this plan because she loved Adam, but she never intended to hurt Joel. This was not what Adam had promised her.

"I told you, he can help me."

"But we were also supposed to help him, remember? You get what you want, and we cure him."

"I never agreed to that." He hovered a few inches off the floor.

"What?" She couldn't believe what she was hearing. At first, the idea of stealing blood for Adam seemed harmless, but as she got to know Joel and his brother the only thing keeping her from feeling guilty had been the fact she was helping Joel too.

"That was all your idea. I never promised I would help cure him. I just need to keep him alive, keep him close."

"But yesterday…" Adam was so frustrating lately. Talking in riddles. "Why did you tell me it was a cure?"

Adam laughed. More of his games. "His blood is more powerful now. Why wait all that time? Why keep us apart longer? I was only thinking of us, Gen." His hand trailed down her arm in a cold caress.

She shivered. "Are you saying you can't save him?"

His caress became a tight grip on her arm. "Why do you care what happens to him? He's a stranger. I'm your husband."

For the first time, true fear for her safety hit her. In life, Adam never would have talked to her this way, hurt her. She twisted her wrist to break free. His grip was unyielding. "I can't use him like that. Lie to him and use him. You promised me we'd help him."

"You seemed more than willing to use him that first night."

Gen winced at the memory. He was right. She'd eagerly stolen Joel's blood. And yesterday, when Adam asked her to cut him, she had with little hesitation. "Well, I won't do it anymore. Not unless you promise to help him as much as you can. It seems only fair. His blood for a cure to his curses."

Adam let go of her arm. He drifted away from her. "You promise to continue with the ceremonies, continue collecting his blood without telling him why?"

"Yes." Joel would likely reject her help if she told him about the blood. If this was how she'd get the crucial information she needed from Adam to cure Joel, then she could stay silent.

He smiled. "Then, yes, I'll promise to help him. There's always another brother, if this one doesn't make it."

Gen froze at the words. To Adam, Joel was just a vessel carrying something he needed. If he couldn't get enough blood from Joel before the final curse, Matt was the backup. It made her sick to think about it.

"You'll see, my love, it will all work out. When we're back together, you'll see it was all worth it." Adam drifted toward the ceiling, his body becoming fainter and fainter until he was gone.

~ * ~

"Is there anyone here who can help us with a bit of history?" Gen asked the female park ranger at the entrance to Cape Perpetua. She had to lean over Joel's lap in order to ask her question. He held his breath when she pressed against him. Her body was warm and soft. A slow flame of desire burned inside him. He wanted to lean into her hair and lose himself in her sweet scent. She smelled like strawberries again.

"Well now, we do have a nice interpretive center." The ranger's voice snapped him back. "Talks about the roads they built through here, the trees and such, the Native American history. Mighty nice little place to stop and visit. Folks usually come for the Churn, the campgrounds. Not many stop at the center. Most people want to see the excitement out by the cliffs."

Gen eased back into her seat, and Joel relaxed. "So there's some history on the roads?" She smoothed her skirt.

"Yep. Spent a pretty penny to connect Calvin City with Florence long time ago. The DeVries family put up half the money, the government kicked in the rest."

"The DeVrieses helped pay for the road? I wasn't aware of that."

"They wanted a throughway south to Florence. Faster connection to Eugene that way. Easier for them to deliver the timber. All about the money, you know."

"That makes sense," Gen said.

"Well, you can learn all about it at the Interpretive Center. Just follow the road a few miles. It'll be on your left. Oh, and the best view is from the West Shelter. First turn on your left. Just follow it all the way up. Worth a stop."

"All right, thanks so much for your help." Gen waved at the ranger. Joel pushed the button to roll up the window and tried to banish the memory of her warmth, her sweet smell.

"You know," Matt commented from the back of the car, "I'm rather enjoying the quiet in here."

Joel could imagine the teasing smile his younger brother had on his face. He quickly pressed on the brake, stopping short and sending his brother's face into his headrest.

"Oh, so cool, *big* brother. Now who's the juvenile?"

"All right, you two." Gen turned to give them both a scolding. "Let's break it up. We're here for a reason."

"We are?" asked Matt.

"Well, I mean, I'm a history buff, and I'd really like to get a chance to find out more about the area before Joel and I have our meeting this afternoon."

"For a business trip, you guys hardly do any talking about business."

"We just don't like to bore you with the details. You know, software, so boring."

Joel, recognizing she was losing control of the conversation, switched on the radio. He tuned it to a country station and turned up the volume.

"Hey, don't you think that's a little loud…and a little too blue collar?"

Joel just cranked it up higher, so that no conversation could be heard in the car. Gen gave him a thankful look.

The Interpretive Center was a low-lying building that blended well with the rough terrain and towering pine trees. Joel pulled into the small parking lot. Only one other car was there. The ranger was right, not a lot of interest in the Interpretive Center. But that meant they wouldn't be disturbed while they found out all they could about the history of this place.

Matt opened Gen's door for her. "Milady." He quirked a smile.

"Thanks, I guess." Gen seemed dumbfounded by the chivalry.

If Joel could have spoken, he would have had a zinger for his brother's attempt at being a gentleman.

"Don't even think it, bro," Matt whispered when they met up on the sidewalk.

Joel gave him a half smile. His younger brother knew him too well.

Inside, the Interpretive Center was dark and stuffed to the brim with Indian artifacts, old photographs, and in one dusty corner a display about the road development through Cape Perpetua. It appeared as if the funding must have run out by the time they got to this part of the park.

A rather sleepy-looking man behind a counter gave them a nod and went back to reading a brochure from the rack next to the cash register.

Curious, Joel scanned the rack. Not much tourist information here. A few motels, restaurants, the B&B where they were staying and a map of the Cape. He grabbed a map and caught up to Gen and Matt who had already made their way to the back.

"Joel, come look here." Gen stood next to the road display, a conglomeration of photographs, maps and a descriptive placard. "They talk about the Silvas and their homestead. The main house used to be right here where the Interpretive Center stands."

"And this would interest my brother because...?" Matt leaned against the wall and crossed his arms.

Joel glared at him.

"What?" Matt said. "What in the hell does this place have to do with anything? I thought we were here to see the sights, not rummage through some old museum. *Hey, Matt, how'd you spend your spring break?*" Matt started a pretend conversation with himself. "Oh, I went to a boring-ass museum. *But I'm sure you finished up your super-important research project, right?* No, I didn't because I wasted my time hanging out in a boring-ass museum." Matt glared at him.

Joel set his jaw. If he only had the ability to speak, he would tell his brother just what an annoying little—

"I'm a big history buff." Gen played mediator. "I thought it was nice you agreed to drive me out here while we had the chance."

Matt hung his head. Joel hoped he was feeling guilty. Guilty and stupid.

"Do you guys mind if I wait outside?" Matt looked up at a stuffed eagle perched on a sawed-off branch above their heads. "This place gives me the creeps."

"I'll only be a few minutes," Gen said. "I promise."

Joel stepped closer to the display case full of yellowed photographs, half-rotten bridles and a large, intricately carved hunting knife. He tapped on the glass to get Gen's attention.

"Your brother. He's so cute."

Joel had no idea what to do with that piece of information. So he grabbed her arm and tugged her toward the case, pointing.

"What?" Gen turned her attention back to the display. The knife gleamed under the dim lighting. "Oh, now that's interesting."

Joel wanted to know why a struggling horse trader would have such a valuable knife. It seemed out of place with the rest of the rotting, dusty artifacts.

"That carving," Gen whispered. "It looks so familiar."

Joel gave her an inquisitive look.

"Just something about it…" Gen shook her head as if she were clearing cobwebs out of her mind. "Never mind. What else can we find here to help us track down any of the Silva descendants?"

Joel scanned the photos. There weren't any familiar faces among them. No one he remembered from the Historical Society. A small placard in the case read "Wm. Silva and Family."

"I'm going to talk to the guy over there." Gen looked across the room at the man behind the counter. Now he was eating a Snickers bar. "You keep looking."

Joel nodded. He focused on the case jammed full of odds and ends. A pair of spurs, a faded ladies' hat, a monogrammed handkerchief. How in the hell would this junk help him out? He wanted to open his mouth and scream. They were wasting time, dawdling around this place, no clear idea of where to go for the answers they needed. Joel banged his hand against the glass in frustration.

"Please don't touch the glass," the man said. He and Gen turned back to an unfolded park map they were scrutinizing together.

Joel nodded, but he really wanted to punch it again. Break the glass. Tear everything out of there. He jammed his hands in his pockets.

Was that a piece of paper?

Joel had banged so hard on the glass case a slip of paper had fallen out from behind a propped-up photo of two men and a team of mules pulling timber. His first instinct was to lift the lid of the case and pick up the paper. A padlock held it firmly closed.

Joel sneaked a glance at the man talking with Gen. He had his full attention on the petite and pretty blonde, their heads leaning in intimately. He centered his thoughts on finding a way to read that letter. He just knew it was something important.

He bumped the case again, this time with some finesse. The letter fell flat. If he could just lean a little bit further he could read it...

Dearest Sabina,

I'm sorry to say, my darling, that we can no longer meet. It wouldn't be prudent to continue such a liaison. I will be leaving for the Army in a few months. I think it would be best if we end things now. I am sure you will find someone more suitable. It had never been my plan to marry...

The rest was too faded to read in the dim lighting, but there was no mistaking the signature: Calvin. So Calvin and Sabina Silva, one of William Silva's three daughters, had a love affair? A love affair which ended badly. Could it be Sabina cursed her lover when he left her? He said in the letter he would never marry, but yet not too long after he wrote this letter, he did marry...someone else. Perhaps that newspaper article about the road had meant nothing—beyond the fact it was clear the Silva and DeVries families were against a match.

Calvin had left her, joined the army and returned married to another. How that must have hurt Sabina's pride. How humiliated she must have been. Then, a few short months after his wedding, he and his new wife had died.

Even though he was in the clutches of the same family curse that had killed his distant relative, reading this letter somehow made it more real. More evil. More insidious.

This letter and their earlier research convinced Joel Sabina Silva had made those people die and was still ruining lives from the grave. The timing was right. The history was right. It had to be her doing.

He scanned the display case with an intensity he didn't have earlier. He found a scrap of paper in his jacket pocket and a pen and began writing. All the photos were marked with white ink. The names of people possibly associated with the Silva family. He took them all down, knowing one of these names would be the answer. A relative they could track down. And then Gen would know what to do.

Gen spoke with the man behind the counter for a few minutes, trying to coax him into divulging any facts that might be helpful in their search for answers. Just when she was going to ask about the knife in the case and its history, she sensed Adam's presence.

"Ask him about the old homestead." Adam's voice rumbled in her ear, a bare whisper, like a puff of air.

"Was there something else I could help you with?" When the man smiled, she noted his teeth were yellowed, most likely from the cigarettes he smoked. His clothes reeked of them.

"Ask." She could feel Adam right behind her.

Gen cleared her throat. "I was wondering about the old homestead. What can you tell me?"

The man leaned his elbows on the counter and wiped his thumb across his shiny forehead. "Well, now, the place sat right here where we're standing until 1963. At the time—"

"Not this homestead. The other one," Adam breathed.

"—they were short on funding, but the Historical Society—"

Adam's invisible body pushed up against her. "Tell him you want to know about the other one."

"Th-the other one. Not this homestead. I want to know about the other one."

The man stopped talking, his mouth open in mid-sentence. He frowned. "Now how'd you know about that? The university just sent people up here last week when someone stumbled across the ruins. Are you with the university?"

How did Adam know about this newly discovered homestead? "Uh, yes. The university. Could you tell me how to get there?"

"Very good, Gen," her husband said soothingly in her ear.

The man pulled out a park map and unfolded it. "There's no trail, you understand, so it might be a little hard to find. You can park here." He showed her a dead-end road at the far end of the park. "Then you can hike in a mile or two. It's in a clearing. Not much left of it, I guess you know."

She studied the map.

"So are you with the archaeology department?"

"Hmmm?" She looked up. "Oh, uh, yes. Archaeology. Here to do a preliminary survey before we bring in all of our equipment."

"Nicely done, Gen." Adam's presence faded. His words echoed in her head.

"Well, good luck with your work, and let me know if you need anything else." The man patted her on the back of the hand.

Gen appeared at Joel's side with the park map. "The guy over there told me that we might try the… What's wrong?"

If only he could speak. He could tell her his discovery and ask her all of the questions he'd been thinking. He stared at her, hoping she could see the knowledge in his eyes. He longed to be done with this and back to his normal life. He thought of his home, the way Bluto used to wait out in the bushes to be fed every night, the comfortable recliner chair he would sit in to read the paper.

Sabina Silva had taken that away from him. A dead woman had ruined his life. He had no enemy to face. Nothing to conquer. He could do nothing to save himself. Nothing. He had never felt so helpless in his life.

"Are you all right?" Gen touched his shoulder lightly. "It's okay. I can do this."

He nodded.

"I haven't yet found a way to help with—" She touched her throat. "You know. At least this one isn't so bad…"

He shrugged. Bad compared to what? Burning, painful boils? Yes, not being able to speak was certainly an improvement, if he had to choose.

"I'll keep looking, though." She played with the map, folding and refolding it. "Did you find anything?"

He tapped on the glass, trying to get her to notice the letter.

"What?" She leaned over the case. "That picture?" She indicated a photograph of several men on horseback.

He shook his head and tapped again on the glass, right above the faded stationery paper.

"The hat?"

Joel tapped harder on the case.

"I said, no tapping on the glass," the man behind the counter barked.

Joel scowled.

"I can ask you to leave, you know." The man got up from his stool.

She stepped in front of Joel. "No, we're okay. We were just leaving." She tugged on his sleeve.

He pulled his arm out of her grasp and tapped again on the glass. He wanted her to see the letter. Read it. Know that Sabina was the one. It made sense. It fit with what she'd told him.

"We have to go," she whispered sharply. "We can always come back. Come on."

Joel stood there for a moment. He looked down the display case. The clues were there inside, if only he could put all the pieces together in some logical order. The strange knife, the pictures, the letter. It all meant something, and he wanted to know what. Right now. Not later on. Not tomorrow. Not next week. Now.

The front door opened. Matt stood in the doorway. "Hey, guys, I've got something I want to show you."

Joel gave one last look at the case and reluctantly headed toward his brother. If need be, he could always come back later. By himself. After everyone else was gone. He had to get inside that case.

CHAPTER SIXTEEN

If they had been at Cape Perpetua for any other reason, hiking the colorfully named Captain Cook's Trail would probably have taken Joel's breath away. But he wasn't here to sightsee. Too bad his brother didn't know that.

"And then I saw this marked path that takes you this way…" Matt led them through a glade of Sitka spruce down a pine-needle-covered trail. Off to the right, as they entered the woods, a sheer drop from the cliffs to the ragged coastline below appeared through the trees. Low-lying gray clouds created a murky sky.

Gen stopped. "This is absolutely spectacular." She took a deep breath of the damp ocean air. "It probably looks exactly the same now as it did a hundred years ago."

"Just wait," Matt said, stepping farther into the woods. "You haven't seen the best part."

For a moment, they broke free of the trees. The sun peeked through the murk and lit up shoulder-high salal bushes with their glossy green leaves. They could see the whole of the ocean now. The gray sky meeting the roiling black waves in the distant horizon. Wind whipped at them. Whitecaps gathered and bobbed, heading toward the shore as they built into boulder-sized waves and crashed on the desolate beach.

Matt pointed at a ragged tip of land, barren of any trees or bushes, straight across an inlet. The waves surged up against the crags, and a fountain of water and sea spray shot into the air like a geyser.

"Amazing, isn't it?" Matt stood near the edge of the drop-off.

"Wow," commented Gen. "That's incredible."

"They call it the Spouting Horn."

The two of them stood there, in awe of the sight.

Joel wished he could enjoy the beauty of this spot, but he thought only of the letter and the clues it might contain. Answers. One step closer to a cure, perhaps. He couldn't talk, he couldn't cure himself, and he depended on Gen to help him. They needed to stop wasting time and find some answers. Do something.

He picked up a good-sized stone and tossed it over the side of the cliff into the water below. He imagined it was the curse, bouncing down and away from him to be swallowed up by the ocean. How he wished it were that easy.

Gen watched the stone and glanced at him. She must've sensed the tenseness in him, the worry.

"Let's get back to the car, shall we?" Gen linked her arm with Matt's. "I'm hungry. I'd like something for lunch." She brushed past Joel.

Another plume of water spewed up behind him, kissing the sky, like a burst of violent emotion.

When his brother passed by, Joel followed. He ran a hand through his hair and thought about the letter in the glass case. How he would come back tonight, once everything was closed, get back inside and take the letter. What other secrets did it contain? Perhaps something that might lead them to a cure or to the descendant they so desperately needed to find.

He never would've guessed he'd stoop to stealing. How did he go from his mundane software-testing job to petty thievery in just a matter of weeks? He barely recognized himself. And how much further would he be willing to go to find a cure and save his brother? The unanswered question chilled him.

CHAPTER SEVENTEEN

The clock struck midnight when Joel sneaked out. Bluto almost gave him away, meowing. An extra bowlful of food quieted him down.

He parked on the shoulder outside the entrance to Cape Perpetua and turned off his headlights. The park had closed hours ago and the gate was shut, but he knew he could still get onto the grounds. Since campers could overnight here, the park never officially closed. A night ranger probably made sure campers stayed safe for the night, but beyond that, heavier security was unnecessary.

He opened the glove box and pulled out a flashlight. He hoped it still worked. He hadn't needed to use it in years. He snapped it on, and the light wavered from bright to dim. Joel shook it. The batteries clacked inside, and the light brightened.

He hoped it wouldn't take him long to break in, get what he wanted and leave.

He climbed over the gate by the ranger booth and kept the flashlight turned off. The Interpretive Center was only a few miles south. His eyes adjusted to the dark. Luckily, the clouds, which had earlier muddied the sky, had thinned. The glowing orb of the moon shone down, giving enough light for him to navigate the spruce-lined road that curved through the park.

A cracking of twigs caught his attention. The moon didn't pierce the dark of the woods. He couldn't see a thing, and he worried that if he turned on his flashlight, he might draw attention to himself. Instead, he slipped into the even deeper shadows on the edge of the road.

He held his breath, waiting. But nothing happened.

He stayed in the shadows just in case. This was not his kind of thing— sneaking around in the dark, breaking into places. His hand shook slightly at the rush of adrenaline to his system. He needed that letter. After taking a deep breath to calm his nerves, he headed for the center.

In the dim moonlight, Joel could make out the hulk of the Interpretive Center beyond the edge of the trees. From a distance the building reminded him of a sleeping giant. Its double glass doors were like two eyes, a row of hedges across the front like the grim line of a mouth.

The cool ocean breeze made him shiver.

Get over it, Joel. It's just a damn building.

Now that he was only a few feet from the entrance, he snapped on the flashlight to help guide him. A heavy chain looped through the handles on the front doors. There was probably an entrance in back, but he could get through this way much faster. He couldn't believe he was going to do this. Break in and steal something. A sourness in his stomach almost made him turn around. This wasn't him.

He thought of the letter and the answers it might hold. To steal it might be the only way to get a look at it. One moment in his life, one bad moment, did not make him a bad man. Did it?

Underneath the hedges were good-sized rocks as part of the landscaping. Pushing past his guilt, he picked up the largest one he could find, aimed and hurled it at the door. A loud clang echoed into the night. The glass cracked, but didn't break.

Damn it.

He let go of the breath he'd been holding.

What now?

He hefted the flashlight in his hands. Grabbing it by the lens, he stepped up to the window and smashed it against the cracked glass. With two hard hits, his fist and the flashlight punched through the glass. He kept smashing until he'd made a big enough opening to crawl through.

He was now officially a criminal. A cold sweat broke out on his brow. He wanted to turn and run, but he forced himself forward. This had to be done.

Ducking through the ragged hole, he turned on the flashlight again. He knew right where to go—the very back corner. In his peripheral vision he caught the flicker of a shadow. He snapped his head toward it. Was someone else there? A park ranger?

Near the counter a trash can fell over with a clang.

His heart in his throat, Joel ducked behind a topography display in the middle of the room. Without a voice, he couldn't call out and ask who was there. Without a voice, he couldn't tell someone who he was and that he was unarmed. Without a voice, he couldn't scare off any wild creature that may have wandered inside.

He turned off the flashlight and pressed himself against the veneered wood of the display. If it was a ranger, he hoped he could get out unseen. If it was an animal, maybe he could scare it away with his flashlight.

There were footsteps. Definitely footsteps and not animal movement.

A ranger.

He froze. His heart pounded.

He had to give himself up. Put his hands in the air, stand up, reveal himself. They might take his silence as aggression or just plain craziness.

But whoever it was wasn't talking. Wasn't asking him why he was there. Maybe it wasn't a park ranger. Then who else...?

Joel peered around the edge of the display. A door to his right stood open. To his left, a figure dashed across the room, hunkered down and crawled out through the hole in the glass he had made.

Another thief?

He stood, flicked on the light and shone it through the door. The reflection of the flashlight beam on the glass momentarily blinded him, but he could hear the distant echo of footfalls on pavement. Whoever it was had gotten away.

It was now more urgent for him to get what he needed and get out of there. What if that person wasn't a thief, but someone who worked there? Or someone who would call the police?

Joel trotted over to the Silva display. He needed to move quickly. To his surprise, the padlock on the case had already been broken. The other intruder was also interested in this case? What were the odds?

The letter.

He lifted the heavy glass top. With his flashlight beam, he located the letter, still safe next to the picture. But something else was missing from the case—the knife. The intricately carved knife which looked so out of place in the case of junk and old photographs. That must have been what the other intruder had been after. It had looked like a valuable piece. Probably pure silver.

He snatched the delicate stationery, tucked it in his jacket pocket and carefully lowered the lid.

The minute he turned from the case and headed toward the broken glass door something happened. A very strange something. His throat felt hot and then cold. Something came unstuck inside. Instead of an emptiness in his throat, there was a sensation of being whole.

"H-h-ello?" he whispered. His voice was back.

CHAPTER EIGHTEEN

After only one day Joel's voice was back. But what began as joy turned into fear and confusion. He'd made it through this curse in one day without any help from Gen. What did that mean?

Climbing through the hole in the glass door of the Interpretive Center, he mumbled to himself to make sure he wasn't dreaming. "I'm Joel. Joel Hatcher. I live in Portland." He started off at a quick clip down the road and toward the exit from the park.

He touched his throat. Everything seemed normal. It didn't feel like anything was going to change.

His toes and fingers began to tingle.

Joel's mind grew muddled. Cloudier than it had been moments before. The adrenaline pumping through his body had kept him on high alert. Every movement, every shadow, he'd noticed. But now, he couldn't seem to think straight.

His hands and feet were leaden. Dead weights on the ends of his limbs. He lifted his hands and looked at the tips of his fingers in the moonlight. They were white. Deathly white. The rest of his hand was not.

What was happening?

He stuffed his hands into his pockets to warm them.

He stumbled a bit. His car sat down the road a piece, past the gate near the guard shack.

He tripped and almost tumbled to the ground. Why was he so clumsy and slow?

He remembered. The curses. Yes, he could talk again. Much sooner than he expected, but why was the next curse taking over now? Just a day later.

He ran through the list of curses in his head. Loss of Livelihood, Trial by Fire, Painful Pox—and got stuck. His brain couldn't process the information. Which one was this? Number six? Seven?

He couldn't think.

Oh, his hands were so cold now. He took his left one out of his pocket and shook it to get the blood circulating. He couldn't bend his fingers. They were stiff, bloodless, painfully cold.

Cold. That was it. The Bone Chill curse.

His car waited beyond the last line of spruce. To retrieve his key, he dug his hand into the front pocket of his jeans. His fingers wouldn't grasp the key.

His legs were like solid frozen chunks of meat. He took steps like Frankenstein, stiff and slow, his knees unbending.

And he was cold. So very cold. Violent shivering took over his body.

Although his car sat only a few feet away, his pace had slowed to less than a crawl. He had to get warm, but he couldn't get the key out of his pocket.

He stumbled. His palms bit into the pea gravel on the shoulder. In defeat, he clasped his hands together and beat on the side of his car.

"Open up!" A tingling sensation spread across his back. Instead of crawling on the gravel, he imagined he was on an ice floe, surrounded by arctic waters—his bare hands on the ice, the wind blowing steady and strong, stealing what little warmth he had left. "Please, open." His voice was hoarse and raw. He needed to get inside, to get warm.

His energy sapped, he sagged against the car. The metal was warmer than his own skin. He pulled his knees into his chest, trying any way he could to preserve body heat. The tingling spread from his back, up his neck and into his scalp. He was a human-sized block of ice.

CHAPTER NINETEEN

In a daze of cold and aching joints, Joel heard a steady squeak. Like an old machinery part that needed oil.

Squeak.

Squeak.

Squeak.

Bicycle wheels whirred rhythmically.

Someone was passing by. In the night. In the middle of nowhere. His lucky break.

Joel huddled in a ball next to the front tire of his car, shivering. Wishing to God he had a blanket or a bonfire or something warmer than the cold ground.

"Help," he said, surprised at how raspy and weak his voice sounded. If anyone could hear him above the rattle of the wind through the trees and the crash of the waves beyond, it would be a miracle. "Please help me."

He heard a gasp, then the whine of air brakes. "Joel, is that you?"

The figure was hidden from him, on the other side of the car near the road, but he recognized the voice instantly. "G-Gen." His teeth chattered.

"G-Gen, p-please help m-me." With all his strength, he pushed himself upright and leaned against the tire. "I c-can't get the k-key—"

Gen skirted the hood of the car. "What are you doing down there? Why are you out here?"

Joel wondered the same about her, but was too miserable and full of pain to ask. He just wanted warmth. To curl up and be warm.

"Th-h-he curse," he said, stumbling over the words, his tongue like a lump of dead flesh in his mouth. "Bone Chill. N-n-next on the l-list." He held his fingers in front of his mouth and blew on them. Even his breath was like ice.

She knelt beside him, picked up his hand and rubbed it between both of hers. "But how—? You couldn't speak. That was only one day…and now this? So quickly? What happened? What's changed?"

The warmth of her hands gave him a small amount of relief from the bitter cold invading his body. "I don't know. I just—I just w-w-want to get inside. The keys are in my p-p-pocket."

"We need to get you back to the inn. Under some blankets. In a hot bath. Something." Gen helped him to his feet. "You can't just curl up in your car for the night."

Joel looked across the hood at the beat-up ten-speed bike propped against the front end with her oversized purse strapped to the back. What was she up to? Why was she out here so late on a bicycle?

She circled an arm around his waist, and her body heat warmed him. Just slightly. Just enough to take away a bit of the misery. A bit of the hopelessness. "I'll drive you back. Get you in bed."

"But the b-bicycle…"

"I can come back for it tomorrow morning. Chain it up to a tree."

"The k-keys." He touched his right front pocket. "And don't f-forget your bag."

Her head snapped up, and an odd look appeared in her eyes. "Yes, I don't want to forget that." She dipped her delicate fingers into his pocket, fished out the keys and unlocked the passenger side door.

She helped him inside. His body quivered like a junkie needing a fix. While he huddled on the passenger seat, she grabbed her bag off the bike.

Even in the grip of the Bone Chill curse, he hadn't lost his ability to figure out the obvious. "That was you b-b-back there. In the c-center. Wasn't it? You t-t-took that knife."

Gen turned the key in the ignition and the engine roared to life. Fiddling with the heater, she cranked it up to high. "Yes. I took it."

"Why?" He rubbed his arms with his hands, more for his own mental health than for any physical comfort it gave him. "Was it hers?"

"Whose?" Gen nervously grabbed at the shifter and slipped it into drive.

"Sabina Silva's. Is that s-something she used to c-curse my f-f-family?"

As she drove Gen shimmied out of her jacket and covered him with it. Hot air blasted out the vents, warming his cold skin. But it wasn't enough. The heat only gave him a moment of relief before the chill set back in.

"I told you, I thought I recognized the symbol on the knife…I thought it might have some kind of significance…" She slowed down to take a particularly sharp curve. "Why were you there?"

Joel reached into his jacket pocket, but his fingers were useless. "In my p-p-pocket…there's a letter."

Keeping her eyes on the road, Gen felt her way over his chest to the pocket where he had stashed the letter. The light touch of her fingers made him forget about the chill. She snatched the letter and spread it open on the steering wheel. "What does it say?" She slowed to take another treacherous curve.

"It's a letter from Calvin to Sabina." He forced each word out of his mouth. It took more effort than breathing. "He b-b-breaks it off with her. Says he can't continue their love affair."

"Just like we thought. It has to be Sabina then. She placed the curse on your family." She grew quiet.

"What is it?"

She folded the letter. "Nothing. I'm just thinking about what our next step should be."

She wasn't telling him something. Something important. Why would she sneak out here all alone? Why wouldn't she have told him she was coming back for the knife?

Same reason you didn't tell her you were coming back for the letter. You still don't trust her.

"I was h-h-hoping the letter would g-g-give us some direction to go in…a name, something. I haven't r-r-read the whole thing yet." He shivered uncontrollably and then cursed. "How am I supposed to get anything done when I'm fr-freezing to death?" He kicked at the floor. "I can't th-think straight. My head's working like it's full of m-molasses."

Sweat beaded on Gen's brow. "But it's so hot in here. You don't feel even a little bit warmer?"

He shook his head and settled deeper under her jacket.

"When we get back to the B&B, I want to try something."

"Another one of your 'c-cures'?" he snorted. Now he had to worry about her "help" possibly making things worse. "Why do you think the curses sp-sped up? Now they're coming every day instead of once a w-week—"

She shrugged, her mouth a straight line.

"I don't know if I want you to t-try anymore."

"What?"

"I th-think you might be making things worse."

"Worse? I helped you. The sores? I fixed you. Who knows where you would be now if I didn't help."

"You mean that b-book helped. Without that s-salve and the spell oils…"

"The book may have taught me a few things." She kept her eyes trained on the winding road. "But I was the one who opened the door for you, took you in."

He reflected back on the first night they met. How scared he'd been. How alone. The thought of not having Gen nearby to help him through each curse, to reassure him things would be okay, paralyzed him. She was right, he might be dead now if it weren't for her. "I'm gr-grateful that you helped, and I'm grateful you're st-still here, but I just can't r-risk it. We don't know what caused the curses to speed up. The Bone Chill curse is number five on the list. Only four more to go…can't you see why I would be worried?" He made a concerted effort to speak slowly and clearly without stuttering. "I can stand being cold for now. If it gets to be too much for me, I'll let you know. And then we can try…but for now, I want to stick it out."

"But, Joel…"

"Trust me. I can do this, Gen. I can. We need to spend our time finding out more about Sabina Silva's family, track down her relatives, and then—"

Gen shifted in her seat. "—and then we fix it. Forever."

He nodded at her words, but her statement was empty. Without conviction. What wasn't she telling him? Maybe they couldn't fix it. Maybe she already knew that, but didn't want him to sink deeper into hopelessness.

He shivered again and did his best to keep his leaden limbs covered under Gen's jacket. Not that it made him feel warmer.

He would have to trust that if he didn't make it, Gen would take care of his brother. If hope was lost for him, maybe they had enough time to save Matt. Figure this out.

Determination settled into his frozen bones. The foggy night encroached on Joel's car and made the drive even more dangerous. If it weren't for Gen driving, he might just decide to miss one of those sharp curves. To break through the barrier and drive over the edge. It would be an easy way out.

But where would that leave Matt?

Joel shook off his morbid thoughts. He could do this. One day at a time.

CHAPTER TWENTY

Joel, wrapped in a quilt, sat inches away from a roaring fire in Gen's room. The flames from the gas fireplace threw off heat, but it didn't penetrate his body. The surface of his skin sensed it, but inside he was as cold as a meat locker.

"What else does the letter say?" Gen handed him a mug of hot tea—the only hot drink she could find. It was either a mug of Earl Grey or some kind of herbal menthol-smelling stuff. "Any clues as to who else might have been involved? Any other family members?"

Joel took a sip of the steaming liquid. He burned his tongue, but the searing heat was a balm to his innards. "Here, you read it. My hands are shaking too much." He handed her the expensive piece of stationery on which Calvin had written his message.

"...*It had never been my plan to marry. Not until after the War. Father has always disapproved of my relationship with you and your family. Meet me at the Overlook tonight one last time. I want to see you before I ship out next week. Mirela can come along if you'd like. I've thought of her as my younger sister. The sister I never had. I know she would enjoy a night out, away from the work at home. Your father works all of you too hard. Please tell me you'll come. I'll meet you at our 'darling' spot after sunset.*"

"It sounds like he was still in love with her," Gen said, setting the paper in her lap.

"At least he might have been before the war. But remember what Mrs. Leach said? He was different when he came back. Maybe he fell out of love with Sabina. Realized there was no way for them to be together. It sounded like Sabina's father hated the DeVrieses."

"And Calvin's father wasn't happy with the relationship either."

He nodded.

She read the letter over again. "What do you think he meant by 'our *darling* spot'?"

"Who knows?" He shivered. "It could be anywhere."

She had a thoughtful look on her face. "Maybe..."

"Can you crank that thing up any higher?" He jerked his chin in the direction of the gas fireplace.

"God," she said, leaning toward the fireplace controls, "your lips are blue." After she turned up the flame, she captured his hand in hers, rubbing it vigorously. "Are you going to be okay?"

A different kind of warmth filled him when she touched his hand. "I guess I'll have to be."

Her hand lingered on his. A cloudy expression came across her face. Did she pity him? Or feel something more? He fingered the gold band on her ring finger. Gen jerked her hand away from him.

"Did he hurt you?"

"What?" Her eyes snapped.

"Your husband. The way you reacted I thought maybe it was because there were bad memories there."

"You don't know anything about my husband."

He grew quiet. "No, I don't. I'm sorry if I misunderstood."

She turned away from him and folded the quilt at the bottom of her bed, smoothing out each wrinkle. "He's dead."

"I'm sorry. I—I didn't know."

128

She ran a hand along the brass rail at the bottom of her bed. "I'm just not ready for…" She sighed. "I've been alone for a long time now." She faced him, two spots of red on her pale cheeks. From the heat of the fireplace or could it be something else?

He caught the meaning behind her words. She did feel more than pity for him. He hadn't been wrong about the attraction he'd felt between them since that first night. "Sit with me." He reached out a hand to her. "Keep me warm by the fire. I don't want to be alone anymore either."

She blinked. Then, she moved a tentative hand in his direction. They locked fingers, his hand cold and clammy, hers warm and dry. All the while her eyes remained locked with his.

He forgot for a moment why they were here. He saw only her face. Her hand in his hand. Her body next to his. She let go of his hand and snaked her arm around his waist, holding him close. Her body was so hot against his chilled skin. He turned toward her, needing more of her warmth. He kissed her hard, pressing his mouth against hers, demanding she give him what he needed. She kissed him back and ran her fingers through his hair, fisting it tight, not letting him go.

He pushed her down to the floor and they tangled together. It all happened so quickly, with a desperate need he'd never felt before. When he tugged on her blouse and bared her skin, she didn't resist. He was swallowed up whole by her heat, even as he shivered, even as the ice inside him repelled what comfort she could give. The fire in the fireplace was nothing compared to the warmth he found in her arms. And he would take it all. Take whatever she was willing to give. Just this once…

Joel had only just fallen asleep when Adam appeared.

Gen grabbed the quilt to cover herself. She trembled at what her husband's reaction might be to her infidelity.

Adam ran a gentle hand up her leg. "Nice. Have you been waiting for me?"

"We have company," she whispered. She glanced over at Joel's sleeping figure. He looked so peaceful. She wanted him to rest. "He might hear you."

Her husband drifted over to Joel. "Yes, I know you brought him here. Your new plaything." He spat the word out in disgust.

"It was a mistake." Remorse filled her. She was torn. Adam was her husband, true, but somehow he wasn't the same man she remembered. Their marriage had been full of life and joy, not this darkness the new Adam seemed to bring with him wherever he went. "I didn't mean…"

"Were you even thinking of me?" His presence came closer, suffocating her. "How that might make me feel…to see my wife with another man?"

"I'm sorry, Adam. I'm sorry." Tears coursed down her cheeks. "I've missed you so much…" Joel had reminded her so much of the Adam she'd loved and lost months ago. Kind, gentle, loving. And Joel had needed her so badly tonight. She'd given him comfort with her body, and he'd given her a taste of real emotions, real human contact. Sensations she'd forgotten could be so exquisite.

He hovered over Joel's sleeping figure. Gen held her breath. He turned back to her. "Did you get the knife like I asked?"

She grabbed her purse and dumped the contents on the bed. "Yes, Joel almost saw me."

"What was he doing there?" Adam asked. "Still trying to stop the curses?"

"There was a letter. He wanted to read it."

"Hmmm…" He floated back to Gen. His pale watery eyes lit upon the silver knife. He grabbed for it, but his transparent fingers went right through the gleaming metal. "Dammit!"

Gen shushed him, worried Joel might stir.

Adam raised an eyebrow. "You'll have to cut him for me still."

"What?"

"I need more blood. This knife holds special powers, stronger powers. A sacred ritual knife used in the Resurrection Spell to draw blood will yield better results. I can't be like this anymore. I need to be whole again. Cut him for me, Gen."

The silver knife glittered in the firelight. She got a better look at the carving on the blade. It was just as she thought. But what did it mean? She picked it up, turned it over in her hands.

"You broke your vows to me tonight." His tone grew sharper. "But I can forgive you if you prove your love to me."

The shame of what she'd done with Joel weighed on her. "What do you want me to do?"

"Take the knife and cut him."

She looked across the room at Joel, his peaceful sleeping figure. The suffering he'd gone through, and he'd done nothing to deserve it. She deserved every bit of suffering from Adam's loss. The accident had been her fault. Adam's death her fault. But Joel? He'd done nothing at all. He'd woken up one day and had his life turned upside down all because of a few strands of DNA. A distant relationship to some long-dead man. "I can't."

Joel stirred in his sleep.

Her husband rose above her, his phantom-like presence smothering her. "I need his blood. You will do this for me."

"Adam, please, don't ask me to." She pushed at his unformed body, her hands sinking into his odd coolness. She needed him to move away. She couldn't breathe. "Please."

"You want him more than you want me."

"No, that's not true."

"Yes, you do. You don't miss me…you like him. You want this cursed man more than your own husband." His voice grew weaker, his presence more nebulous. "I need more blood, Gen." He disappeared.

When she was certain he was gone, she hid the knife between the mattresses. As much as she loved her husband, as much as she wanted to help him, clearly he'd lost his mind. Taking small amounts of blood secretively was hard enough, but attacking Joel with this dagger-like knife while he slept? Adam asked too much.

Better that she keep the knife hidden, safe. Adam would come again, and she'd prove her love for him, but on her own terms. In her own way.

~ * ~

The pain in Joel's fingers and toes woke him, but the rest of him was oddly warm. A light weight lay across his chest. A warm, soft weight.

Gen lay curled up next to him, her head on his shoulder, one arm slung across his body.

Last night replayed in his head. He'd never intended to let things go that far. He shook from a riot of chills that ran through his body. The damned curse had weakened his resolve, made him seek comfort when otherwise he may have stayed away. And she had been so sweet…so giving…

He didn't want to move for fear of waking her, and the feel of her body next to his was intoxicating. The only warm part of him was where her body pressed up close to his.

She stirred.

He wanted to touch her, but his arm was like a dead, frozen weight. It took all his effort just to lift it a few inches. Instead of a light touch, his hand landed on hers like a billy club.

She pulled back from him. "Hey, what was…?" Her words were choked with sleep. "Are you okay?"

Joel tried to push himself into a sitting position. His whole body creaked like the boards of an old sailing ship. Every movement caused pain, searing cold. He shivered.

He stretched out his hands to the gas flames that played across the ceramic logs. "I'm fine. I hope you managed to get some sleep." He flicked his eyes away from her tempting figure beneath the quilt which covered them. What did she think of last night? He struggled to find the words to ask about what happened between them.

"Yes." Her cheeks were red. She gathered her clothes, turned her back to him and got dressed.

"Right." A mistake. She thought it was all a mistake. He knew it. She'd only given him the comfort he sought and nothing more. He pulled on his shirt.

"Today do you feel well enough for some more research?" Her practical words ended any fantasies. She was only thinking about him as someone to save. "I could do it without you, if you don't think you can..."

"I can. I'm fine. It's just mind over matter." A new wave of cold surged through his body that begged to differ. He hunched his shoulders, as if it were a physical blow. Any ideas about a relationship with Gen beyond this bedroom left his head in a flash. "This is my life we're talking about. You can't shut me out."

"You're right." Gen folded the quilt. "But what are we going to tell your brother?"

"I'm sick." He picked up the pillows and set them on the divan. "Yesterday I lost my voice, today I've got a cold."

"But won't he wonder...?"

"Just tell him that, Gen. Please. For me."

"I think we should tell him. He has a right to know."

"He's my brother. I'll decide when and where. Or if. Maybe he never has to know. Maybe we can fix all of this..."

"I'm sure we can."

But Joel could tell by the tone of her voice she didn't believe her own words. She was scared for him. Worried for him. That chilled him inside more than any curse could.

He stumbled forward on heavy, frozen legs. She reached out to catch him. He stopped his fall by grabbing onto the mantel. "I don't need any help." She'd already told him with her body language that last night was forgotten. Any reminders of how soft she was, how comforting, and he'd fall apart. "We'll meet you downstairs for breakfast. Maybe Stella knows something about the Overlook or a 'darling' spot. She seems to know just about everything else."

The weight of her worried gaze rested on him. "If you're sure..."

"Let's just get this over with." He knew deep down he couldn't escape this curse, but he would be damned if he'd give up. Walking was like stepping on broken glass. Each step painful, slow, terrible. But he wouldn't let her know how much it hurt. He couldn't stand to see that sad sympathy on her face. He was a man, goddamn it, not some child she needed to take care of. A grown man.

He left her in the room. He just couldn't stand being near her anymore. One more minute, and he might kiss her again and make her see beyond the curses, beyond the pity...

He banged on the door to his room. "Wake up, numbskull. Let me in."

Matt opened it. "Where have you been?"

"Just let me in, dammit."

His brother swung the door open wide, and Joel stumbled in.

CHAPTER TWENTY-ONE

"Are you sure you're all right?" Stella hovered over Joel at the breakfast table with a plate of sausages. "My Stan had the flu a few weeks ago. Looked about as peaked as you. Sure you don't have a fever?" She touched the back of her hand to his forehead, but Joel ducked away.

"I told you I'm fine. I just need another cup of coffee." He struggled to keep the stutter and his suffering under wraps. Thank God Matt knew the last thing his older brother wanted was to be coddled.

Stella bristled. "Why, of course you do. Let me get that for you." She bustled over to the pass-through from the kitchen, picked up the silver coffee pot and tipped it. "Darn it. Looks like it's empty. I'll be back with a refill in a sec."

The three of them sat stiffly at the dining table. Joel clutched a fork in his club of a hand and tried to scoop eggs into his mouth. Half the forkful fell onto the tablecloth. In frustration, he let the fork drop with a clang onto his plate. "I've had enough." He pushed away from the table.

"You need to eat something," Gen said.

"I'm fine."

Stella waltzed through the kitchen door with a fresh pot of coffee. When she saw his plate full of food, she frowned. "Is something wrong with your breakfast? If you're not an egg person, I could whip up some pancakes or a smoothie. Stan just loves my smoothies. They keep him regular—"

"Do you know a place called the Overlook?" Joel's patience waned. He needed to get out of this place and look for answers.

Stella set the coffee on the table and smoothed her hands down her apron. "Everyone knows the Overlook. It's down the coast a piece. Past Devil's Churn a few miles. Best view in the area. Fantastic food."

"So it's still open?"

"Of course. That place has been in business for going on a hundred years now."

"Do we need a reservation?"

"I can make it for you, if you'd like. They're only open for dinner. Five to ten."

"As early as possible, then."

"All right." Stella picked up his plate and took it with her into the kitchen.

"Business dinner?" Matt asked. "Or are brothers invited?"

"You can tag along," Joel said, wishing the curse crap was over and done with. Perhaps after tonight they would find some more information. Get another clue. If Calvin and Sabina met at the Overlook, dined there…? "I think we've earned a nice dinner out. Don't you?"

Gen took a bite of toast and chewed thoughtfully.

Joel wasn't sure if she was upset at him for pressing the issue or glad to have him take control. A wave of cold shuddered through him, and he curled and uncurled his aching fingers. "I'm going to take a shower." He directed the rest of his words at Gen. "I'll meet you on the porch by nine. Be ready."

"Is this your last business thing?"

Gen nodded.

"Then can you drop me at the library this time? I've got a bit more research to do."

Joel left them in the dining room and plodded with painful footsteps up the stairs. He hoped taking the hottest shower possible would help the numbing, biting cold. He could sense the gentle creep of madness settling in his body, and it terrified him.

~ * ~

Gen waited on the porch. Her watch read nine thirty.

Matt pulled open the front door. He was alone.

"Where's Joel?"

"Asleep." He shook his head and smiled. "He took a shower and then just passed out on the bed. Guess he was sicker than he thought. I didn't want to wake him, he looked beat. Do you think you can handle the customer issues without him?"

"I guess I'll have to." Inside she was relieved. The pressure of keeping Adam a secret, of balancing two selves between these men weighed heavily on her. Doing research on her own would free her from worrying about revealing too much to Joel.

"This is the spare." He handed her a car key. "Keep it for now."

She took it. That might come in handy. "We were supposed to be here all week. Hopefully your brother will feel better tomorrow."

"Yeah. I've never seen him like this. Usually he won't even take an aspirin when he's sick."

"Tough guy, huh?" She thought about him shivering against her last night. She'd soothed his aching body with her own, and he'd soothed her too. Yet he probably didn't realize it. They were two lonely souls seeking comfort, nothing more. At least that's what she had to believe. Although he'd tried to pretend he could handle these curses alone, she knew deep down he was terrified.

"Stubborn is more like it."

They drove toward town. Sun shone through the Sitka spruce that lined the road, making for a beautiful day.

"Joel tells me your parents died when you were young." She wasn't sure why those words spilled out. She hadn't meant to dig into Joel's background.

Matt fiddled with the door lock. "Yeah. I was nine. Joel was in college." He sighed. "We don't talk about it much."

"I'm sorry."

"No, no it's okay." He smoothed his hands down his thighs. "Those memories for me are pretty faint. It was harder for him than for me. He was like my second dad. I still had someone to be a parent, you know?"

Gen nodded.

"He quit school. Well, didn't quit exactly, but transferred from the University of Washington to Lewis & Clark—so he could be at home with me every night. For those first few years, we were lucky enough…he didn't have to work. My mom had insurance. My dad…"

Gen squeezed his hand. "Joel's a good brother. You should be proud of him…"

"He's always taken care of me, never let me worry about anything. I don't know what I'd do without him." He paused. "We're pretty close."

Gen pulled up to the library. "I'll pick you up around one?"

Matt gave her a salute. "Yes, ma'am." He shouldered his backpack and tucked his laptop under one arm. "See you later."

She drove away from the library and watched as Joel's younger brother walked inside. Her heart ached for him. He had no idea what was happening to Joel, no idea he was next in line for the curse. The two of them were so close, and to think that Joel might not be around for his brother anymore…

"Nice kid." Adam appeared in the passenger seat.

"Why did you tell me the other day you'd given me a *cure* for the Curse of the Mute?"

Adam laughed. "I never told you it was a cure."

"You said it would help him. All it did was speed everything up. You only made things worse."

"I said it would help. Help *me*, that is. The faster we can get through these curses, the better." His face wavered in and out—his familiar features clear one moment, a blur the next. "His blood is stronger each time."

"You lied to me." She gripped the steering wheel so tightly her knuckles turned white. "I thought we were going to help him, make a fair trade. His blood for a cure."

"Gen, I almost think you care more for this stranger than your own husband. I need you to be with me on this."

Her husband, who claimed to love her and need her, had deceived her. She wasn't the kind of person who wanted to harm another just for her own gain. "It was supposed to be a fair trade."

"Can you blame me for wanting to be alive again? Be with you again? I'd do anything for that, Gen. I thought you'd do the same for me. You owe me."

She thought about the night of the accident. Her eyes on the dark road ahead, Adam sleeping in the seat next to her. It had been late, so very late. She didn't realize she'd drifted off to sleep until… "I can't take any more of his blood without something in return." Her resolve to stand up to Adam's demands was slipping.

"What if I told you I could help him?" His voice grew seductive, sensual. The same voice he'd used to whisper to her in bed. "That I could save his life after saving mine?"

She blinked. Hot tears gathered in the corners of her eyes. "I don't believe you."

"Once I'm cured, I don't need him anymore. I don't care if he lives or dies." He brushed his hand against her cheek. "But I don't want you unhappy, feeling guilty. I want my wife back. The same wife I've missed for months. You know how much I want to touch you again…really touch you." He swept his fingers across her lips.

Gen couldn't breathe. She pulled over. Her hands trembled on the wheel. "Can I tell him about you? Explain? It would be so much easier if he knew."

"No."

"But why not?"

"The trust he has with you would be broken. He might leave us, and then where would we be?"

Adam was right. Any help she offered Joel after revealing Adam's need for his blood would be rejected. Especially after what they'd shared last night in front of the fire. He'd think it was all a lie, even her growing feelings for him. She couldn't hurt him like that. Not now when he was so vulnerable. "I have the knife now, and you say that will make the spell more powerful?"

"Yes."

"So just one more time? And then we can help him?"

"Yes, Gen, I promise."

Her heart told her to trust her husband. She understood Adam's desperation and why he had sped up the curses. It didn't sit well with her, but it was done. If that meant everyone was closer to the end of this whole thing, then she could live with it. One more ceremony, one more cut with the special knife, and both men would be healed. Adam would be alive again, and Joel and Matt would be saved.

~ * ~

Joel answered the knock at his door. His eyes wouldn't focus, and exhaustion rested on him like a weight. "Hey." When he saw Gen standing there he gave a faint smile. "What're you doing here?"

"I'm here to help. I've done some research and found a way to end this curse."

He let her inside. "We know how well that's gone lately."

She brushed past him, her full skirt swirling when she faced him. "Do you trust me?"

He shut the door and leaned against it, scanning her face for a moment. "I'm not sure."

"What other choice do you have?" She sat on the rumpled bed and pulled her purse across her lap. "Either you believe I can help you or…"

"Or I believe you'll hurt me."

"Yes."

Joel thought back to last night. It was clear to him she wanted to forget what had happened between them. She'd avoided the topic entirely. Call it a lapse in judgment or two lonely people connecting for just a fleeting moment. If she wanted to move past it, so could he. He wouldn't let this wisp of a woman get to him. He had the curse to worry about. That should be his main focus. "Are you here to try again?"

"Yes. If you'll let me." She pulled the knife from her purse, the one she'd stolen from the case.

He eyed the glittering silver blade cautiously. "What do you need that for?"

"Don't worry, Joel. This will help, I promise you." She set the long knife in her lap and reached out to him. "Come, sit down. I'll show you. It won't hurt."

The cold caused his bones to ache, his muscles, even the outer layer of his skin. He was so tired of it. He wanted it to be over. Her words were soothing. She could help. She promised. His head had been fuzzy ever since the Bone Chill curse set in. He couldn't think as clearly as he did before. The help she offered was so tempting. A way out.

"I just need a little blood. That's all. I can fix this for you." Her hand was outstretched, waiting for him to reach out. "*Av akai.*"

"What did you say?"

"*Av akai*—'come here' in Romany. My grandmother was a gypsy."

"Is that where you learned these things?"

"Yes." Her warm eyes drew him in. He saw hope in their depths. "Come, Joel."

"I don't know…" He'd adjusted to the leadenness of his limbs. Instead of shuffling forward like Frankenstein, he took a few small steps in her direction. "Just a little bit of blood?"

His fingers touched hers. She wrapped her hand around his and drew him toward her. "Just a little." Her voice was like honey.

With the warmth of her hand enveloping his, he found the courage to give in, trust this woman and do whatever necessary to feel normal again. She'd comforted him once with her body. If this was all she could give him now, he would take it. "Where do you need to cut me?"

"Here." She touched the tip of the knife to his forearm. "Just a knick."

"Do it." He tightened his abdominal muscles in anticipation.

With a slash of the blade, she cut him. He felt no pain, the knife was sharp and she had done it so quickly.

"I'm sorry. I just need a little bit." She produced a small glass vial and caught the blood in it.

The blood ran down his arm. It was hot compared to his icy skin. He looked up at her, but her eyes were hidden beneath her lashes. After a few seconds, she capped the vial and pressed a tissue to the cut she'd made.

He pulled his arm away and kept pressure on it. "Now what do we do with it?"

"Now we can heal you." From her bag she produced several more vials, these filled with clear liquids. "A mixture of oils, some blood and hair. May I?" She touched a lock of his hair near his ear. "I just need a little."

He nodded.

With a pair of manicure scissors, she cut off a few strands. He wanted her to keep her hands on him, soothe him, like last night. She placed the bit of hair in an ashtray on the nightstand. To that she added several drops from different vials and some of his blood. She stirred it with a finger and chanted aloud:

Dosta armaya

Za trushal odji

Drab, bal, rat

Drab, bal, rat

Za trushal odji

Dosta armaya

Within moments Joel's arms felt lighter, less stiff. A warmth inside his core radiated out to his limbs and digits. "It's working." He took a deep breath and the icy grip on his heart melted away. The shivering stopped. Joel opened and closed his fists. The rush of warm blood through his body was intoxicating, empowering.

"My God, you did it." He hugged her tight. "You did it. Thank you."

Without her knowing, he gently kissed her hair. If he couldn't have her again, he would at least have this moment with her. This little bit of closeness.

CHAPTER TWENTY-TWO

"I made my famous Buffalo Meatloaf." Stella chased after Gen, Joel and Matt as they headed for the door, a wide smile plastered on her face. "It's Stan's favorite. He likes his with horseradish on the side. I say that ruins the flavor. But he won't listen. He always has to go and ruin a perfectly good dinner with all that crazy sauce stuff." She waved her hands. "I probably have enough for five, if you'd like to stay. Always nice to have company for dinner."

Joel imagined sitting through two hours of Stella's chatter. "Thanks for the offer, but we're really looking forward to eating at the Overlook."

"Well, then you best hurry. Taking that coast road through the park in the dark is quite a doozy."

"We'll be careful." Gen smiled.

"We always have at least one or two cars drive off the cliff this time of year. Fog gets real thick sometimes, you know. I'll keep the door open for you. I usually lock up at nine, but just in case—"

"Thanks, Stella," Joel cut her off before she could ramble on.

The threesome made their way onto the porch and out of earshot.

"Thank God." Matt let out a sigh.

They headed for the car.

"I thought you liked good old Stella and her six-packs." Joel unlocked it, and everyone climbed in.

"It was free beer," Matt said, as if that were the only explanation needed. "But she talked my ear off about Stan's guns, the neighbors, the guests she's had…"

Gen laughed. "Better watch out, Stan might get jealous."

"Shut up." Matt slumped down in the backseat.

They drove toward the coast road that would lead them past the Devil's Churn to Florence—the road the DeVries family had built.

"How many years did they say this road's been here?" Matt peered out the window at the sheer drop on their right-hand side. In the growing dark they could only see the outline of the rocks, but the last glow of the setting sun reflected off the foam and spray that played below on the writhing ocean.

"Eighty, ninety, something like that." Joel did his best to pretend he hardly knew a thing about the history of this place.

"Do you think the safety standards were the same back then?"

"Don't tell me you're scared." Gen sat with her back against the door so she could look at Matt. "There's a wall there to keep us from going over."

Joel eyed his brother in the rearview mirror. He looked a little green in the gills. "Since when are you afraid of heights?" He laughed.

"I'm not. But when a foot-high rock wall is the only thing keeping us from plunging into the ocean, and *you're* driving, I think I have a right to be a little bit queasy."

Joel shot his brother a look. "I'm a good driver."

"Who told you that?" Matt asked.

Gen snorted.

Joel focused his attention back on the road. "Now I'm going to get grief from you too?"

"I'm just here to get some food," Gen said. "Not debate about everyone's driving skills."

"Thank you." Joel had a bit a triumph in his voice. He gave his brother another glare in the mirror.

Matt rolled his eyes. "So what's so special about this Overlook place?"

"Yes." Joel picked up his brother's line of questioning. "What *is* so special about it?" He wondered how Gen would manage this explanation on her own.

"I've heard it has historical photos on display. A lot of locals used to come to the Overlook for romantic dinners. I've got a thing for history." She gave Joel a knowing look.

"Whoa, wait a minute, did I get in the way here?" Matt asked.

"What do you mean?" Gen's brow wrinkled.

"You two. The Overlook. Did I invite myself on a date?"

"No," said Joel with a scowl. Leave it to his little brother to get mixed signals and embarrass the hell out of him.

"Matt, we're here solely on business. Where did you get the crazy idea there was something more?" But he heard a catch in her voice.

Joel's heart skipped a beat.

He gave a sidelong glance, but Gen had her gaze squarely on the winding road in front of them.

~ * ~

Joel stood next to the podium. They had been waiting thirty minutes to be seated. So much for their reservation. The Overlook was a spectacular place, though. Rough-hewn logs, most likely from the timber stands harvested by his family, made an imposing entrance. The interior was dark, smelling of pine and wood smoke. With a soaring entrance and vaulted ceiling held in place by more monstrous timbers, he could easily imagine Calvin and his family spending time here. Once he stepped through the double doors, it was as if he'd walked back in time to 1919.

Gen and Matt scanned the rows and rows of black-and-white photos that lined the waiting area. Men in tuxedos, women in beaded gowns. The heyday of this beautiful lodge. Gen studied each photo. Her features were small, like a child's—a turned-up nose, pink cheeks, a glow to her eyes. She was a woman and a young girl at the same time. She brushed a finger across a photo. She sucked in her breath, and even from this distance, he could see her face blanch.

"What is it?" Joel crossed the room to stand behind her.

Gen had a hand to her mouth. Her eyes were wide and unblinking. "I've seen this necklace before. But it can't be…"

Joel stepped closer to the photo. "That's Calvin." A young man in an Army uniform sat smiling at a table, a drink held high. Beside him was an exotic-looking woman in an evening dress, sloe-eyed, dark lips, black hair. "I wonder if that's his wife?"

Gen froze.

He whistled. "She was a beauty."

She traced her finger around an unusual necklace the woman wore.

"You said that looked familiar?" he prompted.

Her mouth was set in a hard line. She turned abruptly away from the photo. "No, no, I was mistaken." But she was pale and shaking like a leaf.

"Mistaken?" Joel searched her face. He knew she recognized the necklace, but what did it mean?

The maitre d' approached them. "I can seat you now."

"Thank the Lord. I'm starving," Matt said.

The maitre d' eyed his jeans and sweatshirt. "I think we can seat you near the back."

"That will be fine, thanks." Gen was still ashen.

Before she could follow the maitre d' into the dining room Joel grabbed her by the arm. "What has you so spooked? The necklace Mrs. DeVries was wearing, did you see it at the historical society?"

"That's not Mrs. DeVries." Her voice trembled. "That's Sabina Silva. That's the woman who cursed your family."

CHAPTER TWENTY-THREE

Before Joel could process what Gen told him about the woman in the picture, a sudden thirst struck him. He wanted to scrutinize the photo and get a good look at Sabina Silva, but the need for water overtook him.

He pulled his arm out of Gen's hands and followed Matt and the maitre d' to their table. A pewter pitcher of water sat in the middle. Joel poured himself a glass of ice water before he sat down. In seconds, he downed the entire glass.

The raging thirst remained.

This time, he picked up the pitcher and drank out of it. The cool water soothed the dryness in his throat. Sweeter than any water he'd ever tasted. More. He needed more.

Matt stared at him. "What in the hell is with you?"

Gen caught up to him. "Joel, what are you doing?"

The waiter approached the table, wine list in hand. "Would you care for a drink?"

"Water." His need to slake his thirst overtook him. "I need water." His throat burned for liquid relief.

"Certainly, sir." The waiter left the wine list on the table and scurried to the kitchen with the empty pitcher in hand.

"Joel." His brother's voice had taken on a serious note. "Are you okay?"

Joel knew what was happening. The Unquenchable Thirst curse. Right in front of his little brother. He couldn't hide it. No explanation would make any sense.

Gen's eyes widened. He knew her mind was racing to come up with a plausible explanation. But why? What was the point? They both knew that without an effective cure eventually it would come to this. Matt would find out the truth. Why hide it any longer? Matt was his brother, the only family he had left. He deserved to know the truth.

The waiter arrived with another pitcher of water. Joel snatched it out of his hands and gulped it down. For a few moments, his thirst would hold. Now was the time.

"Gen's not my coworker," Joel explained. "She's a palm reader." Matt's brow wrinkled. "I hired her to help me because I'm cursed."

"I don't understand." Matt leaned back in his chair. "What are you talking about?"

"Let me start at the beginning." Joel guzzled the rest of the water. The thirst grew more intense, but he battled through it. Matt had a right to know. Keeping him in the dark had done nothing but put off the inevitable. He'd been a coward not to tell his brother from the start.

"I'm cursed. I'm going to die. Gen was supposed to help me find a way to stop it. If we don't, you're next on the list." His tongue was like dry cotton in his mouth. He took another long drink of water.

"Supposed to help?" she balked. "I *am* helping…"

"What?" Matt laughed. "You're cursed? What in the hell, bro? Are you high or something?" He looked over at Gen. "Please tell me he's high."

"I'm not on drugs. I'm not nuts. I'm telling you the truth." He could see the disbelief bloom on his brother's face, the lines of worry deepening between his brows. Matt thought he'd lost it. "I didn't want you to stop by the house, because there is no house left. It burned to the ground…" He choked, dryness taking over his mouth. "And before that I lost my job. The sores, Gen, tell him about the sores."

Gen couldn't speak. She couldn't believe Joel had confessed to his brother. One look at him, though, and she could see Joel had gone past the breaking point of most human beings. The Unquenchable Thirst curse had caught up to him—this time within hours rather than days—and was likely draining away his sanity every second. She didn't blame him for breaking down, for confessing his secret.

Joel lowered his voice. "Tell him."

He needed her help now more than ever. Clearly, Matt thought his brother had lost his mind. She had to stand up for him, help Matt believe. "Joel's telling the truth. He came to me a few nights ago covered in these terrible sores. Some kind of pox. I don't know. I'd never seen anything like it before."

Matt's gaze flicked back and forth from Gen to Joel. "You two are serious. Completely frickin' serious."

"I know it sounds insane…" Gen began.

"Oh, it sounds a little more than insane." Matt pushed his chair away from the table. "I have to get out of here." He ran a hand through his hair and looked around the restaurant full of quietly talking diners. "I'm going back home. I'm leaving you two here and going back to Portland."

Joel got up after him. "How are you going to get there? You don't have a car."

"I don't care." The diners stared at the spectacle. "I just need to get the hell out of here, away from you two, and back to sanity. You can take your trip to La-La Land without me." Matt stumbled out of the dining room, tripping over chair legs and waiters.

Joel grabbed the water pitcher off a passing waiter's tray and downed the whole thing in several large gulps, choking on ice.

The dining room grew quiet. All eyes were on Joel. Water dribbled out of the sides of his mouth and wetted his shirt. To someone who didn't know what he suffered, he appeared out of his mind.

He dropped the pitcher and backed away from the diners. He reacted like an animal in a zoo—eyes wild, motions frantic. He tripped over his own feet.

Gen grabbed his arm. "Let's go," she said quietly. He needed her. She put an arm around his waist and led him out of the dining room and into the lobby. "We need to find Matt. Forget about them."

He sagged against her supporting arm. "I'm so thirsty, Gen. So thirsty."

"I know."

"It's the curse. They're coming faster now," he croaked. "I can't do this anymore. I can't."

"Yes, you can." She opened the door and led him outside.

Joel's tongue had swollen to what felt like the size of a grapefruit. It pained him to even try to swallow, but his throat burned. He thought about the drive back to Calvin City, the low barrier along the cliffs. How easy it would be to just take a step over that barrier and let himself fall into the ocean, its salty coolness enveloping him. And for a split second he would feel normal again. The water would parch his tongue for just a moment, and he could be free of this curse. Free of this life. Free. Free. Free.

"It's not worth it." He shoved against her slight form. "Just leave me."

She held him fast. "What are you saying?" Gen sounded panicked. She dragged him into the parking lot. "I can fix this. I promise. I can fix it."

Then somehow he was in the back of the car, and his brother was sitting up front with Gen. Where did he come from? How did he get in the car? Didn't he run away?

He could hear them talking as if from a great distance.

"I can help him," said Gen. "But I need you to do what I tell you, no questions asked."

"Was it true what he said?" asked Matt. "Is he cursed? Am I next?"

"Yes. He wanted to keep it from you. He didn't want you to worry—"

Joel looked out the window as they drove, waiting for the right moment. As Gen and his brother talked about ceremonies and healing oils, Joel thought about the dark waves of the ocean, the spray of saltwater, the relief death would bring. It was all he could focus on.

The car took the first turn and climbed up above the rough Oregon Coast. The distinctive rock barrier came into view, and Joel knew this was his chance.

His throat was on fire. He couldn't stand it one more second. He had to. He needed to.

He pulled the door lever and it popped open.

A light flicked on the dashboard, and a buzzer sounded. "Joel, what are you doing?" asked Gen.

He unlocked his seat belt.

"Grab him, Matt! Grab him!"

But it was too late. Joel tumbled out of the car and rolled painfully onto the gravel shoulder.

The car braked hard, the red taillights lighting up his path to the wall.

He crawled. His hands bled, gravel embedded in them. He had to get to that wall. Relief was just on the other side. The waves crashed below like a symphony of cymbals—discordant and deafening. To Joel, it was a Siren's song. He could end it, be done with this suffering once and for all.

A firm hand grasped his shoulder. "You are *not* going to do this, bro." Matt hauled him up from the gravel and yelled right in his face. "You are not going to do this."

An animal sound erupted from him. He fought against his brother's grip.

"I'm sorry." Gen stood next to the trunk, the lid popped open. "I'm so sorry, but we have to. It will all be over soon. I promise."

He gave an anguished cry. Not in the trunk. He couldn't go in there. "No!" He bucked as hard as he could.

But Matt, younger, stronger, bigger than his older brother, wrestled him into it.

The lid slammed closed, and all Joel knew was the dark. The dreadful dark. And the misery of his thirst.

CHAPTER TWENTY-FOUR

Joel smelled the fire before he saw it. The ride had been short, but that hadn't kept him from scratching the interior of the trunk, wailing in misery. His throat was a desert, his tongue choking him.

When the trunk opened his brother handed him a gallon jug of water. Joel snatched it from Matt's hands as if it were gold, snapped off the cap and poured the entire container down his throat. The relief lasted mere seconds. He needed more.

"You need to hurry, Gen," said his brother. "I can't keep him in here much longer." Matt handed him another jug.

"I have what I need. Just keep him still."

The smell of burning incense brought Joel out of his stupor for a moment. Gen was going to save him. The next gallon of water went as quickly as the first. But hope stirred in his chest. Maybe he could stand it just a few more minutes. The swollen tongue, the sandpaper of his throat. He could bear it if he knew relief would come.

"Quick." Matt handed him a smaller water bottle. "I'm out."

Joel's sanity returned in small fragments. Instead of drinking the entire bottle, he squirted short bursts into his mouth. He had to make it last. He had to try.

Beyond the trunk, he could see a larger flare of light. Gen appeared behind his brother. She spread some kind of scented oil under his lips, then touched her oil-coated finger to the tip of his tongue.

"*Pani, pani, pani,*" she whispered. "*Piav pani. Piav pani. Bater!*" Her voice rose above the crackling of the fire, the gusting of the winds.

"Is that it?" his brother asked.

She didn't answer him. "Does he look any better?"

It became preternaturally quiet. So still, so perfectly still that Joel thought he had gone deaf.

"I'm not sure," said Matt.

Joel knew it had worked. His tongue shrank to its normal size, and his salivary glands began pumping again. Moisture filled his mouth. He even began to drool.

"Thank God," Joel mumbled, and then promptly threw up about two gallons of water.

Joel sat in the front seat as Gen drove the car back to the bed and breakfast. His mind whirled at the memory of coming so close to jumping over that wall and into the ocean. He would've done it. If his brother had not restrained him, he would've done it. That thought chilled him. Just like many of his relatives before him, he would have ended the string of curses himself by committing suicide. The worst part was, he still didn't dismiss the idea as beyond the scope of reality. Thinking about the curses left in the dead Ms. Silva's arsenal, he didn't know if he could manage. Blindness was next. Then the Fatal Touch. Whatever that meant. And then the Ninth Curse. The one he wouldn't survive. The Ninth Curse would end it all. For him anyway.

He stared out the window unable to discern anything outside in the inky blackness. Occasionally the headlights bounced off a cliff face or the twisted trunk of a cypress tree as they made it around another curve, but for the most part it was too dark.

"So," said Gen. "Have you thought about the next one?"

Joel glanced over his shoulder at Matt. His brother leaned forward on his knees to listen in. Joel looked away. "I try not to." He didn't want to let his brother know the fear that grew inside.

"Maybe if we planned…maybe if we prepared for it…"

"The only thing I want to prepare for is stopping it," he snapped, his nerves setting him on edge. "Do you have any ideas, *Madame*?" Even as the words came out, he regretted them. He'd wanted to forget he'd ever spent the night in her arms, ever kissed her, but whenever those brown eyes gazed at him, all he could do was remember and wish things were different. She'd just saved him from insanity back there, and he had to cut her down. What a bastard this curse had made him.

She took a few moments to answer. "I might. I'll look through my book tonight."

Did her voice tremble? Did she sound frightened? He didn't blame her. Getting involved with him and the curses was probably the worst mistake she'd ever made. He wouldn't blame her if she left. Disappeared. She had no good reason to stay.

"All right." He watched her silhouette as she drove. Her small, turned-up nose, the slight curve of her cheek. If it had been another time, another place, and he were his normal self, he could love her. He really could love her. He spied the ring on her finger and wondered if she was still in love with her husband.

He hated that a dead man occupied a place in her heart. But what did Joel have to offer her? He was ruined. Jobless. Homeless. Cursed. And probably dead soon.

He turned toward the window and the darkness beyond.

After a few minutes of quiet, her warm hand gripped his. A reassuring squeeze. He leaned his head against the window and squeezed her back. He imagined her touching his body, caressing him, and in the darkness of his mind it gave him sanity.

CHAPTER TWENTY-FIVE

"So tell me more about this family curse," Matt said.

The brothers were back in their room. It was late, and Joel was more tired than he'd ever been. Each curse seemed to wring more out of him.

"There's not a lot to tell." Joel pulled off his shoes and set them parallel to each other on the floor. He lay back on the bed and closed his eyes. To get some much-needed sleep was all he wanted.

"Well, you're going to tell me." Matt nudged Joel's legs over and took a seat next to him. "I deserve to know what's going on, don't you think?"

"Hey." Joel opened one eye. "I'm tired. Can't this wait until morning?"

Bluto, who must have sensed Joel needed comfort, leaped onto his stomach and kneaded his claws into his flesh. He tensed at the pain, scruffed the cat and set him down next to him.

Matt got up and paced the room. "No, it can't wait until morning. I want to know now. When did this happen? Why didn't you tell me? And what the hell does Calvin City have to do with everything?"

Bluto purred as Joel stroked him. He sighed. "Fine. I guess you won't let me get any sleep until I've told you everything, huh?"

Matt continued to pace.

"Calvin City is where it all began. We traced the curse back to the DeVries family and some woman named Sabina Silva."

"Who's she?"

"The woman we think did this to me…us." Bluto rubbed his head against Joel's fingers, demanding more attention. "Gen thinks if we find out the why and the who, maybe there's a way to end this."

"So why didn't you tell me what was going on? Did you think I couldn't handle the truth?" Matt stopped in his tracks, his neck and jaw tense. "You think I'm some little kid?"

"No. It's just that—after Mom and Dad—you're all I have left."

Matt ran a hand through his hair. "And you're all I have left."

"I'm supposed to be the one taking care of you." Joel sat up. Bluto climbed into his lap, purring." You're my little brother. I'm supposed to handle this stuff—"

"I don't seem to recall part of your older brother duties involving taking on supernatural curses and battling evil forces."

"I'm not battling evil forces."

"Yes, you are."

Joel scoffed.

"Tonight? You frickin' scared the hell out of me." Matt fell heavily onto the divan under the window. "Jumping out of the car. What were you going to do? Climb over the wall? Kill yourself?"

"I just had to get some relief." Joel rubbed Bluto between the ears. "If you knew what it felt like—my mind wasn't my own."

"If you don't call that battling evil forces, I don't know what is. You're risking your life to save me. Going through who the hell knows what, trying your best so I don't end up the same way. Can you see why I would want to help?" Matt's brow furrowed with worry. "Don't you think I want you to stick around for awhile? You think I want you to die of some family curse? Suffer for me? I would do anything for you, Joel. Anything. Don't you know that by now?"

"I couldn't do that to you, Matt." He picked up Bluto and held him close to his chest. "I just couldn't. I wanted to handle it myself."

"Well, too bad. I'm going to handle it now. You're in no position to—"

"I don't want you anywhere near—"

"Who? Gen?" Matt gestured at the door, as if Gen would walk through it any minute. "The evil forces? There's nothing to stay away from. If you don't survive…if you don't figure this out and make it, I'm next. Don't you think I deserve to be part of this? Don't you think I deserve to find out everything I can? Don't you think I want to help fight this too? Don't shut me out, Joel. Don't you dare fucking shut me out."

Joel sat quietly for a moment. Bluto's purring grew louder, filling the room with its rhythmic noise. "You're right."

That stopped his younger brother short. "I am?"

"Yes. You're right. I've been treating you like a kid, and I could use you right now. The curses seem to be speeding up. I don't know if it was something Gen did, or if it was the fact that I came back here where it all started. But instead of the weeks I thought I had, I only have days to figure this out." If the Unquenchable Thirst was curse number six, he only had three left before it was too late. That meant three days or less to figure out this mystery. And there was no way in hell he was going to let this curse touch Matt. No way.

"Well, good." Matt didn't sound too sure of himself. "Tomorrow we're going to tackle this thing head on."

"Yes, tomorrow." Joel laid back and closed his eyes again, exhaustion setting in. He knew what was coming for him tomorrow. Curse number seven: Blindness. Not being able to see scared the hell out of him. How would he get around? What if he lost his mind again? Went crazy before they could help him? What if Gen couldn't help him this time?

~ * ~

Gen waited in the dark cemetery. Alone.

Adam would come to her soon. He'd be pleased she'd done as he wanted. Her deception bothered her, but Adam had proven himself with the cure for the Bone Chill curse and the Unquenchable Thirst. He was living up to his end of the bargain. So she would live up to hers.

She held the vial filled with Joel's blood. Hard to believe something as simple as blood could be so powerful. With the knife she'd tucked in her bag, it would be even more so.

Considering she only had enough of the special leaves for one more Resurrection Spell, this one had to work. Then Adam would be free from death, and they could save Joel together. Her husband had so much more knowledge than she did. She was merely a beginning student, but he had been a master of the magical arts. Experimenting with spells, tweaking them to get them right.

Her mother hadn't liked that—bringing magic into the house. Not at all.

Adam appeared in front of her. "Did you get it?"

She held up the vial for him to see. "Yes, and thank you for the cures. They worked."

"Of course they worked. I made a promise, didn't I? To save your new friend?" A tinge of jealousy filled his words.

"We owe him that much."

"We don't owe him anything. He's just a means to an end. You know that."

Her heart told her differently. At the beginning, yes, Joel had been something she needed to help her husband. But over the last few days she'd seen his strength, his loyalty to his brother. He wasn't only a cursed man with useful blood. He was a living and breathing man with worries and hopes and dreams, just like her.

She looked at the misty features of her husband's face. She wanted Adam back with all her heart, but to use Joel grew harder and harder. Although she was torn between the two, she couldn't turn her back on her husband, not now when they were so close to bringing him back.

He floated closer. "Let's not waste time. You have the knife with you?"

"Yes."

He smiled. His teeth were like the rest of him, white and semi-transparent. "Good. Let's get started."

She laid out the bag of ashes, the candle, the vial of blood, the handful of leaves and the knife. Following the spell, she started a small fire in the pit she'd used the other night. When the flames were high, she added the leaves, creating a thick smoke. The fire burned through the leaves quickly, and the flames changed from yellow to dark red. Opening the vial, she tipped it to pour Joel's blood into the flames.

"Wait," Adam said. "This time, you must do it differently."

"How?"

"Dip the knife in the blood and sprinkle it over the fire."

The power of the knife. She'd almost forgotten. Following her husband's orders, she dipped the tip of the knife into the vial. The blood, cool and thick, clung to it. She held it over the fire, and large droplets fell into the flames.

"The ashes…"

Only a small quantity of ashes could be used in a ceremony, she'd discovered, otherwise the fire would go out. She carefully shook out a small handful of Adam's ashes from the baggie she kept in her purse. The flames caught the dry material and sparked with a strange green glow. Time to light the candle.

She tipped it into the flames and uttered the words she now knew by heart.

May angle sar te merel kadi yag, opre, Adam!

May angle sar te merel kadi yag, opre, Adam!

May angle sar te merel kadi yag, opre, Adam!

The old Romany words—*Before this fire burns out, arise*—echoed in the cemetery.

She looked up from the fire. Adam was more solid than before, but still very pale with those watery blue eyes.

"You did it, Gen." Adam's voice was stronger.

He scooped her into his arms. Instead of warmth and solidity, he was

160

still cool to the touch. But his flesh had the feel of real human flesh, not the smoky apparition who'd been appearing and reappearing for the last few months.

They embraced, and she smiled against his neck. They'd done it. They'd really done it.

Adam held her face between his cold hands and kissed her.

Gen's stomach rebelled at the odd sensation. Like kissing a corpse in a coffin. Not only was he cold, his lips like rubber, but he smelled of death. She pulled away in horror.

"What's wrong?"

Gen took two steps back and touched her lips. "Something's not right. You're not...you're not alive."

"What do you mean? My body's solid." He pounded on his chest with his fist. "I can walk on the ground." He no longer floated. "I can even pick things up." He grabbed the handle of her bag and held it in the air. "I'm alive just like you, Gen. You did it. I'm back."

"No."

"I am."

"There's a smell—and you're cold." She wanted to gag. "There's no blood in your veins. You're white as a corpse."

"You're wrong." Adam scowled. "I'm alive. I'll prove it to you." He picked up the silver knife and slashed at his palm.

"No!" Gen started forward.

No blood flowed from the fresh cut. Adam stumbled back and dropped the knife. "It can't be. We had his blood. We had the knife."

Gen stared at the bloodless gash in his palm.

"You have to get more blood." He stalked toward her. "Much more. All of it." His face became a white mask of horror, angry lines cut on either side of his mouth. "Get Joel, bring the knife and bring him to the ruins."

"No. I can't...you promised." This was not the man she knew. This was not the man she'd married. The loving, smiling man who couldn't pass up a starving animal on the street. Now he was asking her to kill for him?

161

"You'd choose a stranger over your own husband?" His hand locked down on her arm like a vise.

"You're hurting me." She struggled to get away from this thing who called himself her husband. This wasn't Adam. This wasn't the man she wanted back. This was someone—some*thing*—else.

"Bring him to me. I'll give you one more day."

"How can you ask me to do that?"

"One more day, Gen." Although his body had seemed so solid only moments ago, it faded quickly. He looked down at his hand and saw the change. In a rush, he grabbed for the knife, but his fingers passed right through it. "Dammit. Bring Joel, bring the knife. You will do this for me. As my wife, you'll do this for me." His presence wavered, even fainter now.

Gen picked up the knife and the rest of the implements from the Resurrection Spell and shoved them into her purse. He was stronger now. He would be back.

She ran out of the cemetery and into the woods like the devil was on her tail.

CHAPTER TWENTY-SIX

It was dark when Joel woke up. Pitch black.

"Matt!" Panic filled him.

The distinctive elephant roar of a snore cut short. "Wha—?" Matt said sleepily.

"I can't see." The Blindness curse. Barely a night of relief this time before the new curse set in. "God help me."

A light snapped on. Matt stood at the foot of his bed in a pair of boxers. "That's 'cause it's the middle of the night." His brother rubbed his eyes.

Joel let out a breath. "Thank God."

"Is it okay if I turn this off and go back to sleep?"

"Would you mind leaving a light on? Just so I know—"

Matt turned off the floor lamp. "Would this work?" He flicked the bathroom light on.

"Yeah, thanks." Joel hadn't slept with the light on since he was a boy. He hadn't been afraid of the dark in years, but it all came flooding back. If he were to go blind tonight, he'd rather be awake with his eyes open. To sense the dimming of his vision and watch the colors and lights and objects blur into nothing. He didn't want to wake up in the dark. Not again.

Joel propped himself up in bed. Bluto gave a meow and padded from his spot on the empty pillow to Joel's stomach.

"So you're going to keep me company, are you?" Joel scratched his head, and Bluto purred in response.

The cat hunkered down, and the two of them kept each other company until dawn.

CHAPTER TWENTY-SEVEN

The rich smell of browning sausage woke Joel. His eyelids were heavy, his eyes dry as dust, but he had his vision. Blindness had yet to curse him.

"Get up, Matt," Joel said. "I'm hungry." Stella might be a little talkative, a little annoying, but she sure could serve a mean breakfast.

Matt groaned and rolled to one side. "I'm asleep."

He rubbed the grit out of the corners of his eyes. "No you're not. Breakfast. Let's go."

Bluto jumped from the bed and wound his soft body around Joel's legs. He meowed. "All right, all right." Bluto wanted his breakfast too. "Matt, where'd you put the cat food?"

Matt grumbled.

Joel prodded him. "Get. Up."

Matt shook his shaggy hair out of his eyes. "Okay, I'm up. Are you satisfied?"

"Where'd you put the cat food?"

Matt pulled open a drawer in the bureau. "He would have eaten it all if I hadn't hidden it. Your cat is a pig."

Joel took the box and shook some food into the glass ashtray they'd been using as a dish. "Here you go, cat." Bluto hopped up onto the side table and buried his nose in kibble. He purred and nibbled at the same time. Joel stroked his knobby back. Bluto was still too skinny.

"So what's next on the agenda?" Matt stepped into the bathroom and opened his shaving kit.

"Gen was supposed to do some research in her book." Joel sat on the bed and watched Bluto gobble up his food.

"Her book—you mean that black leather thing?"

"Yes, it's been helping with the curses."

Matt lathered up his face. "So the book tells you where to go?"

"No, it just helps with the cures." He left out the fact that sometimes Gen's cures didn't work.

"So if this book has all the cures, why can't she stop this whole thing?"

"It's not that simple. We have to find a descendant of the Silva family."

Matt paused mid-shave. "And then what?"

"I don't know." Bluto finished his meal and rubbed against Joel.

"You're putting an awful lot of trust in a stranger." Matt turned up the tap to rinse his razor and wiped the last of the shaving cream off his face.

Joel raised his voice over the sound of the running water. "Um, I think you failed to remember she has now officially saved my life twice."

"Okay, well that was nice." Matt squirted toothpaste onto his toothbrush.

"Nice? That was frickin' amazing, and if she wants me to climb a volcano…"

"Okay, okay." Matt held up his toothbrush in a mock surrender pose. "So you trust her. And you haven't paid her anything?"

"Not yet." He couldn't share with his brother how close he'd grown to Gen. How much he cared for her. Besides, the focus was on a cure—not on his feelings.

"Do you think she's only in this for the money?"

If Matt only knew how little money he had. "If she were, don't you think she would've asked for something up front?"

Matt spit toothpaste into the sink. "I don't know—she seems nice enough, but something doesn't add up."

"She's on the up and up." Her latest cure proved that.

"I guess if you trust her…" Matt pulled a shirt on. "Let's go have some breakfast."

"Exactly." Joel started toward the door. His vision wavered. He grabbed at the bedpost. "Matt…" Now he had tunnel vision, and the tunnel was rapidly growing smaller.

"What's wrong?" His brother's solid hand settled on his shoulder.

"The Blindness curse." His voice was strained. The room darkened, and he could only perceive shapes. He clung to the bedpost, an anchor in a world of dark. "God help me, Matt. Help me."

"Jesus, let me get Gen."

Joel sensed the panic rising in his brother. The fear in his voice. Like when he was a little boy. Even though inside Joel was frightened out of his mind, he knew he needed to stay calm. He grabbed his brother's arm. "I'm fine. You go get Gen."

The world was steeped in blackness, but he wouldn't let himself be engulfed by it. This time he wasn't going to let the curse win, take away his sanity. He was stronger than that. He had to be.

"Are you sure?"

He felt his way to a chair by the door. "I'll be fine."

"Stay there. Don't move. I'll be right back."

Joel gripped the arms of the chair and closed his eyes. It would feel more natural that way. That everything was black.

The door closed. Matt was gone.

Bluto jumped into his lap, his bony, furry body a comfort.

The cat meowed and dug his claws into him. Joel scratched him behind the ears. "You don't care, do you? I could be a troll and you'd still sit on my lap." He leaned his head back, took deep breaths and concentrated on the soft fur beneath his fingers. In his mind's eye he could see Bluto—the torn ear, the scarred face, the too-skinny body. He was a mess. But he was Joel's mess.

In a matter of moments Matt returned with Gen. Joel wanted to open his eyes, to see her sweet face and the short, boyish hair. The panic he'd tried so hard to tamp down rushed through him. He reached out for her.

"It's all right, Joel. I'm here." Gen's hand grasped his. "Can you see anything at all? Light? Shapes?"

He opened his eyes. The blackness was still there. A riot of neon colors flashed before him. As if he were pressing his fingers against his lids. "I see color. Like streaks of colored lightning."

"Your brain is still trying to figure out what's gone wrong," Matt said. "The circuits are firing, but there's no information being sent back to the brain."

Leave it to Matt to give a scientific explanation for a curse.

"There's something I can try." Gen tugged on his hand. "Come on."

When Joel stood up he teetered. Without a visual sense of where he was, his balance was shot.

"You have to rely on your other senses now," Gen said. "Pay more attention to what your body is trying to tell you."

"My other senses are telling me to sit down." He gave a tight smile.

"You can do this. I know you can."

Every instinct told him to stay put. Just curl up in a ball and stay put. The warmth of her body so close to his was intoxicating, though. He didn't want that warmth to leave. He slid his free hand down her arm. There were goose bumps there. He wasn't the only one who felt something.

Gen gave a gasp. "We need to get you outside. See if this works."

He managed a few shuffling steps forward. His balance was coming back to him bit by bit.

Joel wanted to grab her, pull her back into his room and kiss her. Kiss the breath out of her. Lean his body into her from shoulder to hip. But

Matt was there, close behind.

She led him down the stairs. In the black, it felt as if he were stepping off into nowhere. As if he would fall any second. Tumble down and down and down. Like falling off a cliff or into a bottomless pit.

He knew they'd reached the open front door because the stiff, salty breeze blew into his face. "Is it foggy out?"

"Yes."

Wet prickles of fog touched his skin. "I can feel it."

"Where are we going?" Matt's voice came out of the blackness. Joel had forgotten he was there. His world had been reduced to what he could feel, and that was Gen. Her softness. The scent of her. The warmth of her body against his. Nothing else in the world existed but the two of them.

"Just a little bit farther." The gentle scratch of a pine branch came across his arm. They must be in the woods behind the house.

Gen nudged him to the right. "Here, sit down."

Joel awkwardly lowered himself to the ground, which was strewn with pine needles. It was damp here. The fog penetrated even this far into the woods. Her warmth left him, and the darkness was empty and terrifying again. He took slow deep breaths to quell the panic.

He sensed his brother sitting next to him.

"Close your eyes," Gen said.

He had thought they were closed. He lowered his lids and waited.

"What is that stuff?" Matt asked.

"Dirt and some other things."

Joel's mind raced. As much as he wanted to see again, he was afraid of what might happen. What if something went wrong? What if this sped up the curses even more? Blindness was curse number seven. There were only two left.

"Wait," Joel said. "Wait."

"What?" asked his brother. "What's wrong?"

"I don't want to do this."

"It's okay, Joel," Gen said, her voice soothing.

"I said, I don't want to do this." Joel unsteadily got to his feet. "Take me back to the house."

His brother grabbed him by the shoulder. "Sit down, Joel. She only wants to help. Let her help you."

He shrugged off his younger brother's hand. "Take me back. If you won't do it, I'll find my own way." Joel stumbled forward and put his hands out in front of him. The pine branches poked back at him. Which direction had they come from?

"Please let me do this. Please." Her hands were on him again. He couldn't stand it. He couldn't stand to have her touch him that way. With pity. He didn't want pity, he wanted more from her. Something she didn't want to give.

"I said, take me back. I don't want your fucking help. I don't want it. Don't you get it?" Just like last night, the fear was taking over. The fear that it was unstoppable. Unbeatable.

Iron arms grabbed him, pulled him back down to the ground. He landed with a thud. "You are going to let her do this, Joel," Matt yelled in his face. "You are going to let her help you or God help me I'll beat your ass into the ground."

Joel struggled in the dirt. The scent of wet pine surrounded him. The dark closed in. He was trapped. Like an animal.

"Do it!" Matt's heavier weight rested on him, a knee in his gut, his arms pinned.

"Goddamn it, Matt," Joel gasped with a painful breath. He fought against his brother. "Let me up. Goddamn you, let me up!"

A cool slickness covered his eyelids. The scent of earth and ash filled his nostrils. He struggled. Some of the mixture smeared onto his cheek.

"Hold still," Gen soothed. "Hold still." She muttered some of her strange words again.

"Get it off me! I don't want it," Joel yelled. Matt's knee pressed harder into him, choking the air out of his lungs.

Gen chanted.

His eyelids burned. The scent of death surrounded him. A presence bore down on him, smothering him. He couldn't breathe. His brother held him down so tightly he couldn't move, couldn't get away, couldn't get a breath of air. A scream rose into his throat. Pure terror.

"It's done."

Matt let go of him. The pressure of his knee was gone. Joel scrambled to his feet and backed away. "Goddamn it, I told you to stop." He rubbed off the mud mixture and opened his eyes. A dim light. A pinpoint of light which grew stronger every second. An instinctual relief flooded through him.

"Did it work?" Matt asked.

Joel didn't answer. His vision cleared. He could see the opening in the trees where they'd come from. He headed toward it. "I'm going."

"It worked," Matt said. "You fixed him, Gen."

"Yes, I suppose I did." Her voice was quiet.

Joel pushed through the pine boughs and tramped into the woods.

"Wait up," Matt called out and caught up to his brother.

"How dare you," Adam growled in her ear. His presence lurked right behind her, invisible, yet still there. "You used *my* body to save him?"

A phantom hand slid around her throat, choking off her air.

"Stop," she croaked out.

His lips were right against her ear. "He's nothing. Do you understand? Without him, I am gone. Forever. He's the key to everything, and I won't have you wasting *my* body." His grip tightened. "Do you understand?"

"What are you doing, Adam?" She tugged at the ghostly fingers. "I love you. Why are you doing this?" The tears came in a hot rush. Fear and love co-mingled in her heart.

"Soon he'll be dead, and he won't be any good to me. You know what you must do."

His fingers slid down her skin. "I won't do it." His touch used to set her on fire, but now those dead fingers repulsed her.

"We always have the other one."

"Matthew?"

"You know he'll be next. If I don't get what I need from Joel, I can get it from Matthew."

Her breath caught in her throat. Not only would Joel be dead, but she would have to use Matthew too? "No..."

"Joel's a dead man already. There's no hope for him."

"There must be a way to save you both..."

"The only cure for the last curse is to kill the descendant of the Silva family." He laughed. "If you can't kill Joel for me, what makes you think you have the courage to kill an innocent for him?"

"No, that can't be true." A prick of fear and disbelief struck her. She thought about the knife she'd stolen and the picture of Sabina Silva. All the clues coming together...

Adam stroked her throat, his ghostly grip lessening. "You'll do this last thing for me and then we can be together. Don't you want that?" His voice lowered. "Remember how it used to be? Just the two of us. So much in love." He slid one hand down her body in an intimate caress. "Joel was a dead man the minute he walked through your door. There's nothing left to save."

The cold hand across her throat disappeared. Adam vanished. But he'd be back. He'd make sure she followed through on his plan, or Matthew would be next. Unless she could find the courage to defy him and do what she knew to be right.

She tucked the bag of ashes into her skirt pocket. Just like Adam knew a cursed man's blood was stronger than regular blood, she knew a dead man's ashes held their own power.

She touched her throat. Her Adam never would have threatened her so. The Adam she knew, loved and lost had been gentle and smart. A brilliant scholar of ancient magic.

Guilt hung on her. Adam wouldn't be in this state if it hadn't been for her. Since he wasn't fully human, could it be part of his humanity, what made him the man he was, had yet to return? Could this be the reason for his short temper, his aggressive behavior?

Adam would've done the same for her. He wouldn't have let her remain dead. She knew it. Why else would he have wanted to research the Resurrection Spell, perfect it, if he didn't intend to use it?

She owed it to her husband to bring him back, but she couldn't do what he asked of her. There must be another way.

CHAPTER TWENTY-EIGHT

Someone knocked on Joel's door. Bluto sat on his lap, purring. "Come in." He watched the fog drift by outside his window, swirling through the spruce.

His brother hadn't returned to the room after the events of the morning. Joel had skipped breakfast, and lunch had passed him by. The cat had kept him company.

The door creaked open. "Can I talk to you?" Gen stepped inside.

"As if anything I said would stop you." Bluto dug his claws into Joel's lap. The pain felt good. Life affirming. Pain was the only thing that let him know he was alive anymore.

"About this morning…"

"Did you and Matt enjoy ganging up on me?"

"That's not fair, Joel."

"It's not fair? Is this family curse fair, Gen?" Anger that had been boiling just under the surface spilled out in a rush of words. "Is it fair that my family is being wiped out one by one because a jealous girl couldn't see past tomorrow? Did she have any idea what she was doing? Did she know back then what kind of havoc she would bring down on innocent people?"

"I don't think so." Gen sat on the edge of the bed and reached to scratch Bluto behind the ears. "She was probably like you said, a naïve girl who had little experience with black magic. She probably had no idea what she'd done until it was too late. Until she saw the rest of the DeVries family fall victim too. Oh, perhaps at first she was happy to see it happen…Calvin's wife then his father. For those were people against whom she had some kind of hatred. But later on? I don't think she meant for it to go on like it has. The waste of life it caused."

"Then why didn't she stop it? Why would she just sit back and watch it all happen?"

"I don't know. I haven't been able to find out very much about the Silva family after the 1920s."

"You've been researching without me?"

She shrugged without giving him an answer. "Perhaps they left the area because of the curse. If the whole family was practiced in the black arts, they would surely know one of their own had caused the DeVries curse. Perhaps they knew it was only a matter of time before someone pointed a finger at them. You have to remember, they were outsiders. Gypsies."

"Gypsies? When did you figure that out?"

"I had an inkling when we found out her name—Sabina Silva. A very traditional gypsy name. But some other things gave me a clue…"

"Like?"

"Does it matter? This helps us quite a bit. I think I may know now what needs to be done."

"You do? You've found a cure?"

She wouldn't look him in the eye. "Possibly."

"Then tell me, what do you we need to do? Can we start tonight?"

"You don't want to know the details." Her gaze drifted away from his.

"Why?" He made her face him. "What's wrong, Gen? What don't you want to tell me?"

"I just don't want you to worry anymore." She kept her eyes on the cat. "Let me worry about it, okay? This is my responsibility now. My choice.

Not yours."

He tipped her chin up. Her eyes met his. "I don't understand. I brought you into this. You don't owe me anything. If anything, I owe you my life several times over. Tell me what you need to do. I want to help. I have to help."

"You can't." Her voice wavered. "Just trust me when I say you can't."

"I don't understand..."

She turned her face away. "Just know that I want to do this for you, Joel."

"Why?" He grabbed her wrist. He wanted to hold her, touch her, kiss her. But she wouldn't look at him. "Are you afraid of me?"

She shook her head and gave a slight smile. "No, I could never be afraid of you. Never."

"Did something happen with your husband?"

Her eyelids twitched. "I told you, I don't have a husband anymore."

"Did he hurt you?" He'd asked her the same question before, but the way she behaved made him wonder if she'd lied to him earlier. She was so reluctant to let go, even scared by the prospect. "Is that why you won't let me in?"

"I don't want to talk about this." Her voice was a harsh whisper.

"Why? What are you so afraid of?" He held her by her shoulders, his face leaning close to hers. His thoughts returned to the night he spent in her arms, in front of the fire. There'd been more between them than two lonely people comforting each other. He'd sensed a deeper connection that even now made him determined to beat this curse. For his brother and for her. "Are you afraid of what I'm feeling for you?"

Gen's body tensed. "What?" Her face was ashen.

Confessing his true feelings felt like parachuting out of an airplane—terrifying, but also exhilarating. With the curses charging at him full speed, he didn't have much time to think through everything. He just knew he had to tell her. He wanted her to know. "I'm falling in love with you, Gen." Bluto meowed and jumped off his lap. "Every time I touch you, I..." He touched the side of her face.

"Please." She leaned away from him. "Don't say any more."

"Why not?" His fingers curled into the fabric of her blouse. He wanted so much to hold her close, lose himself in her body one more time. But fear radiated from her in waves. "What are you hiding from me?"

"Nothing."

Their gazes met. "You're lying."

"I tell you it's nothing." She looked away. "I can't love you, I don't…"

"You can't?" He tilted up her chin and forced her to look at him. "You can't or you won't?" His stomach dropped. "Is it because of the curses? There is no cure, is there? I'm going to die, and you can't watch."

There were tears in her eyes now. "You don't understand. I can't love you, Joel. I can't." She wrenched out of his grasp and dashed to the door.

"Wait!" Joel got up from the chair.

Matt met him at the door. "What's going on? Why's she so upset?" He scanned Joel's face. "Did you say something stupid again?"

Joel watched her retreating figure disappear down the stairs. "I told her I loved her."

CHAPTER TWENTY-NINE

"You did what?" Matt closed the door behind him. "One minute you're about to throw yourself over a cliff and the next you're in love with Ms. Fortune Teller?"

"Spiritualist."

"I knew there was something up with you two." He crossed his arms and leaned against the bureau.

Joel picked up his jacket and slipped it on. "I have to go after her."

Matt stopped his brother with a palm to the chest. "You don't want to do this."

"Do what?"

"Just let her go, man."

"I can't let her get away without explaining…"

"Do you really want to bring her further into the mess? Just let her go."

Joel weighed his brother's words. He *should* keep Gen at a distance. He'd opened his heart to her, and she'd rejected him. Even though he knew his brother was right, Joel pushed past his brother and chased after Gen.

Joel couldn't love her. He just couldn't. Gen never should have succumbed to the overwhelming loneliness she'd felt the night she brought Joel to her room. Why did he have to make this harder for her? Although Adam was not the same man, was frightening even, she couldn't leave him half dead. That would be two times she failed him. To deny him both life and death, to leave him somewhere between the two would be cruel. Adam needed her, but she also wanted to save Joel, give him a life to live. But when Joel told her that he loved her, it all became much more complicated.

She raked a hand through her hair. All the clues had been coming together over the last few days. She reached for the chain around her neck and pulled out the necklace her mother had given her on her fourteenth birthday. A "family heirloom" she'd called it back then. But now Gen knew the truth. Her necklace was the same one in the picture at the Overlook. To see that photo had startled her. Maybe on some deeper level she'd known. When she stole the knife, she didn't do it just because Adam had told her to, but because she sensed something about that knife. Adam, without realizing it, had given her the answer. She knew what she had to do. What she had to prepare for.

She was the descendant of Sabina Silva. Her family caused all this grief and sorrow and death. And now this curse would end with her. From her skirt pocket she pulled out the spare car key Matt had given her the other day. She'd had a feeling it might come in handy. Before she'd be ready, she had one more place to go. She didn't have much time.

The fog settled in. She switched on the low beams. The passenger door opened.

"Not so fast." Joel slid into the empty seat. "Where do you think you're going? In my car?"

She couldn't look at him. The words wouldn't come. "I have to go somewhere."

"Where?"

"To a place near the Silva homestead."

"When were you planning on telling me about it?"

"I wasn't." Why not be honest with him for once? What could it hurt?

He flinched.

It killed her to pretend she didn't care. Pretend she wasn't falling in love with him too. A man who might die if she couldn't pull off her plan. Another life in her hands. And this time, she wouldn't make that fatal error.

"I see." He crossed his arms. Unlike her dead husband, Joel was solid, real, alive. Here with her. Caring for her. Worrying about her. Her chance to do the right thing this time. Save him before it was too late.

She drove down the lane, leaving the bed and breakfast behind them. "And Matt?"

"He'll be fine. He's working on his paper."

"I don't believe you."

"Someone has to believe everything's going to turn out all right," Joel said. "I don't think I could stand it if Matt were moping around."

"I'm not moping around."

"No, you're not." He seemed hurt that she wasn't. He took a deep breath. "So, where are we going?"

"The guy at the Interpretive Center told me about a new archaeological dig in the woods. The Silva homestead was torn down years ago, but this new site is something older."

"You think it might have some significance to tracking down the Silva family?"

The sun hung low in the sky. The fog thinned and the red orange rays of the setting sun lit up the wisps of lingering fog in a brilliant display.

She nodded. They both took in the beautiful view in front of them. Gen wondered how many more sunsets Joel had left.

He broke the silence with a sigh. "So I wanted to ask you, this next curse. The Fatal Touch. What does that mean?"

"Do we have to talk about it now?"

He bristled. "Yes, we do. I'd like to know what's in store for me. It can't be too far off. I want to be prepared."

The lowering sun burned into her eyes as she headed toward the coast.

Her eyes teared up from the brightness. "I don't know."

He didn't believe her. She could feel it. He thought she was keeping something from him. "Just take me to this homestead. Let's see if we can find some real answers there."

She nodded.

Gen drove along the winding road, which led them back to Cape Perpetua. She thought about the special knife in her bag. The knife Adam had been so anxious for her to steal. Now she'd seen with her own eyes the power it held. A few weeks ago, she would have done anything to use that power to save her husband. But she was beginning to realize the Adam she knew would never be coming back.

A heavy sorrow settled in her chest. Her breathing was tight, like the day of his funeral. It had been a mistake to conjure his ghost, to find out how to bring him back to her. This was black magic she was dealing with. Ancient magic that ruined lives, devoured souls, and never gave anything for free.

~ * ~

"Are you sure you know where you're going?" Joel fought through the underbrush, which was thick and wet with fog droplets. "We left the trail ten minutes ago."

"It's just up ahead. I can see them."

"See what?" Joel peered through the thick green growth. What was she talking about?

"Look." Gen pointed to the sea of strange plants in front of them. "It's Darlingtonia. This is their 'darling' spot."

"Darlingtonia?" Joel asked. "What's that?"

In the middle of a clearing, a host of unusual plants surrounded them. Like Jack-in-the-Pulpit, only larger, taller with a heavy drooping bulbous head.

"These plants. They're called Darlingtonia."

Masses of them spread out under the canopy of trees. He picked one, and his feet sunk into the moist ground beneath them. "I've never seen a plant like this before. Strange, isn't it?"

Gen tucked a few of the stalks into her bag. "It's a carnivorous plant."

Joel examined the head of the plant. "Like a Venus Flytrap? Luring bugs to their doom?"

She plucked one of the strange-looking buds and tipped it upside down. "See this opening in the top of the plant?" She pointed into the plant's hidden maw. "The back is translucent, making the fly or bug that's attracted inside think he can fly back out again. When he tries, he hits the back wall of the plant and falls into this hollow stalk, where he's digested." She traced a line down the throat of the plant, where its coloring switched from pure green to green streaked with red. She gathered a few more.

"What are you going to do with those?"

"They're very powerful plants. Meat-eating plants are the closest thing to human in the plant world."

Carnivorous plants? What would she need those for? He shivered at the morbid thoughts that came to his mind.

They continued past the clumps of Darlingtonia. An old stone chimney rose toward the early night sky. Framed against the brilliant deep blue of twilight, it looked like an ancient ruin. Half-rotted timbers from what used to make up the roof lay on the ground, and all around them stood the strange plants.

"This must have been their meeting place," Gen said. "Before it fell apart."

"What kind of place was this?"

Gen held on to a roof beam and swung herself underneath to get to the other side of the ruin. "Maybe a logging cabin or hunting cabin built well before this area was developed."

Joel lost sight of her for a moment, and in the gloom, he worried about losing her altogether. "So now what do we do? This seems like a dead end. No one lives out here anymore. Shouldn't we go back into town tomorrow and research the Silva family? Find a descendant? Isn't that the way to stop it?"

Gen reappeared farther away from him, standing on top of one of the beams. "I already know how to stop it."

"You do?"

"Yes."

"Well, why didn't you say something before we came all the way out here?"

"Because I..." Her words seemed to catch in her throat, and even in the encroaching darkness he could see a shadow pass over her face. "The descendant is me, Joel."

"What?" But he couldn't hear anymore. The rush of blood to his ears sounded just like the crash of the surf against the Devil's Churn. Loud. Pounding. Deafening. It couldn't be true. Gen couldn't be related to the Silvas.

"It's me." Gen disappeared behind a moss-covered beam, leaving Joel alone in the darkening woods.

CHAPTER THIRTY

Gen passed underneath the beam, her stomach in knots from the truth she revealed to Joel about her relationship to the Silva family. Adam was here. She could sense him.

"Why did you tell him?" Adam's voice was harsh in her ear. "You've ruined everything."

"Stop it. Please, stop it."

Joel was on the other side of the ruin, but he would join her soon. Adam needed to leave before Joel overheard them. The guilt was swallowing her up.

The touch of his fingers trailed down her arm like pinpricks of ice. "Now he won't trust you. Now he won't give you the blood we need."

"The blood *you* need."

The ghost fingers clamped down painfully on her forearm. "I've been helping you. All along I've been the one who saved your precious Joel. He would have killed himself the other day on the cliff side if it hadn't been for my spell."

Fear spread through her like wildfire. Adam was gaining strength. Soon he would inhabit his body completely.

"Adam, you have to leave." Gen peered over his shoulder. "He's coming." Joel held on to the underside of a beam to balance himself as he negotiated the dilapidated structure.

"You want to be with him, rather than with me, don't you?" Both hands gripped her now. They looked like flesh and bone, but they were so cold.

"Adam, you're hurting me. Let go," she whispered, terrified Joel would hear them. "He's almost here." She looked past Adam to see Joel passing underneath the beam. "*Adam.*"

Joel's eyes met hers.

Adam was gone.

"Did you say something?" Joel stepped clear of the mossy, rotted wood.

Gen stumbled over her words. "I was just talking to myself…thinking things through. The next step." She could barely catch her breath. That had been too close. If Joel saw Adam how would she ever explain…

"Considering you're the descendant of Sabina Silva, I was hoping you'd be the next step." His brows crimped together. "Why didn't you tell me it was you?"

The night was settling in, and Joel was obscured in shadow. She was grateful for that so she wouldn't have to see the hurt on his face. "I just found out myself. I haven't even had time to process it…"

"Where have I seen that before?" Joel lifted the necklace from Gen's neck. The pure silver piece had an intricately carved intertwining vine design.

She felt her cheeks heat. He knew. He knew where he'd seen it before.

"The picture at the Overlook. Sabina Silva was wearing the same necklace." He let go as if it burned him. "That's when you knew, wasn't it?"

She turned away from him. "I wanted to tell you, but I didn't know how…" Gen tucked the necklace back into her clothes. She tried to shake off Adam's presence. He still felt so close. "I knew my grandmother grew up somewhere around here, but I didn't know it was Calvin City."

"So what do we do? How do we stop this? If you're the descendant…isn't there something…a spell, a chant, a prayer? What happens now?" He stood behind her, his presence tall and warm. Joel was alive and real, and he loved her. He said he loved her. Adam was dead...or almost dead. And the only way he would be alive again would be to take life away from Joel. What little life he had left.

"We go back and get some sleep."

"What?" Joel's breath was hot on her neck. He was so close. "We need to stop this...you must know something."

"I know something, and I will share that with you when I think you're ready."

His words came out clipped now. Angry. "When you think I'm ready?" He spun her around. "What, you don't think I've suffered enough yet? Or, no, maybe you think I deserve it. Maybe all along you knew you were Sabina's descendant and wanted to watch me squirm. Yes, that's it." His eyes were blue fire. "You even helped speed up the process. Instead of nine weeks, you gave me only days." He let go of her, bit his lip and looked up at the stars just appearing overhead. He massaged his forehead with his thumb and index finger. "I see now. Family loyalties run very deep with you, don't they?"

It couldn't be her. Gen couldn't be the one. Not now. Joel couldn't love the very person who stood between him and life. Who stood between his brother and survival. "I trusted you. I told you things..." His voice broke.

She turned but only halfway, her face a perfect silhouette of shadow in the growing dark. "I never meant to hurt you. If I'd known from the beginning, things might have been different."

"How? How exactly would any of this have been any different? I'm still cursed, and it won't stop. Not for me, not for you, not for anyone. I have so little time left...and now what happens? If you are the descendant...? I thought we would find that person, and they would know what to do. How to handle it. They would have some ritual or spell or some goddamn way to help me." He emphasized his frustration with a hard kick to a fallen timber. "But you? You've been using a piece-of-shit book." He grabbed her by the shoulders and shook her. "You don't know anything. You can't do anything to stop this. The last curse will come, I'll die, and Matt will be next."

"No!" Tears spilling down her cheeks, she wrenched away from him and ran.

As she fled through the woods, Adam called to her. "There's nothing you can do for him now. Why not let his death mean something?"

"No," she cried. "I can't do it. I can't sacrifice him." She wouldn't have the deaths of two men on her hands. It wasn't too late for Joel. She still had time.

"Sacrifice? You make it sound so horrible." Adam now ran next to her. His white face shone like marble in the twilight.

"It *is* horrible." She slowed her pace.

"You'll be sparing him pain. Ask him. How would he rather die? By the hand of someone he loves—?"

His hand touched her arm, and she shoved it away. "Shut up!"

The act didn't seem to faze him. "He loves you, Gen. Isn't that sweet? And he has no idea what you planned for him."

"Me?" She stopped in her tracks. "I haven't planned anything. This is all your doing."

"You were the one who started this. The first time you looked through my notes and found the Resurrection Spell."

"No!"

"You put this all in motion. You made your decision then, that you would do anything to get me back." He smiled. "This is all your fault."

"Get away from me." She felt sick. He hit a little too close to home. "I don't want you here."

"How ironic you're the descendant, Gen. That makes it all the more sweet. Sabina Silva gets her final wish, the end of the DeVries line. And you'll be there to see it."

"I said go."

Adam vanished. He apparently had tortured her enough.

Her heart ached for Joel. She'd crushed him with her revelation. The web of trust between them was now irrevocably broken. How would she get him to listen to her and explain that the only way to stop this curse was if he killed her? Stabbed her through the heart.

She needed to get to Matt. He would be on her side in this. He had to be. He would convince Joel it was the only way.

For a fleeting moment she thought of how much she'd grown to love him. His sweet smile, the care he had for his brother. The determination to live was so strong in him. He would never give up on his brother. He'd never give up on someone he loved.

Adam was truly dead. She understood that now. Whatever she had conjured up was not the same man who died on the road all those months ago. No way would she follow through with Adam's plans. But she could save Joel, and Matt was the key.

~ * ~

As they drove back to the bed and breakfast Joel remained silent, and it frightened her. In the dark she couldn't read his expression. Now that he knew her connection to Sabina, what her family had done to him and his brother, he'd put a distance between them.

She wished she could reassure him she could end it all. Using the knife and its special powers, she knew her plan would work. He must kill the descendant, trade blood for blood.

When they finally arrived at the bed and breakfast, he left her in the lobby. Took the steps two at a time and slammed the door shut before she could even say good night.

Matt entered from the dining room, a beer in his hand. "Hey, where've you guys been?"

"I thought you weren't going to take any more free beer?" Gen gestured at the open can in his hand.

Matt shrugged. "I finished my paper, and after what you two told me, I thought it might help get my mind off of things." His mouth was a straight line. "Where's Joel?"

"Upstairs." She looked at the stairway. "Could I talk to you for a minute, Matt?"

"Sure." He took a sip of his beer.

"Let's go out on the porch." She didn't want Joel to catch them talking When Matt passed by, she grabbed the open beer can out of his hand.

"Hey!"

"You're underage." She let the door close behind them. "Now have a seat."

Matt plopped down on the porch swing and crossed his arms over his chest. On his face was an expression better suited to a three-year-old who didn't get what he wanted. "So what is it? Did you figure out how to end this curse crap?"

"Yes, I have, but your brother won't listen to me."

"What the hell is he thinking?" Matt popped up from the swing and headed to the door. "Let me go talk some sense into him."

Gen caught his arm before he could get past her. "Just listen to me, Matt. I need your help. I have a way we can save him, but I know he'll never agree to it."

"Oh?"

"Promise me you'll make sure he does what I tell you."

He sat next to her on the swing. "Whatever it takes to save my brother, I'm in."

CHAPTER THIRTY-ONE

Joel slammed the door. How dare she keep such important information from him. If the roles had been reversed, he would've told her immediately. Confessed he was the descendant. Worked with her to find a solution. But the minute Gen decided to keep that information to herself, the trust building between them had crumbled. What else was she keeping from him? It was suspicious enough when her "cure" for the Curse of the Mute actually speeded up the curses...but this? How could he ever trust her word again?

A breeze whipped the curtain back from the window, and the full moon peeked out from behind the last remaining puffs of fog.

"Bluto?" His cat hadn't meowed when he came into the room as usual. No soft black shape at the foot of his bed. Where was he? "Bluto? Kitty, kitty, kitty." He turned on the lamp on the bedside table.

Meow.

Bluto slipped out from under the bed. "Are you hungry, kitty?" Joel picked him up. The minute he touched him Bluto went limp.

"Bluto?" Joel shook him gently.

The cat was still. Too still. He pressed a hand to the cat's underside. No

x

190

heartbeat.

The moon's light shifted.

Joel scruffed the cat and held him closer. Still no heartbeat.

Bluto's green eyes were wide open and glassy.

"Jesus." He set the cat's body on the bed. "Jesus, Bluto, Jesus." He couldn't think straight. The poor cat with the scars and the spiky fur, who only a madman could love, was dead.

The Fatal Touch curse. Number eight. Now he knew what it meant. He was like King Midas who turned everything to gold—but Joel brought death.

His knees collapsed underneath him, and he knelt on the floor. "He never did anything to you," he whispered to no one. "He was just a little cat. A stupid little cat who liked chicken livers and tuna, for God's sake."

He ran a hand through his hair, not wanting tears to come. He wouldn't cry for a goddamn stray cat. Not him. He wouldn't let it touch him, this curse. He got up from the floor, grabbed a T-shirt out of his brother's bag and wrapped the limp animal in it, unable to look at the staring green eyes.

He would bury it. Get rid of it. This cat never existed. He would forget the cat by morning. Ex him out of his brain. The food would go in the garbage cans out back, the water bowl in the trash, the carrier...

Hot wetness coursed down his cheeks.

Goddamn it, it was just a friggin' cat.

He burst through the door and immediately reeled back. He'd almost barreled headlong into his brother.

"Don't touch me!" He backed away from Matt and held Bluto's swaddled body like a shield.

"What are you doing?" Matt's face had an odd expression on it.

Joel scanned the hallway and the stairs beyond, terrified Gen or Stella might sneak up on him, touch him. He stood there with the body wrapped in his brother's Timberwolves T-shirt. A stiff, furry forepaw peeked out.

Matt reached for the bundle. "What the...what happened? What happened to Bluto?"

Joel retreated further, cradling the cat's body close to his chest. "I said, don't touch me. I'm dangerous." He headed for the stairs.

"What happened?" Matt followed behind, but gave him a wide berth. "What do you mean, you're dangerous?"

Joel picked up the pace and burst through the front door. He needed to get away, get to the woods. "Don't follow me. Stay back."

"Was it the curse, Joel? Did the curse kill Bluto?" His brother trailed behind him, his big clodding feet stomping through the brush. That kid always had the biggest damn feet.

"Don't let me touch you." No more words would come out. That was all his brother needed to know.

"You have to listen to Gen, bro."

"What?" He shoved a pine branch out of his face. Why wouldn't his brother just go?

"She can help you. She told me. Just trust her."

Joel stopped full force and wrenched his head around to face his brother. "Trust her? After she lied to me about who she is? How do I know anything that comes out of her mouth is real? How can I trust her after this?" He thrust Bluto's body forward, taking care to keep his distance.

Matt, instead of backing down, squared his shoulders and met Joel head on. "She put her life on hold for you. Followed you into the middle of goddamn nowhere. Saved your ass more times than I can count. What the fuck do you want from her? A goddamn guarantee? Well, you aren't going to get one. Either you trust her or you don't. Either you die and leave me to pick up the pieces...or you just try what she's offering. She's going to give her life for you, man, doesn't that mean anything?"

"What?"

"Goddamn it, Joel, didn't you even listen to her?"

"What the hell are you talking about?" What scheme had Gen convinced his brother of now?

"The only way to stop the curse is to kill the descendant. She's offering her life in exchange for yours. Now do you get it?"

Those words hit Joel like a physical blow. Gen wanted him to kill her? She couldn't mean it… No way.

"I don't believe you." He swung back around and pushed into the clearing where Gen had done the ceremony that morning.

"It's the truth. Ask her."

His brain ran on overdrive trying to take everything in. The curses, the revelation of Gen's connection to him, Bluto dying. And now this. "Let me bury him."

"Then we can talk about it?"

"Yes." His response was as dry as the pine needles under his feet. With his bare hands, he dug a grave. For a cat, it didn't have to be deep. Just deep enough.

His brother stood by silently. Giving him distance. Giving him a chance to process everything.

He remembered the day he'd first noticed Bluto in his yard. His skinny, scraggly body. All bones and fur and eyes. And that pathetic meow. Bluto was hungry, but wouldn't take food from him for days. Joel religiously set out a bowl of food—chicken liver flavor—on his back stoop and drank his morning coffee, hoping the cat would come out of hiding and eat.

After a time, the cat had crept out from under the bushes, keeping a wary eye on Joel through the window. Joel had been patient, though. He knew the cat's hunger would eventually become greater than its fear. And he was right.

One morning, he set out the food as usual. Before he went back to the kitchen for his coffee, the cat was scarfing down food. It was gone in three or four bites. Joel stood not three steps away.

That was the first time he'd gotten a good look at the stray. How beat up he was. The scars, the hunks of missing fur. The name Bluto stuck.

Now he was burying Bluto's body in a grave far away from the safety of those bushes in his old yard. The house was gone, the stoop was gone, his supply of cat food gone too. But he'd escaped the fire with the most important thing—Bluto.

"I'm so sorry, buddy," he whispered as he laid the body still wrapped in the T-shirt into the dark hole he'd made. Out of all of the curses he'd suffered through, this one hurt the most, hurt the deepest. His shoulders bunched up and his body bent into itself. He was a full-grown man, but for that moment he felt like a little boy. Small, helpless, in need of a parent's comfort.

"I'm so sorry, bro," Matt said. "He was a good cat."

His brother's words gave him strength. "Yes, he was."

As Joel stood away from the grave at a safe distance, Matt scooped dirt with his bare hands and covered the body. "You'll get all the tuna you want now."

Matt patted down the soil. A small mound of dirt in the middle of the woods. Bluto's short life was over.

Gen watched from behind a stand of trees. She'd heard Joel cry out at the bed and breakfast and knew the curse had struck again. She sensed it now in her bones. Maybe because of her connection to Joel's family. Maybe just because she was more sensitive to life and death passing around her. This new curse meant she didn't have much time left.

Matt had promised he would help, and she hoped his talk with Joel had worked. It would be a shock, the steps they had to take. But there was an end game. Something that might work, if Joel could do it.

As the brothers mourned their cat, tears filled her eyes at the care they took to lay the little body to rest. It pained her to know her family caused all this grief.

"It's not your fault." Adam was suddenly beside her. She could smell death mixed with his cologne. How could that be? Was he getting stronger without her?

"It may not be my fault," she said. "But I can fix it."

"No, you can't." The smell of her husband's cologne used to comfort her, now it frightened her. The scent enveloped her like choking smoke from all sides. He grabbed her by the arm. His hand was almost solid flesh and blood now. His blue eyes were no longer watery and pale, but the strong ice blue they'd always been. Behind them there was no warmth, only an eerie fire she didn't recognize.

"I have to, Adam." She trembled. "My life for the two of theirs. It's the only way."

"What about my life, Gen? What about me?" He dragged her to him. Her purse fell and the contents spilled out on the forest floor. "I need his blood to save me. I won't let you take that from me."

"You're hurting me, Adam. Let go." His grip was like iron. "We would be together in death, don't you see? I can't take someone else's life to save yours. You died in that accident. Your life is over, Adam. And what's left..." She touched his cool arm. "Something's missing. Something's not right."

His face was inches from hers, his teeth strong and white in the dark. "You will do this for me, or I'll kill you myself."

Gen gasped. He'd used her to get close to Joel, to get what he needed. Now that he was so close to his goal, he'd become a demanding and dangerous being who would stop at nothing to live again.

Joel crashed through the trees. "Let her go!"

CHAPTER THIRTY-TWO

Joel wanted to throttle the man in front of him for daring to put his hands on Gen. But if Joel touched this man he'd kill him. He held himself back.

The tall lean man had a death grip on Gen's arm and murder in his eyes. When he saw that Joel hesitated, he smiled wickedly and wrenched Gen toward the woods. It only took a matter of moments for Joel to decide Gen's life was at stake.

Joel launched himself at the stranger and dug his hands into the folds of the man's shirt, but his fingers slipped. He couldn't seem to get any purchase on the fabric. What looked like solid muscle and flesh beneath, was not. His Fatal Touch had no affect.

"I said, let her go!" Joel cocked his arm back and threw a punch, meaning to land it on the man's jaw.

Gen screamed.

Joel's fist sailed through the air.

And landed on nothing.

The man had disappeared.

"What the fuck?" He lost his balance from the force of the punch and stumbled forward. "What in the hell is going on? Who was that?" A shiver ran down his back. A man was there and then he wasn't. Was he losing his mind?

Matt appeared beside them. "Is everyone all right? Where did that guy go?"

"I'm not sure." Gen's voice shook. "But he wasn't human."

"What?"

Joel wanted to tip her chin to meet his gaze. "Who was that...that...thing?" He could still feel the sensation of the flesh that wasn't flesh as his fist flew forward.

"My husband."

Matt and Joel exchanged confused glances.

"He's dead." Her back was to them. "But I was trying to bring him back."

"Bring him back? What do you mean...?" That night in the cemetery—the strange figure he'd seen. It all made sense now. Her odd behavior. The absences. The hesitant answers.

"About six months ago, I had an accident. A car wreck on I-205. Adam was badly burned—he only lived for a few hours." Her voice was thick with unshed tears. She sank to the ground and hugged her knees to her chest, the contents of her purse spread around her. "It was my fault. I'd been driving, you see, it was late, I was tired."

"I'm so sorry, Gen," Joel said.

She took a deep breath. "He'd been a student of dark magic. I never studied more than palm reading and tarot cards. But his studies went deeper. Those books I mentioned when we first met, they were his. I was devastated by his death...I felt so guilty. Then I found a spell he'd been working on..."

"So what does this have to do with me? Was he one of the reasons why you came to Calvin City with me?"

She'd been so willing to take him in, help him. Almost as if she'd been expecting him when he showed up at her door. When he needed to go to

Calvin City, she'd just hopped in the car and left her life behind. Now he could understand why. It hadn't been about him, but about her dead husband. It had never been about him.

"Yes." Her voice was strained. "He told me he needed your blood. The spell has to be done with blood, you see. I'd been using mine, but your blood—the blood of a cursed man—is so much more powerful. I thought that I could just get what we needed and then help cure you as...as payment."

"As payment? You cut me, stole blood from me as payment?" Had she slept with him only to draw him closer, to take more blood from him? Was everything they'd shared a lie? "I should have known. You only helped me because of him. I was just a means to an end. You never really cared what happened to me, did you?" Betrayal cut through him. He spied the black book on the ground next to her and snatched it up.

"Wait, don't! You don't understand." She scrambled in the pine needles to reach for the book.

"Your book. That was all a lie, wasn't it?" He flipped it open. The pages were blank. "What am I, some kind of experiment for you to toy with?" He thumbed through the book, blank page after blank page.

"It's not what you think—"

His hand shook as he held it. "Who gave you those cures? Your husband? Is he the one who told you to speed them up?"

"I wanted to help you, but I wanted to make sure—" She was crying now.

"Wanted to make sure you got my blood." He ground the words out between his teeth. She had betrayed him. This whole trip, all these days, he was just the vessel for an ingredient she needed. Blood of a Cursed Man to save her dead husband. "You used me. You used my blood to save your damned husband. And all the while..." he reeled at the thoughts running through his head, "...all the while, I thought I was falling in love with you. I thought all that care and concern was real..."

"It was!"

"It was all lies." He tightened his jaw. "Every single bit of it."

"No."

"And you almost convinced my brother to help you. I don't know what kind of sick game you're playing…"

"It's not a game, Joel."

"But it's over. I'm done with you. We're getting out of here tonight and as far away from you as possible." He tossed the book at her. "Don't come near me or my brother ever again."

Gen rushed to pick up the rest of her things and stuffed them back into her bag. "I can help, Joel. I can save you both."

"Shut up."

"But…" Her tears came faster now.

If he took a minute to think about it, he'd feel sorry for her. The last thing he wanted to do now was feel anything for this liar.

"Matt, let's get out of here. Let's go home." The words hit an empty place in his heart. There was no home to go to. All he had were the clothes on his back, his car and his brother. He didn't even have his cat anymore. His life had been reduced to almost nothing.

Matt had stood silently by the whole time. His eyes shone with unshed tears. But Joel wasn't sure who they were for: Bluto, Gen's betrayal or the fact that Joel couldn't avoid his fate now.

"Jesus," his brother said. With the heel of his hand he ground away the tears.

"We're done." Joel pushed through the trees. He was on a mission. He'd knock down Stella's door if he had to, pay his bill with what money he had left and then get the hell out of Calvin City.

"I've never had anyone leave in the middle of the night before." Stella stood in the doorway of her private rooms with curlers in her hair.

Joel glanced at his watch. "It's only ten o'clock." Matt had been assigned the job of packing. Since most of what needed to be packed belonged to Matt, it shouldn't take long.

"Stan won't be happy about this. No sir. Slinking off into the night.

We're not that kind of place."

Joel fleetingly wondered what kind of place she thought people checked out of at ten o'clock at night. Nothing good came to mind. "Just the one room. I have a credit card."

"One room?" she asked, looking absently at the credit card he handed her. He took care to make sure their fingers didn't touch. "But what about the girl? What about her room?"

"She'll be paying her own way."

"Oh." Stella took his card and then looked into his face with a new awareness. "Oh, I see. Yes, I see." She retied her wrapper, came out into the living room and closed the door behind her. "My machine's in my office over here. It'll just be a moment."

Joel glanced back at the front door as they passed through the living room. He prayed Gen wouldn't come through the door. He couldn't stand to see her again. She'd hurt him too deeply.

Stella rambled on in her usual fashion. "One time we had a couple a fellas from Portland—you're from the big city, right?"

"Yes, ma'am," he answered, but his concentration was focused on that front door. The stained glass panels on either side, the curlicue molding, the gleaming brass knob. His eyes played tricks on him, as he imagined the knob turning.

"These two took my honeymoon suite, can you imagine? Two men?" Stella ran the card through her little black machine next to the phone. "And they specifically asked for it in the reservation. What do you suppose they wanted that room for?"

Joel didn't have the heart to enlighten Stella about the finer points of homosexual relationships. "There's all kinds, I guess."

The machine spat out a receipt.

"I guess you're right. All kinds." She tore off his copy and set it on her desk for a signature. "Well, it was pleasant having you with us. Sorry I have to charge you for tonight, but you understand..."

"It's not a problem, Stella. You have to make a living." He quickly scratched his name on the line. He sneaked a glance at the door. Nothing.

"Yes, yes, I'm glad you understand. Stan tried to explain that to a tour group that cancelled at the last minute. They just didn't seem to get it. I mean, we're not the Hilton. We had an argument about the deposit. Can you believe that? Even though we state our policy right there on the confirmation letter. Fourteen days and you lose your deposit. No ifs, ands or buts, as Stan would say. The man on the other end got very upset after that. You wouldn't believe the language he used."

"Stella, it's been a pleasure, but my brother's waiting for me."

She reached out to touch him on the arm. Joel yanked it away. Stella frowned. "Oh, yes, I'm sure you're anxious to get going. It's quite a drive back to the city. Don't want you out on the roads too late."

"Exactly. I'm glad you understand."

"Oh, of course, dear, of course."

Stella closed up her office and shuffled back into her bedroom.

Matt dumped their bags in the front hall.

"That everything?" Joel asked.

"Yep."

"Then let's go."

Matt hesitated.

"What?" Joel was afraid to find out what his brother was thinking. "Don't tell me you feel sorry for her? That you believe her?"

"Gen did stop those curses, Joel."

"She also sped them up."

"Did it look to you like her husband—that ghost or whatever the hell he was—was helping her or hurting her back there? Something's going on. Doesn't she deserve the benefit of the doubt?"

Joel's heart hurt. She'd betrayed him. She'd lied to him. He confessed his love for her, and she'd stolen his blood. "I don't have much time left, and she took some of it away from me. I don't know if I can forgive her for that."

Matt flinched. "What are we going to do?"

"First, I want to find out if what she said was true…if we kill her, can we end this thing? Or was that just another lie?"

"Could you really do it, Joel?"

"Yes." Joel narrowed his eyes at his brother. "I'm not going to let this happen to you, Matt, I promise." But Joel knew the weakness of that promise. There was no guarantee. In fact, he was further away than ever from a solution to his problem. The last week had been wasted on a wild-goose chase, and now he had no idea where to go to find any answers.

"But if she's the key to ending this, we can't leave," Matt said. "Not yet."

"We're not leaving town, we're just leaving this place. I can't think straight here." He didn't want to mention he couldn't walk through this house knowing Gen's betrayal. "I saw a motel outside town when we first drove in. I'm guessing we won't need it for more than a night."

His brother sobered at that statement. Matt knew it was only a matter of time before the last curse struck and ended Joel's life.

Would he feel it when it happened? Would it be gradual? Or like a strike of lightning?

"Let's get out of here," Matt said, clearly shaken.

They both walked out the front door together, and when it closed behind them, Joel thought it sounded like the thud of a coffin door closing. Heavy and final.

CHAPTER THIRTY-THREE

Gen raked through the damp ground with her fingers. She knew they had buried him here. Under this small mound of dirt and pine needles. Alone in the dark and the silence of the woods she thought about how things had gone so horribly wrong between her and Joel.

She should have been upfront with him from the beginning, but when they first met she didn't know how her husband had changed or how little he resembled his former self. He was changed by death. Was it his soul that had been lost? Or a part of himself? The Resurrection Spell would bring back a body from the dead, but ashes? When she'd first tried the spell, she wasn't sure it would work. Adam had been dead for several months and he'd been cremated. Maybe a complete resurrection had been impossible.

She understood now the reasons why Adam brought Joel to her. It wasn't a random selection. The choice had been purposeful. The perfect savior for her husband hadn't stumbled upon her accidentally, Adam had lured him there. Drawn him to her.

Even if it would be difficult to make Joel trust her again, she couldn't let him die and his brother suffer because of her. All along she had been the key to saving them both. If Joel hated her, and Adam was no longer Adam, death would be a release for her. The DeVries family didn't deserve such long suffering. If it hadn't been for the incompetence of her ancestor, the curse would have begun and ended with Calvin DeVries, but something clearly had gone wrong. Too much hatred, too much passion. Sabina had created a lifetime of curses. A never-ending string of misery. And now she had a chance to right that wrong—sacrifice her life for Joel's.

First, she had to prove she could help—show him she meant no more harm. Joel could hate her all he wanted, but she hoped she could regain his trust.

She clawed deeper into the dirt and hit a soft object. "Bluto." She lifted him out of his shallow grave and unwrapped the T-shirt. "Let's see if this really works, okay?"

~ * ~

A cool breeze blew in through her window. Gen laid the cat gently on her dresser. Each scar proved how hard Bluto had struggled to stay alive. She touched the tip of one ragged ear, perhaps torn off in a fight with another tomcat or in an altercation with a stray dog. Who knew what trials this small black body had been through only to end up dead because of the curse? It wasn't fair. It wasn't right.

Tears pricked her eyes. This had to work. It was the only thing she could give.

In an ashtray, she shredded bits of the Darlingtonia plant she'd collected near the ruins. Thank God Adam had led her to the plants to replenish her supply for the Resurrection Spell, or she would have been without this necessary ingredient.

With a lighter and bits of torn paper, she started a small fire in an ashtray. It sparked up immediately. She added more bits of Darlingtonia, the odd pink green leaves sparking up blood red in the flame. Next came the blood—her own. She wasn't cursed, but Bluto was freshly dead and whole, unlike her husband. Any blood should do the trick.

She searched through her bag for the knife.

It was missing.

In a panic, she dumped the contents of her purse on the floor. In the woods. Her purse had spilled when Adam had attacked her. He must have seen the knife and taken it.

What would she do without the knife? Not only did she need it to assure the Resurrection Spell would work on Bluto, but she needed it for her whole plan. The knife had proven to be a powerful tool.

She took a deep breath.

Calm down, Gen. It's okay. You can do this without the knife.

She'd done the spell before for her husband without it. Perhaps she wouldn't need such a strong spell.

In the bathroom, she broke apart her safety razor and took out a single razor blade. With the edge of the blade she sliced her finger and dripped fresh blood into the fire.

The flame grew, dimming only when she added the blood to the mixture.

She tilted the stubby, yellowish candle into the flames. The wick sputtered to life. Over Bluto's body she passed the candle three times, chanting the Romany words she'd found in her husband's notes all those months ago.

May angle sar te merel kadi yag, opre, Bluto!

May angle sar te merel kadi yag, opre, Bluto!

May angle sar te merel kadi yag, opre, Bluto!

Each successive repetition, her voice grew a little bit louder. The candle's flame turned from yellow to orange to deep red, sizzling on the wick like a sparkler on the Fourth of July.

Gen held her breath while the candle sputtered. Bluto lay still. After a few minutes, a whisker twitched. Then a paw. His chest rose and fell with regular breathing. Bluto jerked his head up, looked at her with his bright green eyes and meowed plaintively.

Joy flooded her.

Bluto meowed again and rubbed his head against her fingers.

"Are you hungry, kitty?" She scratched him behind the ears, just like she'd seen Joel do. Her heart thumped. This would be her proof for Joel. Her plan would work, if only he'd listen. He would be so glad to have his cat back. But would he be glad she had a hand in it?

Before she could gather up the cat, Bluto jumped onto the windowsill, meowed once and disappeared into the night.

Gen rushed to the window. "Bluto, come back!" His black fur made him impossible to see in the dark. "Here, kitty, kitty." She heard one more meow, then nothing but the rush of wind through the trees and the distant crash of waves on the rocky shoreline.

Her proof just jumped out the window. Her peace offering to Joel that proved she wanted to help and could help.

Now she had nothing.

"Bluto!" she called out again, hoping he would come back. This time, there was no answering meow. In a rush she headed for Joel's room. She had to tell him what she'd done.

She knocked on Joel's door. It creaked open. The sheets had been stripped off the bed and the towels were piled in a heap on the floor. All that was left was an empty cat carrier with the door ajar.

Joel was gone.

~ * ~

The mattresses were lumpy, the bathroom was full of mildew, and the TV only received one channel. From bed-and-breakfast paradise with hot food on the table every morning and free beer at night, to this.

Matt lay sleeplessly in his bed and flipped through the channels. Joel had promised to be right back with the pizzas.

Pizzas.

Why was he so concerned about food when his brother was about to die? He was going to inherit the DeVries family curse. He pulled out his laptop and opened the file for his completed geology paper. Hours of research and writing for nothing. In fact, it seemed rather silly he'd wasted so much time on something so pointless.

He minimized the file and shut down his computer. No wireless internet access at this dump. Stella didn't have any either, but at least she gave him beer.

He heard a scraping sound at the door.

"Who's out there?" Matt shut off the TV.

The scraping grew louder, sharper.

Matt's skin crawled. He grabbed a table lamp and yanked the cord out of the wall. Taking position next to the door, he called out once more, "Who's out there?"

A loud bang. Wood cracked and split. The door flew off its hinges. Matt flattened against the wall, lamp still in hand. Sweat beaded on his brow.

"Joel Hatcher." A dark figure stepped into the room.

Matt held his breath.

When the person turned, Matt swung the lamp with all his strength. It came into contact with the head of his target and exploded into shards of white ceramic.

The figure turned in the direction of his attacker.

Matt screamed.

The man from the woods stood in their motel room. The man who had disappeared. His face was damaged from the impact of the lamp, but no blood. Just shreds of flesh, white like congealed fat.

He came at Matt, a fist pulled back and ready to strike. Before he let go, he said, "I need Joel Hatcher." Matt's jaw exploded in pain from the force of his punch.

His head snapped back and hit the wall. As he lost consciousness, he heard his brother, his voice low and growling, "Here I am, fucker, why don't you come and get me?"

CHAPTER THIRTY-FOUR

Matt's face was a bloodied mess and Gen's dead husband was to blame. That's all Joel needed to know. He had no weapons on him but his fists, and he wasn't sure if that would be good enough to battle some creature who was less than human.

Joel took a step toward the man who wasn't a man, fists clenched more in rage than in defense.

Adam leapt on him before he could react. His grip was surprisingly sure for someone half-dead. He held on to Joel like a tiger taking down its prey.

"Joel Hatcher, you will come with me." The man had managed to spin Joel around and get an arm across his throat in a matter of seconds. Joel burned inside with fury. He faced his brother who was unconscious on the floor.

All the anger in the world wouldn't free him. He struggled against the man's otherworldly grip. The arm across his throat got tighter and tighter. Joel's vision grew hazy.

Some other part of his brain kicked in. He flailed his limbs and bucked against his captor. He did everything he could to stay awake, stay alive. He couldn't leave his brother here like that. He couldn't. Who would protect him? Who would save him? He didn't have much time left...and to waste it with this freak...

"Joel Hatcher, you're the one I need for the final ceremony," the monster whispered in his ear. "Your blood will bring me back from the dead. Your blood will save me. Your death will have meaning. Take comfort in that."

The smell of earth and death was overpowering now. The stench seemed to emanate from the man's skin and clothes.

When his mind grew dark he had one final thought: Gen. Now he knew why she'd done it. It may have started out as the love of a woman for her husband, but this man was no longer human. When he'd come across her in the woods, she'd feared this thing. He recognized that now. He wished he could tell her what he'd realized too late.

Gen. Gen. Gen.

~ * ~

Matt awoke gradually, his mind fuzzy. From the pain in his jaw, it felt as if he'd been hit in the face with a sledgehammer. Gingerly, he touched it. Although it was swollen and tender, it didn't feel like his jaw was broken.

Two pizza boxes, their contents spilled on the floor, lay next to him.

"Joel?" Matt sat up. Adrenaline coursed through his body.

The door stood open. The sun was just beginning to rise. He'd been passed out almost the whole night.

Shards of the ceramic lamp littered the floor. He hadn't dreamt what happened last night. His jaw told him as much, but it was still hard to believe.

That man's face. The bloodless face with the lightning blue eyes and yellow hair. Like a demon, dressed all in black. But where was Joel?

He took a look outside. Joel's car was gone. What happened?

He shuddered at the thought.

He was stranded with no car, no brother and no clue about what happened to him. He went with his first instincts and picked up the phone.

"I need a cab at the Forest Motel & Diner."

As the taxi driver shuttled him back to Stella's bed and breakfast, he wondered if Gen would still be there when he drove up. She was his only hope.

CHAPTER THIRTY-FIVE

Gen gripped Matt's sleeve when he arrived at her door. "Where is he?" She had dark circles under her eyes and her lips were bloodless.

"I don't know. That man in the woods, your husband? He was there at the motel. I don't know how he found us. He knocked me out." He touched a hand to his sore jaw. "When I woke up, Joel was missing."

The worry on her face scared him.

She answered him as if she was talking to herself. "He's going to try it alone. Without me." She reached into the pocket of her skirt and pulled out a baggie full of gray dust. "But he forgot about this..."

"What's that?"

Gen shoved the baggie back in her pocket. "Something he needs. Come on, I think I know where he might be."

Matt stopped her. "What's he going to do to Joel? Where are we going?"

Gen pushed up the sleeves of her blouse. "Do you want to save your brother?"

"You know I do."

"Then promise you'll do everything I ask, without question."

The intensity in her eyes made his gut twist. "I promise."

Gen scanned his face as if she were looking for a crack that would reveal something hidden inside him. "My husband, Adam, needs Joel's blood. Lots of it."

He felt sick. "What?"

"He's trying to come back, all the way back, and your brother has what he needs. A cursed man's blood is uniquely strong when he's close to death."

Fear, worry, hatred all converged inside, raging to get out. "Did you know he'd go after Joel?"

"I had something else I needed to do first. To win back Joel's trust. I didn't think Adam would act so quickly."

He backed away from her. "You knew he'd go after Joel. You knew." Anger overtook him. "But you just let it happen. How could you? He loves you, Gen. He loves you!"

Her eyes welled up with tears. "I didn't know Adam would go this far on his own. Believe me, I didn't. He lied to me, too, to get what he wanted. He told me we could be together again, and all he needed was just a little bit of blood." She twisted her skirt in her hands. "I didn't see any harm. That first night Joel came, he was covered in sores. Bloody, oozing sores. He was in so much pain. I just wanted to help. Honestly I did. Adam may have lured him to the house, but I thought he'd only need a little bit of his blood. That's how it all started. Just a drop."

He wanted to punish this woman for hurting his brother, deceiving him, but the rational part of his brain told him no. She was the only connection to Adam, to his scheme. Maybe she could lead him to where her husband was holding Joel. "So how does it work? How do you bring him back with Joel's blood?"

She pulled out the baggie again. "These are Adam's ashes. All that I have left."

"Isn't that what you used to cure the Blindness curse?" He thought back to the ceremony in the woods and the mud she'd smeared on his brother's eyelids. "Your husband's ashes?"

212

"Yes. The ashes of a dead man have their own powers." She tucked the ashes in her bag. "To bring Adam back, there's a Resurrection Spell I've been using. You need blood and the body you wish to resurrect, and a few other things. I think that's why regular blood didn't work so well. It wasn't strong enough to bring him back since his body was cremated."

"So whose blood were you using before…before you knew about Joel?"

"My own."

Matt shivered at the horror of it. Using her own blood to bring back a dead husband.

"So where are the rest of his ashes?" The baggie held maybe a handful.

"Each time I do the ceremony Adam regains a bit of his human self. The ashes become flesh again. He's somewhere between living and dying right now. For the final ceremony he'll need the rest. Once he figures out he forgot it, he'll be coming for it."

Matt's breathing sped up. "You said you thought you knew where he'd taken Joel."

"Yes, there's one other ingredient there that he needs—Darlingtonia—a very special plant."

"And this place has Darlingtonia?"

"Yes, it's the spot where Calvin and Sabina used to meet. A powerful spot. Generations of magic live there. I could feel the echoes of my ancestors all around me yesterday." Gen started toward the garage behind the house where she'd found the bike the other day. "Stella has an old pickup back here. Let's pray the keys are in it."

"Let's go." Matt ran ahead of her. "Let's get this bastard and save my brother."

~ * ~

The ropes burned against Joel's skin. The friction of pulling against them had rubbed his arms raw. Blood dripped into his palm, warm and wet.

The gray light of dawn barely penetrated the thick stand of trees around him. He was tied down to a wooden beam in the midst of masses of Darlingtonia. Adam had brought him to the middle of the ruins where Calvin had met with Sabina all those years ago.

When Adam had him in the armlock, he was certain he wouldn't wake up. As the blackness came over him, he had found a strange sense of peace. How much better it was to die this way than to let the ninth curse take him. But now his mind railed against that thought. His brother was out there alone without him. If he died, there would be no one to protect him. No one to fight for him.

He tugged at the heavy rope which tied him to the old rotted beam. It lay propped up against another beam, so he lay on a slant. Darlingtonia grew around him, their pink red heads wet with fog.

A fly buzzed by his head. It landed on his arm, its tiny hair feet tickling him. He managed to move his arm under the tight rope. The fly spooked and flew away.

It landed on the tip of a bulbous head of Darlingtonia. Rays from the morning sun broke through the stand of spruce that surrounded the clearing. The fly crawled on top of the plant, explored underneath and crawled into the red pink maw. The fly sat still for a moment, then buzzed furiously inside. The sun shone through the thin membrane, which revealed the shadow of the struggling fly.

The buzzing lasted several more seconds until the Darlingtonia plant easily won the battle.

Joel fought against the ropes even more now. His brother was alone and injured. Looking for him. Vulnerable. The fly slipping inside the Darlingtonia reminded him of that. Free one moment, trapped the next.

Matt needed him.

Joel cried out and pulled against his restraints. His yell echoed through the trees and bounced back to him. He was alone out here. The only one who would come for him would be that horror who needed him in order to become human again. Fear coursed through him. Fear like he'd never had while in the grip of the curses. This new fear was knowable. Tangible. Death hung on Adam like a pall.

He yelled again.

The sun rose slowly, lighting up the field of Darlingtonia around him with a pinkish glow. Joel struggled against the ropes fruitlessly.

"Matt." The ropes cut into his bare arms, scratching, digging, burning. "God, Matt."

His words were carried off by the breeze. No one heard him. No one.

In the silence, alone with his own thoughts, he noticed a change inside. Nothing dramatic, but a slight shift in his core being. Like a gasp, a flutter. Something not right.

Deep within he knew this was the workings of the final curse. The Ninth Curse. His life ebbing away. It wouldn't be a dramatic end. A sudden dying. No, it would be a slow, agonizing march to death. With complete awareness the end was nearer each step of the way.

Pain burned deep within his bowels. He couldn't hold back a cry of agony. He should have known the last curse would be the one to hurt the most. Each twinge, like a hair being pulled out of his head. A needle jabbing into his back. The tip of a knife scraping along his neck.

"Don't go yet, Joel." Adam was suddenly next to him, holding the point of something sharp against his jugular. The edge cut through the first layers of skin and wet warm blood dripped down his throat. Adam angled Joel's head back. The once ghost-like limbs were now solid, but still cool. The hands that gripped him and held the sharp point against his neck had no warmth. "I need you still. You're the one I've always needed."

With his head tilted back this far, it was difficult to speak, difficult to breathe. "I'll kill you, you bastard," he spat out. "You'd better be sure you can do this." He focused his gaze into the bright blue eyes of his captor. Eyes empty of a soul. There was nothing there. No feeling. No emotion. Nothing human. Gen had brought back the body of her husband, but what made him human had been lost.

Adam laughed and, in an unexpected move, let go of Joel. He sat back on his haunches. "She wouldn't let me do this, you know."

"What?" Joel struggled in his restraints. He'd rather die on his own terms than as a victim of this freak.

"Gen wouldn't do it." Adam pricked his thumb with the knife. No blood appeared. His skin was deathly white. Like a cadaver. "How did you manage that?"

"She wouldn't do what? Kill me for you?" His mind flashed to Gen in her fluttering skirts. She'd seen more in her lifetime than most. Curses. Men rising from the dead. Maybe using Gen was his way out. If he could just get under Adam's skin, make him doubt— "She loves me."

"What?" Adam leapt on top of him, the knife back at his throat. He gripped Joel by the hair and exposed his neck more fully to the weapon. "I don't believe you," he snarled.

Joel lied further, gasping the words, "She told me that she loved me. Just before I left." He was the one who'd admitted his love for Gen. And now, facing death, he knew he still did. No matter what she might have done to him. She couldn't go through with that last Resurrection Spell. She'd chosen him over her husband. That must mean something. "She wouldn't kill me because she loves me."

"Shut up!" Adam took the knife from his throat and slashed at Joel's chest, ripping through his T-shirt and into the flesh beneath. Joel flinched at the new sensation of pain, but it was no match for the growing agony deep inside. The curse eating him from the inside out. "You're lying. She's my wife. She loves me. She did all of this for me. Took you in that night like I asked, drew your blood for me, brought you here. You're nothing to her. Nothing."

Adam's eyes lit up like fire now, his face a mask of insanity. Mouth drawn back in an odd scowl, his bloodless lips taut against his teeth, and that white, white skin.

"Then why didn't she kill me? Why did she let me go?" Joel hoped he created enough doubt in this ghoul's mind...whatever mind he had left. "Did you ask her why?"

Another slash to his cheek this time. "Shut up, shut up, shut up." With each word, he made more cuts on Joel's body. The life drained out of him bit by bit. The pain deep within and the blood coursing down his face and arms. All of it brought him closer to the end. And what of Matt? How would this help his brother? Killed by a half-alive madman in the woods? The agony of not knowing the answer to that question hurt him more than any wounds, any curse.

Matt, I'm sorry.

As Adam raged, one final cut slipped across the ties that bound Joel's left arm to the beam, loosening it some. But was it too late to make an escape?

"Give me your blood...all of it...and it will be over. It doesn't matter what Gen said. I'll be alive again. You'll be the dead one. You won't be here for her anymore. It will only be me. Just like it used to be." Adam raised the knife over his head, positioned it above Joel's heart and plunged.

CHAPTER THIRTY-SIX

"Adam, don't!" Gen's voice carried across the clearing.

With a snarl, Adam spun around and whipped the knife in her direction. It sailed through the air and landed with a thwack inches from Gen's face in the trunk of a tree. "You bitch. You lying, sneaking bitch." He flew at her, his footsteps eating up the distance between them.

Joel struggled under his bindings. The nicked rope loosened little by little, but not fast enough. That maniac was likely to hurt her before he had a chance to get free.

"Stop!" She held up a plastic baggie. "Stop right where you are." She tipped it as if to dump out the contents.

Adam stopped short about ten feet from her. "If you do this, I'll not only kill him, I'll kill you. You won't do this to me." He lunged at her.

The crack of a shotgun rang out.

Adam stumbled forward, the shell catching him in the back of the head. He crumpled to the ground.

On the other side of the clearing, Matt stood with a shotgun to his eye. "How do you like that, fucker?"

The pale body in black lay still.

"Untie me!" Joel yelled, struggling with the ropes.

Matt dropped the shotgun and ran over to help.

At the same moment, Adam, his head split open and pale brains exposed, got to his feet.

Gen jumped and backed away from him.

Adam grabbed for her. "You won't do this to me!" He was a wraith of death and destruction, his visage one of pure rage.

In one smooth motion, Gen jerked the knife out of the tree and plunged it into Adam's chest.

His eyes bugged open. He stared at her in surprise.

"Adam!" She fell with him to the ground. "I'm so sorry," she said as the life left his incomplete body. "I'm so sorry."

The knife glowed with an intense blue light, growing brighter and brighter. Gen let go and stepped away. The light became blue fire, engulfing Adam's body. In a matter of moments, the flesh and bone was reduced once more to a pile of ashes.

Gen opened the baggie still gripped in her hand and dumped the rest of Adam's ashes. The breeze picked up the light material and scattered it in the air.

Matt finished untying Joel. Freed, he rushed over to Gen and engulfed her in his arms.

She covered her face with her hands. "I couldn't really save him, could I?"

"No." Joel felt lightheaded. Wrong somehow. Like he wasn't all there. Blood dripped from his wounds and stained Gen's clothes. "I'm a mess. I'm sorry."

Without even noticing the wounds and the blood, she pulled him closer to her. Her mouth sought his and her soft lips gave him a gentle kiss. He answered back with a kiss of his own, wanting to know more of her. Find out everything he could about how she tasted, how her mouth felt against his. Before it was too late.

A pain to his gut made him pull away. He bent over double and leaned against a tree for support.

"Are you all right?" Gen asked.

"The Ninth Curse." The pain gripped Joel so tightly, he thought he'd collapse right there. He'd managed to escape the nightmare of her dead husband only to be right back where he started…on the verge of death.

"You have to help him, Gen," Matt said.

"No, I don't think so." Joel looked her right in the eye. "I know what your plan is, and it's not going to happen. I'm not going to kill you, Gen. I'm not." He collapsed.

"Joel!" Gen knelt next to him and held his face between her hands. "There's no arguing. Your brother knows what to do. I have a way."

"What way?" He struggled to pay attention to her words through a haze of torment.

"I brought Bluto back to life."

"What?" Matt asked before Joel could speak.

"I tried the Resurrection Spell on Bluto and it worked."

"I don't believe you." Joel pushed away from her. "You wouldn't have had enough of my blood to do something like that."

"I used my own." She straightened her shoulders. "And it worked."

"I thought you needed a cursed man's blood to make the spell work." Joel spoke each word with tremendous effort.

"A cursed man's blood is powerful. But Bluto had only been dead a few hours, he didn't need the strength of your blood, Joel."

"So with a recent…corpse…" Matt spoke carefully, "…you could make this spell work? It would be you and not that thing?" He gestured at the pile of ashes that used to be Adam.

"Bluto ran off before I could show you. But, yes, a fresh body is best."

Matt shivered.

"You want me to kill you, and then bring you back to life?" Joel faced her, all of his energy focused on his words. "Are you insane? How could you ever think I'd agree to something like that?" Sweat dripped down his face as the Death Curse ate away at him.

"If you don't, Matt will be next." Gen sat back on her heels. The pleading in her eyes was too much for him to bear. "If you don't stop this curse in its tracks, Matt will be suffering through this alone. Without you. Then in nine weeks' time we're right back to where we are today. My death is the only thing that will end this curse once and for all, Joel. You know it's true. What other choice do you have? You have to trust me. The Resurrection Spell works."

Joel looked from Gen's hopeful face to his brother's. He knew his grasp on his body, on this world, was slipping away with each breath he took.

How could he kill her? How could he kill someone he'd grown to love so dearly? He reached out for her, wanting her body close to his. Her short hair brushed against his lips as he whispered into her ear, "I trust you."

CHAPTER THIRTY-SEVEN

Gen lay down on the wooden beam to which Joel had been tied. "This is how it begins." She couldn't believe how calm she sounded. Although she did trust in the power of the Resurrection Spell—Bluto proved to her it could work—the idea of being stabbed through the heart frightened her to her core. But if she showed fear, she knew Joel wouldn't go through with it, and he had to. He just had to.

She pressed the decorative dagger into Joel's hand. "This is the knife you must use. It's a very powerful instrument."

"I know." Joel stood over her, his hand gently sliding up and down her arm. His cheeks looked sunken, the sockets around his eyes dark. He was dying.

"You have to stab me in the heart." Tears sprung to her eyes. "I'm not afraid. I want you to do this..."

He closed his eyes and grunted. The ninth curse had a tight grip on him. A streak of gray appeared in his hair. "Gen..."

"Shhh, don't say it. I know." She reached up and ran her fingers through the gray streak. Joel opened his eyes, captured her hand and kissed it.

"I don't know if I can do this."

"You have to. It's the only way." She pressed the knife into his hand, and the sharp blade caught the mid-morning light. "It's all right."

"It's *not* all right." His eyes were fever bright.

"It's the way things were supposed to be, don't you see? It wasn't right, what happened to your family, what's happening to you. This is the only way to stop it." She rested her hands at her sides.

"Please don't." The knife hung limply from his hand. "Please don't make me do this."

"If you do everything as I told you, once I'm...once I'm dead..." Gen said.

Joel looked stricken.

"And it works..."

"What if it doesn't work?" His knuckles were white he gripped the knife so tightly.

"*And it works,*" she said more loudly this time. "Everything will be okay. Your brother will be safe. I'll be safe. It will be over."

"How do we know it will work?"

"Remember Bluto?"

"He's a cat, an animal." His hands were trembling and now covered with age spots.

A dark shadow bloomed inside her. A shadow of doubt. "It will work for me too, I promise." But she didn't sound so sure to her own ears. "It's all right, Joel."

He knelt beside her. "How can you ask me to do this?"

"I knew the minute you showed up on my doorstep I would help you." She cradled his face in her hand. He kissed her palm, his lips raspy and dry. "This was how it was meant to be. I know that now. I feel it."

He laid his head down next to her and wept. "Gen, I love you."

"I know."

"I love you, and you want me to kill you."

"It's the only way." The tears came freely now. The hot sting of tears.

She wanted to be brave. She wanted to be strong, but this man had cut her deeply. Not with any knife, but with his love for her. She touched his hair lightly with her fingers, as if she were giving him absolution.

He lifted his head and searched her eyes for something. Forgiveness? She wasn't sure. Then, he leaned forward and brushed his mouth against her lips. Her last kiss.

"You can do this, Joel," she whispered in his ear. "Save yourself. Save your brother."

He pulled his head away and reached for the knife. With a groan of agony, he lifted it above his head and centered it over her chest. "Oh, God."

"It's all right, Joel."

His arms trembled as he held the knife. "It's the only way," he repeated her phrase. "The only way." He closed his eyes and plunged the blade deep into her heart.

Matt's cry broke the silence, the grief, the heartache.

Joel looked up from Gen's body, the knife gripped in his hand. Gen's blood covered it. He wanted to be sick. "Oh my God. I killed her." He let go of the knife and stumbled away from the body. "I had to."

His brother's face was ashen. "I know. Holy fuck, I know."

Even in his grief, he felt a lightening in his body. The deep unbearable pain evaporated. He looked at the backs of his hands. The age spots had disappeared. It had worked. Gen had saved him. Saved Matt.

A sense of purpose filled him. "I have to bring her back." Time was ticking away. He didn't have time to waste.

Matt sank down and retched. His eyes were glassy when he looked up. "Holy fuck."

Joel had to perform the spell. Now. He only had a few minutes to act before it might be too late. Before her grip on life was too far gone, and they took the risk of bringing back something other than Gen.

"You have to tell me what to do," Joel said to his brother, who was still in shock. "She said she told you how."

"Yes." Matt's voice was weak.

"Good. Get it together. We can do this." The knife. He knew they needed the knife.

Gen was still warm. He tried not to look at the blood covering her chest. The knife sticking out. The empty look in her eyes.

Dead. She was dead. If this didn't work...

Joel grabbed the handle of the knife and gently pulled. The sensation of metal against soft flesh and harder muscle disgusted him. But it had to be done. For the wound to heal and life to return, it had to be done.

As he pulled out the knife, he glimpsed the back of his hand. Only a week ago it had been covered in painful sores. Only minutes ago, it had appeared like an old man's. But in the seconds following Gen's death, his hand had returned to normal. Proof the curse was over. He'd survived. Matt was safe. Now he had to save Gen. He had to because he couldn't imagine life without her.

The knife slid out, and he wiped it on his shirt. "God help you," Matt whispered. "God help us all."

"What do I do now?" His brother was too pale. Joel spat out his order, "Matt, tell me what I need to do."

Matt snapped out of his trance and grabbed Gen's bag. The bag she was never without. "We need a candle, the plants, an ashtray and blood." He dumped everything in her bag on the ground. His voice grew more confident. "Get some Darlingtonia." He pointed at the mass of plants that surrounded them.

Joel snapped off several stalks of the odd plant and joined his brother.

Matt grabbed a fat yellow candle and a lighter. "We need a fire. Here." He cleared off the leaf fall on top of another beam.

While he waited for Matt to start the fire, Joel turned back to Gen's body. "I won't let you die." He kept his gaze focused on her face and tried to ignore the gaping wound in her chest. The damage *he'd* inflicted. "I won't. I promise." She'd sacrificed everything for him. He wanted her to be there so that he could remind her every day how grateful he was for that. How much he loved her for that.

Her face was pale, but she still felt warm. He would make it better. He would fix it. He had to.

Matt had a fire going. "Now add the Darlingtonia."

Joel shredded the plant into bits and added them little by little to the growing flames.

The small fire sparked up and ate at the Darlingtonia. The leaves popped in the fire, the bright green turning brown, the odd pinkish red glowing like blood amidst the flames.

"Now what?" Joel asked.

"The blood."

Joel grabbed the knife he'd used to stab Gen and sliced across his forearm. The pain was intense and sharp. "Fuck!" But he cut further, opening up a four-inch gash. The blood spurted out and dripped down his arm. He held the fresh wound directly over the flame and let the blood cover the Darlingtonia in the ashtray.

The flame sputtered, but against all logic, the blood only made the flames grow higher.

"Now we light the candle." Matt tipped the yellow candle into the flames, as more blood dripped from Joel's wound.

The fire turned from yellow to orange to a strange red. Dark blood red. Joel had never seen a fire with such a deep color. The wick caught the flame.

Matt passed the candle three times over Gen's lifeless form. He read words he'd written on his hand. Words that had no meaning. That sounded like gibberish.

Joel hoped with all his heart they would hold the power to bring Gen back to him.

May angle sar te merel kadi yag, opre, Gen!

May angle sar te merel kadi yag, opre, Gen!

May angle sar te merel kadi yag, opre, Gen!

The words rang out in the empty clearing. The sun was now high overhead with not a cloud in sight. The sunniest day since they'd arrived in Calvin City, as if the sun were shining for Gen, telling her to wake up from her death sleep.

The candle's flame turned bright green. Joel picked up Gen's cold hand and squeezed it, hoping she would squeeze back. But her eyes were half-open and glassy, her mouth slack.

His gut twisted. Something wasn't right.

Even after the fire, the blood and those strange words, she was dead.

She'd tricked him. She'd tricked him into believing the nonsense about the Resurrection Spell.

Nothing had happened.

"No!" He threw himself across Gen's body and cradled her close. "Why did you make me do that to you? Why?" He rained kisses down her cheeks and tried to ignore the chilled flesh beneath his lips.

"Joel." Matt tugged at his shirt.

Joel shoved him away. "She lied to me. Don't you understand? She never brought Bluto back. It was all a lie." The truth made his heart ache. "I killed her! Oh, God, I killed her, Matt." He pulled her off the beam and onto the ground with him, holding her in his arms, wishing with all his heart that he had been the one to die. Not her. And not like this. He'd never be able to shake the image of the knife plunging into her chest. The life seeping out of her. The horrid stillness that came with death.

"Come back to me, Gen. Come back." He stroked her hair. Her forehead was so cool to his touch. "You have to come back."

"She's dead." Matt's voice was monotone. "She's not coming back, Joel." Matt took another step toward him. "There's nothing left to save."

He dropped her hand and shook her. "Wake up. You're not dead. You're not. You said this would work. You promised me this would work." He was angry now. She had promised. How could she have made him do that to her? For the rest of his life, he would remember the look in her eye when he plunged the knife into her heart. The feel of her warm blood on his hands. "Oh God, Gen. Please come back."

He sensed Matt kneeling down on the other side of her body. "She's gone, Joel. Let her go."

He shot his brother a look of pure venom. "No!" He rocked her. "You have to come back. You promised me. You promised."

He didn't want to let go of her. He could still smell her sweet strawberry scent in her hair. He wanted to hold on to that smell as long as he could.

Joel cupped her chin in his hands. "Did you bring Bluto back? Did you really do it?" He wiped away a few drops of blood on her pale cheek.

Did her face look less white just now? Joel couldn't be sure.

Gen coughed. Her eyes rolled back in her head.

"Oh my God, it worked!" Joel wanted to jump up and shout it from the rafters.

Pink returned to her cheeks, her eyelids fluttered and, most miraculously of all, her chest wound began to knit itself back together.

"Jesus," whispered Matt as they both watched the strange healing take place.

Gen blinked, her gaze unclear. "Is it you, Joel?" Her voice was barely a whisper. "Did it work?"

"You did it, Gen," he said, cradling her warming body against his. "My God, you did it."

CHAPTER THIRTY-EIGHT

A sensation of falling without ever hitting bottom—that was what death was like. Not empty and black like Gen would have thought, but strange and disturbing. A place she wouldn't like to return to any time soon.

Her chest hurt. As if she had been hit by a bus. But there was no longer a wound of any kind. Just a tear in her blouse and the dried blood staining it.

Joel had held her so close, so tight once she'd woken up, she could barely get a breath. She didn't need to hear the words, she could feel the joy in his limbs, the trembling of his hands. The touches across her face and body, as if he were just making sure she was still there, still breathing.

"I'm all right." Her mind was wide awake, but her body was weak and slow. Guess that's what death did to someone. Robbed her of strength. It would take some time to get it back.

"You'd better be all right." Matt knelt on her other side, a wide smile on his face.

She took in Joel's handsome face. The streak of gray in his hair was gone and the sunken look to his eyes had disappeared.

It was over. They'd done it. The DeVries family curse was over, and everyone was alive. Everyone was going to be okay—except for Adam. He'd been dead a long time. She latched onto memories of the real Adam. A student of dark magic, but a man who understood when knowledge was best left to die. She hoped somewhere out there he forgave her for what she'd tried to do. It was only her grief driving her. Grief that no longer sat so heavy on her heart. She was ready to accept that and move forward in her life.

She struggled to get to her feet. Joel wrapped an arm around her waist to help her up. "So when's lunch?" She smiled weakly at him.

Joel swept her into his arms and carried her away from the ruins and the reminder of what they'd survived. "Whatever you want. Should we find out if Stella's in the mood for some company?" He paused. She could hear his heart thudding. "I thought I'd lost you."

Gen rested her head on Joel's shoulder. "Never." He made her feel secure, safe. Like Adam used to when he was alive.

She touched the back of Joel's neck. This man had helped her heal that wound of Adam's loss. See that there was hope and joy and love left in this world for her. For them.

"Okay, so once we've gotten something to eat," said Matt, trailing behind them, "what's next? Spring break is over on Sunday, but we have no house to go back to. Joel's out of a job. I'm thinking I probably can't even afford next month's rent...can I, bro?"

"Probably not."

"You can stay with me," Gen said.

"What about your mother?"

"She'll be fine with it."

"She will?"

"I'll make her be fine with it." She smiled.

"I'm sure we can find something soon." Joel carried her deeper into the woods. "I can file for unemployment while I look for work."

"Are you saying you're in a hurry to be rid of me?" She felt stronger now. More present in this world.

They reached the road. Matt had parked Stella's truck next to Joel's car. "No, but I didn't know if...that is, I didn't know if you and I. If we..."

"I think she's trying to tell you that she loves you too, dummy," said Matt, only a few steps behind.

"What?" Joel turned red as a beet. He set Gen gently down on her feet.

Gen stopped him from getting past her. "He's right." Their hips met, and she slipped her arms around his middle.

"He is?"

His arm was bloodied, his hair stringy with sweat, but he was hers if she wanted him. "Yes. I'm not asking you to stay for a few days until you can straighten out your life. I'm asking you to stay as long as you want to stay."

Joel gathered Gen into his arms and kissed her. Her lips were no longer cold. They were warm, soft and yielding. He imagined spending hours kissing those lips. Days, months and years stretched out in his mind. Now he could dream again. Imagine. Plan for the future.

When they broke off the kiss, Joel laced his fingers with hers. "I like a view. Do we have a room with a view?"

She punched him in the arm. "I'm the view, and that's the only one you need."

He rubbed his arm. "Ow, are you sure that Resurrection Spell didn't include some kind of steroid treatment?"

She smiled.

A plaintive meow came from the back of Stella's pickup truck. The head of a black, beat-up cat poked out from under a tarp.

"Bluto?" all three of them said.

Bluto shook himself and jumped on the edge of the truck bed.

"It *is* you!" Joel cried.

"I told you I cured him." Gen scratched the animal under the chin.

Bluto purred and rubbed her hand.

"I will never doubt you again." Joel smiled and scruffed his cat, nuzzling his soft fur against his cheek.

Gen looked at Matt. "You're my witness."

Matt grinned and gave Bluto a pat on the head.

"I'll have to get you some tuna, boy." Joel carried him to the car. "I think you deserve it."

"So, when are we eating?" Matt asked. "I didn't get to have any of that pizza last night."

Joel set Bluto in the backseat and closed the door. "By all means, I don't want to keep a man from his lunch." He opened the passenger door for Gen. "Shall we?"

Gen climbed in.

"Thank you." Matt headed for the banged up Ford F-150. "I'll drive the truck back."

"Hope Stella didn't mind us borrowing it," Gen said.

"Considering it had a rifle and a gun rack in the back, I have a feeling it's Stan's forgiveness we'll be asking for." Matt slammed the heavy truck door.

Before they followed Matt back to the bed and breakfast, Bluto jumped into her lap and kneaded her skirt.

Joel started the car. "It took me three weeks to get that cat to come out of the bushes and eat one bite of food. You show up, and he's your new best friend."

Gen scratched the scruffy cat behind the ears. "I think he knows how lucky we both are to be here. Don't you, Bluto."

Bluto meowed and purred contentedly.

"Now let's go get something to eat."

"Yes, ma'am." Joel saluted her. As he drove the car down the road, he thought only of sunshine, lunch and the woman he loved. Those three things made this day just about perfect.

In the shade of the trees in the woods beyond, a man and woman had loved each other many years ago. A love that never was meant to be. And now, decades later, was it fate or just irony that brought together a descendant of Calvin DeVries and a descendant of Sabina Silva?

Joel squeezed Gen's hand.

He didn't care. Those two names would never cross his mind again. He'd sacrificed everything for this moment. For this chance at love, and he wasn't about to look back.

ABOUT THE AUTHOR

K. J. Gillenwater has a B.A. in English and Spanish from Valparaiso University and an M.A. in Latin American Studies from University of California, Santa Barbara. She worked as a Russian linguist in the U.S. Navy, spending time at the National Security Agency doing secret things. After six years of service, she ended up as a technical writer in the software industry. She has lived all over the U.S. and currently resides in Idaho with her family where she runs her own business writing government proposals and squeezes in fiction writing when she can. In the winter she likes to ski and snowshoe; in the summer she likes to garden with her husband, take walks with her dog, and try her hand at gold panning and huckleberry picking. She has written several paranormal suspense books and plans on writing more..

Check in with K.J. at her blog: kjgillenwaterblog.blogspot.com or visit her website for more information about her writing, her books, and what's coming next. www.kjgillenwater.com.

If you enjoyed this book, K. J. Gillenwater is the author of multiple books, which are available in print and in ebook format through Amazon.

THE LITTLE BLACK BOX

After the suspicious suicides of several student test subjects, Paula Crenshaw, research assistant and budding telekinetic in Paranormal Sciences at Blackridge University, suspects they may be connected to a little black box designed to read auras. Professor Jonas Pritchard, the head of the department, doesn't believe his precious experiment could be causing students to drop like flies. But when her best friend almost dies after her encounter with the black box, Paula is certain there is a connection. She pulls her cute, but sloppy, office buddy, Will Littlejohn, into the mystery, and they get closer to the truth behind who might be financially backing the project and why. Haunted by memories of a childhood accident, which she believes she caused with her untamed psychic abilities, Paula finds herself lured to the black box and its mysteries.

BLOOD MOON

Werewolves are roaming Northeast High, and Savannah Black is determined to hunt them down.

When Savannah's academic rival mysteriously disappears, she enlists the aid of her two best friends, Dina and Nick, to solve the mystery. Football players with glowing eyes and razor sharp canine teeth may have fooled the faculty, but not Savannah and her friends. These brave students are determined to eradicate a clan of deadly werewolves who threaten to take over their school.

When Dina disappears right before the big Homecoming Dance, Savannah and Nick must act quickly to save her from the werewolf's curse. But will a straight-A student be able to master knives and silver bullets as easily as chemistry and calculus?

SKYFALL

A science fiction short story collection of three flash fiction works.

Skyfall. A miner confronts a devastating future.

Time Travel. A failed engineer tinkers with a matter-energy transporter, which he plans to step into for the first time.

Torch. A man attempts to escape from a futuristic prison.

NEMESIS

K.J. Gillenwater edited and wrote a story for this science fiction anthology entitled, NEMESIS. The idea for the anthology was this: Write a short story between 4,000 and 5,000 words using the word "Nemesis" as your inspiration. Ten writers participated (including K.J.). Here are the short story titles included:

Polarity by Holly Gonzalez

Superhero Comic Girl vs. the Litter Box by Steven R. Brandt

Last Walk by Jinn Tiole

Stagnant by Dave Cardwell

Three Shades of Black by Matthew Thrush

Disciple by Kristin Jacques

Outwitting Alexa by Jesse Sprague

Mordecai by Hannah Ansley

Guardian by Louis Williams

Star Log by K. J. Gillenwater.

ACAPULCO NIGHTS

ACAPULCO NIGHTS was a Write Affair finalist (Kensington Books) on Wattpad as an "Editor's Pick."

Suzie's fiancé, James, is pressuring her to pick a day for their wedding. She's cancelled three dates, and he's starting to wonder if she really wants to get married. But how does she go about telling her fiancé that she's already married to a man in Mexico? She needs a divorce, and she needs one fast. Her marriage has been a secret from her best friend, Janice, her fiancé, even her own mother, and she wants to keep it that way.

When Janice asks her to come along on an all-girl vacation to Acapulco, Suzie leaps at the chance. A search on the Internet gives Suzie all the information she needs to track down her husband, Joaquin, while out of the country and finally get that divorce.

Unfortunately, Joaquin won't give her up so easily.

When James appears in Acapulco unexpectedly, all hell breaks loose, and Suzie stands to lose everything she's ever loved.